THE TREASURE
OF
PONFERRADA

THE TREASURE OF PONFERRADA

JOHN ANTHONY GOODALL

Bombardier Press

Avec Cynthia.

The Kingdom of the Father is spread upon the earth, but man does not see it.

Gospel of Thomas

October 12, 1307

The golden days of autumn were devoted to the French harvest, just as the nights were to sleep. It was on one of these cold October nights, after church bells proclaimed the midnight hour, that an unusual kind of harvest took place in central Paris.

The streets of the city were dark and still—two lanterns cast a soft glow of light across the river from opposite sides of the swirling water. One suspended like a pendulum from the Tower of Nesle. Another above the entrance to the fortress of Châtelet.

As usual, scores of ships were moored along the muddy shore, but on this night, some wore sails blackened with soot, and cloaked figures huddled in the shadows.

The silence was shattered by a rumble and a clatter when a procession of horse-drawn wagons emerged from a narrow lane, hooves and wheels wrapped in burlap to quiet them.

Then, as if on signal, men rose from the shadows and transferred load after load of cargo from the wagons into the ships with black sails.

When the holds could hold no more, the hatches were sealed, and ships, riding low, plied away into the darkness.

1

1

Stop and go, one car at a time, a blast of Seattle rain smears my windshield as I creep up to the Second Avenue stop sign. Spotting a break in the oncoming headlights, I give it some gas, and a soft thump rocks the front of my car.

An impatient driver leans on his horn when I scramble out to help a pasty-faced teenager to his feet. "Are you alright?" I say. "You want me to take you to the hospital?"

"I'm okay, but maybe you could help me out with a fifty?"

"A fifty?" I say, brushing what I hoped was dirt off his jacket. "That seems a little steep."

He pulls out a cellphone held together with Scotch tape. "Maybe I should talk to my lawyer."

I blink. "How about thirty?"

Triple horn blasts from a Puget Sound ferry rattle the air.

A police car cruises by.

He follows it with his eyes.

"Okay, I'll take the thirty."

It isn't until I park across from the auction that it hits me—he flopped on my fender just to earn that thirty.

But I have to let it go. Any minute now, I've got a dicey deal of my own to pull off.

The rising pitch of the auctioneer's chant is coming from Bushell's, a family-run business in a nineteenth century, red-brick building.

People are filing out the door, and I bump shoulders with a man cradling a gold Tibetan buddha. He puts his nose in the air when he sees me and grips the buddha tighter to his chest. Garrison Crowley inherited his family fortune and has hated me ever since I outbid him on a Ming Dynasty robe. If he knew what I was after tonight, he wouldn't be so smug.

Hiding my smile, I slip inside behind the Stanton brothers who are hauling out a weather-beaten Haida Indian totem pole. They run the Old Curiosity Shop down on the waterfront docks.

A seductive crackle of energy fills the wide, high-ceilinged room, and all eyes are fixed on Bill Bushell, a rugged-looking man in his seventies, who is calling out the bids from an elevated wooden podium.

Moving slowly, I'm scoping out the crowd. Familiar faces fill the tight rows of metal chairs facing the podium, others stand against the walls or line the rear.

The out-of-town heavies haven't shown, but some of the local money is seated together in front. Kathy Brown, owner of Globe Antiques, gestures to me with a gold pen before jotting another purchase in her ledger. Two seats over, silver-haired Herm Lebowski is trying to be invisible while bidding on a painting of a Victorian lady with cats on her lap.

Everybody knows Herm collects paintings, but he doesn't get this one. The auctioneer hammers it down for $4,500 to a red-haired lady in sensible shoes and an ankle-length dress. Ms. Cutts runs a second-hand bookstore full of cats called Puss 'n' Books.

A pencil-mustached fellow in a powder blue suit dips me a nod as I move towards the back of the room. Texas Thompson owns an antiques store but earns his real money playing poker.

Normally, I'd stand in the back with Tex so I can see who's bidding against me, but I have a different plan for this sale. After examining it earlier, I left a bid with Mary and Sally Bushell, the gray-haired sisters who run the office. This way, the auctioneer bids for me while I can pretend to be bored stiff.

A hush settles over the crowd when the auctioneer starts selling a painting by Mark Tobey. Off in a corner, flinty-eyed

3

Leo, who buys for other dealers, and hawk-faced Abraham, who peddles cheap Pakistani rugs beneath a faded *50% Off* banner, put their heads together, and come at me, sails spread.

"Brother Tony," Leo says, keeping his eyes on mine, reading me. "What's bringing you out on this dark and stormy night?"

"I'm not here to bid. I just stopped in to watch the show."

He smiles. He knows I'm lying.

"People are saying things about you. They say Tony Shepherd's on to something. That he's got the Midas touch."

"The Midas touches? What the heck is that supposed to mean?"

"Buying things nobody understands and turning it all into gold."

"That's ridiculous. Every time I buy something, I'm taking a chance. Sometimes I win, sometimes I lose."

Abraham moves a few inches closer. "We read about a guy who got two million dollars for an old Navajo wearing blanket."

"Well, that wasn't me."

Abraham places an unwelcome hand on my arm. "What about that knotted pile thing in tonight's sale? The green one with yellow stars."

"Yellow stars? ...I didn't pay it much attention."

"But you're always buying oddball things like that."

I shrug. "Sorry to disappoint you."

"Someone said the seashell border could mean it's a really old European piece."

"Is that right?" I say, inserting a note of surprise. "I'll try to remember that."

He narrows his eyes. He suspects I'm being sarcastic but is not quite certain.

A burst of applause signals the Mark Tobey painting had sold to Herman Lebowski for a healthy $200,000.

When the commotion dies down, Leo leans in and lowers his voice like he's delivering a secret message. "It's got one of the strangest inscriptions I've ever seen."

"Do you know what it says?"

4

"The letters are weird. They don't make any sense."

I give him my thoughtful look. "It's not much use if you don't know what it says."

A quick glance at Abraham. "It's also got a funny looking weave. We've never seen anything like that before."

"A funny looking weave?" I dredge up a grin. "What's that supposed to mean?"

"I don't know. That's why I'm asking you."

"How am I supposed to know?"

"I don't know how you'd know—but you'd know."

I'm growing tired of their game. "A funny looking weave means absolutely nothing."

He puckers his brow. "Are you sure?"

"Damn right, I'm sure. If you think it's so great, you should buy it."

Telling him to buy it is almost certain to give him second thoughts.

The auctioneer is about to sell the rugs and tapestries, so they give up on me and move to the front. I follow behind and position myself to one side where everybody can see me.

Bill Bushell introduces the Spanish piece in a matter-of-fact tone, without any fanciful speculation about what it might be. "Okay, folks, we've got a pretty little handmade textile and it looks to be an old one. Who'll start me out at three hundred? Do I hear three hundred?"

Hands flutter up and down until the bidding stalls at $2000. Leo and Abraham look my way. I shake my head. Kathy Brown bids the $2100. Leo's hand shoots up to bid the $2200, and it goes back and forth until it hits $4000. Kathy gives me an inquisitive glance before dropping out.

But it's not over. The auctioneer squints down at his absentee bids. "I'm bid four thousand one hundred up here, who'll make it forty-two?"

Leo looks my way again. I give a noncommittal shrug and head for the door. Leo bids the $4200 as the door closes behind me.

Outside, with the swish of traffic going by, I can hear the auctioneer calling my bid. "Forty-three...forty-four...forty-five...forty-six...forty-seven."

A silent pause.

"I've got four thousand seven hundred up here, do I hear forty-eight-hundred?

"Who'll bid four thousand-eight hundred? forty-eight-hundred anywhere?"

Another silent pause.

"All done then?"

The bang of the hammer.

"Sold to the absentee bidder for four thousand seven-hundred dollars."

Now it's mine. I had left a $10,000 bid.

I wait for Leo and Abraham to come out the door.

Abraham looks pinched and angry.

Leo is trying to calm him down.

"Did you buy it?" I say, trying to keep a grin off my face.

"I wasn't sure about it, so I let it go," Leo says, as a Bible-black Jeep Wrangler wearing Nevada plates pulls to the curb.

Nobody gets out, but two figures become briefly visible when a match flares, and somebody inside lights a cigarette.

"We were supposed to buy it," Abraham says, his eyes on the Jeep. "Now I'll have to explain why we didn't."

2

Low clouds swept across the sky as I crossed Aurora Bridge on the way to pick up my purchase. After parking in the loading zone behind a battered blue pickup truck, I paused to hold the door for Danny Shine who was carrying out a box of books. Danny, a bearded man with long gray hair, looked like an Old Testament prophet and dealt mostly in books.

"Hey, Danny," I said.

"Leave it open," he said, breathing heavily. "I've got more."

Mary came to the office window. "Are you picking up now?"

"Yeah," I said, opening my check register.

"We haven't seen much of you since the accident."

I nodded. "It's been a few months."

A fleeting look of compassion, then she handed me the invoice. "We'll be happy to get that thing out of here."

"Why is that?"

"People have been pestering us about it. It's been getting more visitors than a rich man on his deathbed."

"Sounds like whiny latecomers trying to grab a piece of something they missed out on. It happens all the time."

Her lips tightened. "Not like this, it doesn't. One of those snooty types said he would pay more than we sold it for and had the gall to wave a wad of hundred-dollar bills in my face. Can you imagine? Then two gals came in wearing saris. One distracted me with questions while the other tried to sneak into our back room."

Sally came to stand beside her sister. "That wasn't the worst of it. A spooky little man dressed like a priest scared the living bejesus out of me. He was bald as an egg and had skin so white it looked like he'd been raised in a closet."

I grinned. "Maybe he's been spending too much time in the confessional."

She looked at me with lifted eyebrows. "He didn't act very priestly. He wanted to know who bought it. When I explained that we never give out buyer information, he got angry and went to badger Mary."

Mary nodded. "Something wasn't right about that man. Two fingers were missing from each of his hands."

"Maybe he was born that way?"

She shuddered. "They were ragged little stubs, like someone cut them off. And none too nicely, I might add."

John Bushell, a man in his thirties, brought the panel out of the storeroom. "What the heck is this? Has it been cut?"

"It's not cut," I said. "It's one panel of an old Spanish table rug that was woven in two panels."

"You mean it was never made to be used on the floor?"

"That's right. Exotic looking table rugs became popular when Renaissance artists began depicting them in paintings."

"How do you know it's Spanish?"

I smiled. "Spanish rugs are woven differently than other rugs. The knots are tied around only one warp thread, instead of the usual two."

Danny returned for another box of books and pointed at the inscription cartouche on the Spanish piece. "Those letters look like the writing on my grandfather's Torah scroll."

I looked more closely at the inscription when he left with the last box of books. "That inscription may be the most unusual thing about it," I said to John. "Do the people who consigned it have the other half?"

"I could ask the lady."

"If she does, I'd like to buy it?"

"I'll be sure to tell her."

8

North of downtown, I exited into the Fremont District, a neighborhood of quaint boutiques, coffee shops, and artist studios stretching along the north shore of Lake Union. Twenty years ago, I was drawn here by a vacant storefront the prior tenant, Fleet Detective Agency, had turned into a suite of shabby office cubicles. I ripped out the seedy offices, put up track lights, and painted everything white. Now I have my own sign above the door. Gold letters two-feet tall reading *ARTIFACTS*.

Going over the panel under a bright light, I saw that the delicate colors had been grayed-out by centuries of dust and dirt. After giving it a quick immersion wash in my back room, I turned on the local classical station, and sat behind my desk just in time for my eleven o'clock opening.

Pachelbel's Canon in D was playing the soaring quarter notes when I felt a prickling on my neck. A pale face with a bald head was squinting through my window. The sweetly sorrowful tones of Pachelbel's Canon seemed to slowly dwindle when he caught my eye and sauntered in swinging a battered black satchel.

There was something faintly menacing about the way he set the satchel on my desk without asking, extended a hand that was missing its last two fingers, and spoke to me in a honey coated voice. "You must be Mister Shepherd," he said. "My name is Mario Orsini. I am an art dealer from Italy."

The accent was not Italian, and his baggy blue suit smelled of mothballs, but I took the hand, and sized him up as a hustler before he sat down.

After glancing quickly at the door, he unzipped the bag and laid four *soumak* bag faces on my desk. "I found these in a villa outside Florence. Except for a few old repairs, they are in pristine condition."

Soumak bag faces are among the most collectible of all tribal artifacts. Their jewel-like weave resembles needlepoint with a shaggy back and dates to 6000 BC. Good examples bring a couple

9

thousand dollars. Exceptional ones could go for the price of a new BMW.

But why had he brought them to Seattle, instead of selling them in Italy where he had a better market?

His violet eyes observed me with a watchful repose as I examined each piece, sort of like an experienced cat might contemplate a less experienced mouse. When he thought I was busy looking, the eyes darted over my gallery walls.

The wool was hand-spun, and the dyes were old, but something didn't feel right. Then it hit me. The designs had none of the whimsey or subtle color changes that a confident weaver puts into her work.

The near perfect copy is the simplest category of fake. It is also the easiest to detect because it lacks originality. And one of the most common tricks of a forger is to add old looking repairs to make people think an object had been repaired in antiquity.

Fakes were rarely a problem with weavings that took so long to make, but these had soared so much in value that it had become worthwhile. Rumors were circulating among specialized dealers that new soumak bag faces were being made by unraveling old *jajims* and *kelims*.

They were 'genuine' all right. Genuine fakes.

"They look good," I said, handing them back. "But I'll have to pass."

The violet eyes narrowed, but stayed fixed on my face. "I can give you a special price."

"Money's a little tight right now."

He pursed his lips as he folded them into his satchel but didn't appear to be particularly disappointed.

"I heard an unusual Spanish piece was sold at auction here," he said, a little too casually.

"Is that right?" I said back, just as casually.

Alert as a bird, he hunched forward. "I assume you've seen the Vizcaya Carpet in the Prado?"

"I don't think so."

His eyes went from me to the door, then back again. "The Vizcaya Carpet has an unusual star design along with mysterious phrases from the Kabbalah that were all written in Hebrew."

"So? What's the significance of all that?"

"The significance, my friend, is that we can be in the midst of great happenings and not even know what is at play."

This guy was working an angle, but I had no idea what it was. I gave him a questioning look.

"You must understand something," he said. "Spies were everywhere in those days. Weaving something with Judaic symbols could bring savage reprisals. Nobody would have taken such a risk unless it was incredibly important."

"If it was so dangerous, why would they use Hebrew writing?"

His quirky grin suggested that I was probing a place where secrets were kept.

"They wanted to conceal what they had written."

"Do you have any idea what the Vizcaya Carpet is worth?"

Something furtive moved behind the heavily lidded eyes, and he smiled a reptilian smile. "Collectors are like vultures perched on a branch. They would fight each other to get their hands on the only carpet from those times that was woven by Jews."

The words *woven by Jews* were ringing in my ears when he went out the door, and I had the uncomfortable sensation that there was a point to his conversation that I had somehow missed.

I knew that Jewish people had been active in the dyeing business, but I knew nothing about them weaving carpets.

Opening my laptop, I surfed for the Vizcaya Carpet. It was an obscure topic, and there were no pictures, but a man named Anton Felton had written an expensive and hard-to-find book entirely about that one rug.

I needed to know all about it, so I ordered the book.

11

3

Salsa music was playing when I crossed the street to grab a bite to eat at the Cuban café before opening next morning.

"Hey Carlos," I said to the wiry man with a frizzy explosion of black hair who was wiping the counter.

"Hey Tony," he said back. "You want the prawn sandwich?"

"Right, and a cup of coffee."

"A guy came in asking about when you open."

"Was he Turkish? My repair guy is coming today."

"He didn't look Turkish."

"What did he look like?"

"He looked like a tough guy. Someone you wouldn't want to get into a fight with."

I tried to imagine what kind of artifact a tough guy might want while eating my sandwich and thumbing through a tattered copy of a local weekly called *The Stranger*. When I was done, I tossed back what was left of my coffee, and went to open my gallery.

Horns started honking when I sat down behind my desk, and I looked up to see a barrel-chested guy crossing Fremont Avenue in the middle of the block. His fixed stare was aimed at my door.

An inch or two over six feet, he had curly black hair, sloping shoulders, and was powerfully built. The kind of guy you remember if you saw him just once.

I sat up straight when he came in.

The gold chain around his neck went well with the tanning salon complexion, but there was something about those scarred up knuckles that didn't peg him as an artifact collector.

He looked more like a debt collector.

"Are you the guy that owns the place? He said, fastening his eyes on me."

I said, "Yeah."

"I'm lookin' for old Spanish rugs. You got any?"

"Spanish rugs? I run across those sometimes, but I don't have any right now."

The ghost of a smile. "Somebody said you just got one. A green one with yellow stars."

"Who said that?"

He made a dismissive movement with his hand. "It don't matter. You have it or you don't?"

I slid a pen and a notepad across my desk. "If you leave your name and phone number, I'll give you a call if any come in."

He looked at me like a bug had just spoken. "Mind if I take a look around?"

"Go ahead. I've got a few minutes before my next appointment."

He shifted position to look past me into my washing room.

I reached back and closed the door.

The smile played on his lips as he walked over to my tall, double-doored safe.

"What do you keep in here? The good stuff?"

"No. Just money. I don't trust the banks."

A cold stare. So much for jokes.

Watching while he poked around in my stock, I was picturing my dad's pearl-handled Colt Lightning revolver resting inches from my hand in the top drawer. An antique gun with lethal accuracy.

"You'd never get it out in time."

He said it without looking up from the tapestry fragment he was examining.

"Then it's a good thing I don't have to," I fired back.

13

A wrinkle of amusement lingered on his face, and it crossed my mind that it wasn't his physical presence that was most intimidating. It was his unequivocal self-confidence.

Seconds later, my restorer came in. I was keeping a loose watch on the big guy while greeting Alaydin when the man stopped to look at me with one hand on the door.

"You see anything you can't live without?" I said,

"Not so far."

"Maybe a guy like you could use a nice prayer rug?"

The muscles around his eyes tightened. Then he flashed a smile. "Maybe I should come back when you're not so busy."

"It's always best to call first."

He held my gaze with a twinkle in his eyes. Then he turned abruptly and left.

It's funny how much information can be exchanged without a word being said.

"Is that guy a client of yours?" Alaydin said.

"I've never seen him before."

He squinted at the broad-shouldered figure crossing the street. "We run across a lot of shady characters in this business."

"It's a good thing most of them are harmless eccentrics."

He gave me a penetrating look. "I not so sure about that one."

"What do you mean?"

"I saw him at Abraham's yesterday."

"What were they doing?"

"They were nose to nose arguing."

"What were they arguing about?"

"I have no idea. They clammed up at the sight of me."

4

The transformation was stunning when I brought the panel out of my drying room at the end of the day. The colors glowed with a luminosity that seemed to come from within.

For a moment, I tried picturing it as a complete piece. Then I went to work shooting photos front and back, along with close-ups of the white seashells in the blue border, and the lattice of yellow stars on the green field.

I was focusing my camera on the inscription when I realized the shape of the cartouche was odd. Most are symmetrical, but this horizontal oblong, no bigger than a playing card, had one rounded end and protrusions sticking out on both sides like little wings.

Then something caught my eye that was almost hidden inside the writing. It was a small white circle outlined in blue. Leaning in for a closer look, I saw a squat red T shape in the center. I had never run across anything like that before.

Anomalies always help to sell things, so I got on the phone to a client with a burning passion for the old and unusual. Doctor Paterson picked up on the fourth ring.

"Hi, Jim, I found a piece that might fit into your collection. I hope I'm not calling too late."

"Not a problem, Tony, I'm catching up on some paperwork. What have you got for me?"

"It's just one panel of a two panel Spanish piece, but it's the only medieval table cover I've ever found."

"I've never run across one of those either. But I better ask how much you want. My wife says I've been spending too much on my little hobbies."

"I'll have to do more research, but it might be worth around fifteen thousand."

"That could be a bit out of my range, but I'd like to see it."

"I'll e-mail you some photos and give you first refusal."

"I always appreciate being first, and the photos might help persuade Claire that I'm not being frivolous."

"How soon can you come look at it?"

I heard a shuffling of papers. "I've got a convention coming up. Could you hold it for me until a week from Saturday?"

"Consider it done."

A quick sale in ten days was just what I needed to cover some upcoming insurance bills.

I was locking the panel in the trunk of my car to bring it home with me when sudden movement drew my eye to the laundromat across the street when. Two women were watching my every move from inside the window.

I smiled to myself as I drove two blocks up the street to do some quick shopping at Marketime Foods. Maybe they thought I was cute?

I was shoving my grocery sacks into the back seat when I saw the same two women were watching from the bus stop across the street.

Okay, I'm tall, and in good shape for a forty-year-old, but I'm not cute enough to follow around.

Trying for a better look, I did a quick U-turn in the middle of Fremont Avenue, but dark glasses and heavy scarves concealed their faces.

I puzzled over it a few seconds but put them out of my mind when I pulled to the curb across from the Buckaroo Bar. A squad of Harley-Davidson motorcycles were angle-parked beneath a flashing neon sign depicting a cowboy riding a horse. Every time the neon blinked its pink and turquoise colors, the horse bucked, rocking the cowboy back and forth.

Threading my way through the tightly packed motorcycles, I opened the door to the sweet smell of beer, the soft click of pool balls, and the nods of familiar faces.

I hadn't been in since the loss of my wife, but Scully, the bearded bartender, didn't say a word when I hoisted myself onto a stool at the bar. He just started pulling a creamy pint of Guinness.

I was washing away the cares of the day, and grooving on Bessie Smith singing about careless love, when a young woman slid onto the stool next to me. She wore a pale green scarf, a matching sweater, and gold hoop earrings. She looked good in green. Even smelled good in green.

After a few exploratory glances, a scarlet-tipped finger pointed at my beer. "What's the brown stuff?"

"The brown stuff?... It's beer. Irish beer."

A twinkly blue-eyed smile. "Is it any good?"

I didn't know what to say to that, so I shrugged.

She pointed again when Scully came to take her order. "I'll try one of those."

Scully turned away to pour it, and she pulled off her scarf. "You're kind of a tall fellow, aren't you?" she said, shaking down a glossy mane of blond.

I reached for my beer. "Other people have pointed that out," I said. "But I don't notice it so much when I'm sitting down."

She looked at me, a little baffled. Then switched on the high-voltage smile. "Do you come here often?"

I took a slow sip while I thought that over. "Isn't that supposed to be my line?" I said, smiling like I didn't mean it—though I really did.

Scully set a pint of beer in front of her before she could come up with an answer. "Oh my," she said, pulling it closer. "It's so big. Won't this get me drunk?"

17

Scully gave her a questioning look. "Only if you're one of those people with a strange metabolism."

I watched in the mirror as she took a hesitant swallow. "It's not bad," she said, glancing my way. "It's sort of creamy."

I nodded, as a Lightnin' Hopkins song started playing. "Next to the music, the beer here is the best."

She was taking another sip when something beeped in her purse. After a quick look at a text message, she slid off the stool and twinkled another smile.

"Don't go away, big guy. I've got to go powder my nose."

My mind was immersed in the metaphysical implications of the scent of green when she slid back onto the stool. The twinkle was gone, and she had acquired a bad case of the sniffles. I read somewhere that powdering your nose could do that.

"I hardly ever drink this much," she said, sniffing again. "But it's half gone, so I should try to finish it."

"A Taoist would say the glass is both half-full and half-empty, that neither half could exist without the other. The Irish, on the other hand, would say you should drink it because Guinness is good for you."

She was mulling that over when the sharp sound of a horn honking came from the street. "That's my ride," she said. "I've got to run. It's been fun talking to you. Maybe I'll see you again sometime?"

"That would be great. I enjoy discussing meaningful things."

A puzzled look was followed by a sudden thirst, and she polished off her beer. Then, ignoring the *No Smoking* sign, she lit a cigarette, tossed some money on the bar, and headed for the door.

Amusement flashed in Scully's eyes as we watched her climb into a luxurious green SUV. "Are you ready for another one?" he said.

I nodded toward the SUV as it pulled away. "Do you mean another one of those, or another Guinness?"

"I'm not allowed to serve you one of those, but I can pour another Guinness."

"Another one of those would be one too many. Did you notice? The color of her clothes matched the color of the SUV."

"Yeah. And it was one of those Cadillac Escalade models that go for a hundred and twenty-grand."

I froze in my tracks when I started across the street to where my own car was parked. All four doors were open wide. As I got closer, I saw the back seat upside down on the sidewalk, and a metal hook was wedged in the trunk where it had been twisted back from the rear window.

Car pilfering happened so often that I had traded in my new car for an old Nissan with a strong trunk. Now I was glad I did. They had managed to get it part way open, but not far enough to reach inside.

After calling 911, I looked around for clues. A broken string of polished wooden beads was coiled on the ground beneath the shattered driver's side window. They smelled of sandalwood.

The police arrived twenty minutes later. A man and a woman. The woman searched my car with her flashlight as if she were expecting to find some kind of contraband, while her partner wandered up and down the street.

He came back dragging a broken length of rusty chain. "Look what I found," he said. "Whoever did this must drive a car that was big enough to break a heavy-duty chain."

That much was obvious.

A more pressing question was what the hell had I gotten myself into.

5

Two men in gray suits were waiting for me when I came to open the next day. The pudgy one looking at his watch had wavy black hair, a mustache, and steel-rimmed glasses. The one with a cellphone to his ear was a long-legged blond with ice-blue eyes, a buzz cut, and a face so thin he didn't have room for a smile.

"I'm Officer Sparrow and this is Officer Crane," the mustache said. "Are you Mr. Anthony Shepherd?"

I nodded as I unlocked my door. "That's what it says on my birth certificate."

"Do you mind if we come in and take a look around?" Crane said, brushing past me to do just that.

"Not if you're interested in buying something," I said to the back of his head.

Sparrow took out a little gold pen and a dog-eared notebook. "We just have some routine questions."

I smiled. "Has my driver's license expired?"

"Nothing like that. We're investigating a crime and we hope you can help us out. You do want to help us, don't you?"

"Maybe I better see some ID."

Enameled badges with an American flag identified them as detectives for S.I.O.P.S., the Smithsonian Institution Office of Protection Services.

"Aren't you a little out of your jurisdiction?" I said, politely.

"We're a federal agency that protects American museums. The Seattle Art Museum got robbed yesterday. Three valuable

20

canvases went out through a service elevator while the guard was distracted."

"What does that have to do with me?"

He flipped open his notebook. "We just want to talk to you."

I sat behind my desk. "Okay, go ahead and talk."

Sparrow sat in one of my client chairs while Crane stalked around my gallery squinting at price tags.

"Have any suspicious characters been coming around your store recently?"

I almost laughed. "Let's just say I've acquired a varied clientele during twenty years in business."

"Do you know a man named Johnnie Radic?"

"Never heard of him."

"How about Mario Orsini?"

"He came by a couple days ago."

"Have you known him long?"

"I never met him before."

"Do you know him by any other name?"

"No, why do you ask?"

"We think he changed his name."

"You mean legally?"

He raised an eyebrow. "If he did do it legally, that would be the only legal thing he's ever done."

Crane interrupted from across the room. "It looks like a museum in here. Are these things valuable?"

"I like to think so," I said back.

"Are they works of art?"

"Some are."

Sparrow turned a page. "Did Orsini try to sell you anything?"

"He tried to sell me some fake saddlebags."

"How do you know they were fakes?"

"The same way I know your partner doesn't know much about art."

He blinked. "Did he try to buy anything?"

"No, he didn't try to buy anything."

"Did he invite you in on any kind of a deal?"

21

"Well…not really."

His little gold pen stopped in midair. "What is it?"

"It's probably nothing."

"Let me be the judge of that."

"He asked if I'd seen the Vizcaya Carpet in the Prado."

Sparrow adjusted his glasses. "Why did he ask about that?"

"I have no idea, but he seemed kind of nervous."

He scribbled something in his book. "We think Orsini's an alias and that he's actually a Serb."

"English wasn't his native language."

"His native language is money. Did you notice any accent?"

"He had some kind of accent. It could have been Serbian."

"We can't locate any photographs of him. Could you describe his appearance, how he was dressed?"

"Bald head, guillotine pale, and a loose-fitting suit."

"Was he missing any fingers?"

"He had ragged little stubs on each of his hands."

Crane angled back to me. "Would you have any objection to letting us see what you've got in your safe?"

Now I was getting annoyed. "Unless you've got a warrant, that's none of your business."

"We could make it our business." He said it with a look that implied 'civil rights violation'.

I smiled thinly. "You wouldn't like my business very much."

"Why not?"

"You have to put up with too many ill-mannered paper-shufflers."

He glowered before shooting a look at his partner.

I turned back to Sparrow. "Why are you asking about Orsini?"

"We think he's an art thief with an unusual interest in medieval manuscripts."

Crane tossed one of his cards on my desk. "The only thing we know for sure about Orsini is that his name is not Mario Orsini. If you hear from him again, you better give us a call. This guy is so crooked he could eat soup with a corkscrew."

6

Tyson sprang from the floor to check out the Spanish panel spread across my breakfast table. Since the death of my wife, this feral Russian Blue cat has been my most reliable drop-in friend. His face was scarred, and he was missing half an ear, but the look in his cool green eyes said, 'You should see the other guy'.

After stroking him slow and careful, the way he likes, I gently shooed him off the table so I could examine the colors. I needed to verify that all the dyes dated from the Middle Ages.

White lamb's wool had been used for the scallop shells decorating the pale blue border, but at least a dozen other colors were dyed with natural pigments that were being used six hundred years ago.

The soft yellow used for the field of stars was derived from pomegranate or larkspur, but several brighter stars, arranged in a curious pattern, had been dyed with a sunny yellow tone that only came from the precious saffron flower.

Subtle shadings in the green background to the stars signified a green that had been made by over-dying yellow yarn with blue, and I counted four different shades of blue. Sky, Cornflower, Aquamarine, and Denim. Some of these were derived from indigo leaves, others from a flowering plant known as Dyer's Woad.

Most of the red tones were made from the root of the madder plant, Rubia Tinctorum, but a more bluish shade of red had been used for some of the smaller motifs. Known as carmine, the only source of this color was two types of insects: cochineal beetles that thrive on a cactus that grows in Spain, and female lac bugs that live on a tree that only grows in India.

Two shades of brown had been used: a chocolate tone as an outline color, and a softer shade as background for the inscription cartouche. These had been dyed with walnut husks or oakbark.

A confirmation of great age was that the black pile used for the writing inside the inscription cartouche had lost most of its nap. The iron oxides used to produce this type of dye caused the wool to slowly deteriorate.

I was surprised to find that the triple-corded selvedge along the side had been wrapped in silk, and that it was dyed a distinctive shade of purple. Known since the days of ancient Greece as *The Color of Kings,* the only source for this color was the glands of tiny sea snails found in the Mediterranean.

Tyrian Purple has always been highly prized. Ten thousand snails had to be sacrificed to produce just one gram of the precious dye.

I got another surprise when I flipped it over to examine the weave. The wefts, the horizonal interlocking threads between the rows of knots, had been woven in alternating shades of red and gold silk. Normally these were undyed wool or cotton yarn.

All the colors had the profound depth and clarity of great antiquity, but I had to put it aside. It was time to take my nearly undrivable car to Gus's Auto Repair, a block up from my gallery.

Tammy Wynette was singing about standing by her man from a tinny sounding radio as I pulled into a stall smelling of oil and grease. A matched pair of legs was poking out from beneath a white pickup truck parked in the space next to me. Leaning over the legs, I shouted, "Hey, Gus, you got time to fix my car? I'm a working man too."

A metal tool hit the floor, and a *bzt* sound was followed by a curse. "If you come down here, I'll show you what real work looks like."

I waited while a long-limbed man rolled himself out on the little wheeled thing car guys call a 'creeper' and stood to wipe his hands on a greasy rag. A sweat-stained baseball cap was turned backwards on his head, and 'Gus' was stitched on his blue coveralls.

"What did you do to your car this time?"

"I didn't do anything. Someone tried to pry my trunk open with a hook and a chain."

"What do you keep in there, gold?"

"Don't I wish."

"When did it happen?"

"Last night."

"Someone stole a chain off my tow truck last night. It had a hook at one end."

He kept talking, but I didn't hear a word. I couldn't take my eyes off the Ottoman-era cushion he was using on his creeper. It was a *yastik*. One side was silk pile with a classic sickle leaf design. The other side was a richly decorated flat weave.

"How about selling me that little cushion before you totally wreck it?"

"That old thing's worth some money? How much?"

"A collector would pay two thousand bucks, maybe more."

"Two thousand bucks?" he said, his eyes widening. "I better ask my wife. It's from her family."

"Does she know what you're using it for?"

"No, she doesn't. And you better not tell her."

"I won't tell her if you promise to fix my car."

"I'll have it ready this afternoon, if I can find a trunk lid to match your faded blue paint."

Two women wearing high heels, fur coats, and sunglasses came in shortly after I opened. The redhead seemed perplexed by my Angkor Wat buddha head. "Could it really be a thousand years-old?" she said.

"It was part of a Buddhist temple in Cambodia."

"How do you know it's not a fake?"

25

"Nobody lasts twenty years in this business if they can't tell the difference between a real one and a fake."

The blonde fingered the tag. "The price does seem rather high."

"It took several years to carve it."

"How could you possibly know how long it took?"

"Professional stone carvers have tried making one without using any mechanical tools."

"Well," she huffed, "I know enough not to be had."

A short man with rosy cheeks and a halo of wiry-gray hair glanced around the gallery as he approached my desk. The sagging pockets of his loose-fitting tweed hunting jacket were stuffed full of small objects.

"You buy old watches?"

"Nope."

"How about jewelry?"

"Nope."

"Coins?"

"I'd be interested in a Brasher Doubloon with an EB on the eagle's breast."

He was halfway out the door when he stopped. "What might one of those be worth?"

"The last one that turned up brought seven million dollars."

Bushy eyebrows came down across the rim of his glasses in a sudden look of shrewdness. "I'll keep an eye out."

Half an hour later, a man in his twenties came in. He was cradling a small Pakistani rug of the cheapest quality. "Abraham marked this down from twelve hundred to five hundred. I'm wondering if I should buy it."

"I can't tell you what to do."

"I just need to know if it's a good deal."

"I charge a hundred and fifty for an appraisal."

He was angry when he left, but he should not have been.

I was getting ready to close when Jay and Stanley pushed open the door. Jay, round-faced and chubby, always wore a dark suit, white shirt, and a skinny tie. Stanley, thin with hair that stuck up on top, dressed casual and never spoke much.

They used to run a fancy antique store, but now they scoured garage sales, estate sales, and auctions for things they could sell to other dealers.

Jay led the way while Stanley struggled in with a bundle of rugs and textiles draped over his shoulder. I grinned at the sight. "It looks like Stanley hijacked a caravan."

Jay rested one hand on his ample hip. "We talked our way into an estate sale a day early."

Stanley gave a timid nod and began rolling out an assortment of bazaar-quality weavings from the 1950s.

"Sorry, fellows. I can't sell anything that has synthetic colors."

"But they're old," Jay said.

"Not for my clients. They want things that were made before Thomas Edison lit up his first lightbulb."

Jay frowned and glanced at Stanley. "OK. You like a good deal. How about a hundred bucks apiece?"

"It's not about the price. It's the age and the bright colors."

"We also bought this," he said, reaching into his jacket and pulling out a knotted pile weaving that looked like a face mask.

"I can pay you two hundred bucks for this one," I said, turning it over in my hands. "It's a *tek hab*, a headpiece for a Tibetan pack horse. The Tantric Buddhist symbols are meant to provide magical protection. Not many survive the hard use they get up in the Himalayas."

Jay's eyes lit up at getting that much for a such a small piece, but he turned it into a grimace of distaste when I handed him the check.

The expression on his face changed to one of intense curiosity when he spotted the Spanish panel on my desk. "Where'd you get this?"

"It's a half panel of a medieval Spanish table cover."

"I know what it is. How much are you selling it for?"

27

"I'm holding it for a client."

Jay leaned in for a closer look as Lee came to stand beside him Lee pointed at the shell motif in the border. Jay met his eye, nodded, and turned to me. "I assume you know that's the Shell of Saint James."

"What do you mean?"

"Those aren't just any old seashells. Those are scallop shells."

"So?"

"At the time this was made, scallop shells symbolized the Camino, the pilgrimage route going through France and Spain to the shrine of Saint James."

"Thanks for the tip. It's the first medieval textile I've ever found."

Jay made a little waving motion with the check as he followed Stanley to the door. "I hope you've priced it accordingly."

"I'm still thinking about that."

"If I were you, I'd be thinking more about what scallop shells are doing on a table cover of that era. Of course, if I tell you everything I know, that might end up being a free appraisal."

7

I discovered that Jay had been right about the scallop shell motif while nuzzling my morning cup of coffee and flipping through a musty opus on medieval history. A full-page picture of a white scallop was titled *The Shell of Saint James.*

James acquired the honor of becoming the first Christian martyr when King Herod had him decapitated in Jerusalem in 44 AD. He made the news again later when his body was dug up and his head had miraculously reattached itself. Then, for unexplained reasons, his magical remains were transported to northern Spain in a stone boat blown across the sea by angels.

It wasn't clear why they reburied him in Galicia, but Saint James illustrious bones were lost or forgotten for hundreds of years until a hermit-monk named Pelagius rediscovered them in the year 813. Out wandering around one night, he came upon a mysterious star hovering over a green field and hurried off to tell the townsfolk. After arming themselves with pitchforks and shovels, a mob of people came and dug up the bones of St. James.

As word of the miracle spread, Christian armies gloriously reunited beneath the banner of Saint James took back all of Spain from the Muslims. Some reports said that James reappeared and joined in the final battles.

It was difficult to understand how such celebrated bones could become lost for so many centuries, but it didn't seem to bother the people who built a cathedral to house those bones on the field where they were found. Even more interesting was what they named it. Santiago de Compostella means *Saint James of the Field of Stars* in English.

Christians who managed to travel to Rome or Jerusalem had always been assured of extraordinary blessings, but once the Cathedral of Santiago de Compostela was built, it became the world's most popular pilgrimage site. Every year, half a million pilgrims would march along the old Roman roads now called The Way of Saint James, The Way, or simply The Camino.

Some towns along The Way witnessed thousands of pilgrims streaming through every day with their four Way of St. James Essentials: a big hat, a long staff, a gourd to drink from, and a scallop shell. Scallop shells were also attached to posts marking the trail, and those who carried one were entitled to food and shelter at churches and abbeys along the way.

But why a scallop shell? It's because the grooved lines from the outer rim that meet at the base represent all the different pilgrimage routes that eventually come together at the tomb.

I was having a hard time picturing anybody plodding along for months on end just to pay homage to some dubious old bones until something occurred to me. It's not the destination—it's the journey.

The adventure along the Camino was its own reward, the people you met and the lessons you learned along the way. Then again, maybe you could say the same thing about life?

I stopped on the way to my store to order 8 x 10 glossy prints of the photos I had taken, and the phone started ringing as soon as I unlocked my gallery door.

"Artifacts," I said, with the emphasis on 'art' as I always did when picking up.

"This is Mrs. Eskenazi. The auction told me you asked about the weaving you bought. I'm sorry to say I sent it in by mistake. I must have accidently put it into a box with things I wanted to get rid of. I'm calling to tell you we can't sell you the other piece because our daughter Laura has it."

Those were not the words I had been hoping to hear.

"Is there any chance your daughter might be willing to sell me the other half?"

"Oh dear." She sighed. "All I can do is ask. She's teaching three classes a day on religions of the world at a commune on the other side of the state near Walla Walla. They offered her a job there three months ago and now she's so busy we hardly ever hear from her."

"Is that the place the newspapers call Rancho Sutara? Swami something-or-other? One of those guru guys from India who drives around in vintage Cadillacs and has his followers wearing lime green?"

"That's the one. They came from India and built a small city on the old Wheeler cattle ranch. But they don't all wear lime green. The leadership wear a more emerald green."

"Would I be able to call her? I'd like to find out if she might be interested in selling her piece to me."

"I do have a number you can try, but I wouldn't count on her selling it. The Swami said it was full of spiritual vibrations when Laura's friends showed it to him."

I pictured an image of the woman at the Buckaroo Bar while punching in the number.

"Taja-Sutara Ashram."

"I'm trying to reach one of your members, a woman named Laura Eskenazi."

"One moment, please."

I heard people talking, then a scraping sound followed by laughter as someone picked up the phone.

"Hello, this is Laura."

"My name is Tony Shepherd. I spoke on the phone with your mother about one panel of an old table cover that she consigned to the auction. I purchased the panel and I'd like to buy the other half from you if you're willing to sell it."

There was such a lengthy emptiness on the line that I thought she had disconnected. "Are you there?"

"Yes, I'm here," she snapped. "I've heard nothing about this. Who exactly are you?"

"I'm an artifacts dealer in Seattle."

"And you're telling me my mother put the other half of our family heirloom into an auction?"

"That's right."

A brief silence.

"I can't discuss this right now. Give me your phone number, and I'll get back to you when I can."

After giving her my number, she hung up.

I stared at the phone for a few seconds before putting it down.

8

Shafts of sunlight poking through the morning's mass of gray motivated me to put on my sweats and drive up to my favorite workout steps running down the woodsy west slope of Phinney Ridge. If I got there early, I could have them all to myself.

I got there early but didn't exactly have them to myself. Bradley the Bum was seated on the top stair taking in the view of the Olympic Mountains on the other side of Puget Sound with a quart of Colt 45 in a brown paper bag.

Bradley was pushing forty, had a shaved head, and wore layers of clothing topped by a hooded sweatshirt. I met him here about a year ago and learned he had been a top Greco-Roman wrestler at college before changing his lifestyle. After finding out I had done martial arts, he gave me training tips, such as:

"Don't stoop. Keep your back straight and your arms up high to focus more on the legs... One step at a time helps for quick moves because it works the lower legs...Two at a time helps for power moves because it works the thighs."

He nodded a silent greeting.

"How's it going?" I said. "I haven't seen you in a while."

"I'm good. I spent a few weeks over at that Swami ranch with all the people in green. They were bussing some homeless people over, so I figured I'd take a crack at free room and board."

I could hardly believe my ears. "I saw those yellow school buses on the news. Why were they doing that?"

"It was a scam to get us registered to vote. Hardly any people live in that dry part of the state, so they thought they could take over the county by running their own people."

"What was it like over there?"

"I was hoping for one of those yoga and yogurt kind of places, but they had people spying on you all the time."

"What do you mean?"

"You couldn't take a piss without somebody reporting it to that Sheena broad who runs the place. My buddies thought she had the whole place bugged. They were in the can talking about smoking weed and got busted right off by the Peace Force cops."

"Did they give you work to do?"

"They treated us good until the county said we couldn't vote. Then they put us in a Physical Worship Group and ran us like dogs digging in rocky ground twelve hours a day. I don't mind hard work, but they'd only let us have one beer. Not only that, but they slipped something into it that made me feel doped up."

I walked to the bottom and ran back up, thinking about how to pry more information out of Bradley. "Are there still lots of people over there?"

"You better believe it. Thousands show up whenever he gives one of his talks. You gotta go to those. No choice. And they always gave us one of their funny beers before he did his spiel."

"Are they letting people come in and visit?"

"If they think you've got money, they'll welcome you in. Might even let you meet the Swami. Otherwise, it's a bunch of control freaks checking people in and out."

"Did you get to meet him?"

"Hell no, just the show he puts on for his lectures."

"How come they buy him all those vintage Cadillacs?"

"The old guy likes to drive them, and it brings tons of free publicity."

"They feed you okay?"

"That's the other thing. Soggy vegetarian sandwiches for lunch, and dinner was always a dog fight with tired people standing in endless lines. I guess if you love the Swami, you don't mind stuff like that."

"How'd you get out?"

"They told me there wouldn't be another bus back to Seattle for two weeks, so I decided to sneak out and hitchhike back. I was mostly scared of the rattlesnakes, but a guy told me rattlers sleep at night when it's cool. I just waited for a cool night."

"How'd you do it?"

"Except for the guard houses and the Swami place they call Jesus Grove, they cut the electricity from midnight to six. I waited till three in the morning and snuck out back where there aren't any roads. They don't guard that part because it's a national forest. Then I circled around past the main guard tower and hiked out to the highway. It was a long hike, but I got a ride about sunrise with a farmer hauling hay. Why are you asking all these questions?"

"There's a woman living there I'd like to see, so I'm wondering what it's like. What's the deal about joining up?"

"I don't know exactly, but the people who live there are all joined up. Some of my buddies joined because it was easier than living on the street. All it took was to say you want to go the Swami route, something like that. Then they give you a Swami name and some beads called a mala."

"Are they wooden beads?" I said, picturing the broken string of beads from my car break-in.

"That's right, round ones with the Swami's picture. If they're wearing the beads, they're joined up even if they aren't wearing the green."

"What did you think of the Swami?"

A thoughtful pull on the bottle. "Just another guy trying to explain the inexplicable."

"Did he explain it?"

"Not really. But Einstein already nailed that. He said everybody should just accept that we're surrounded by a great mystery."

35

9

She swept in shouldering a white tote bag over a black sheath dress. She wore no jewelry. She didn't need jewelry. The creamy skin, ebony hair, and eyes the color of a clear blue sky said it all. The feminine curves drew my attention, but it was her intelligent eyes that reeled me in. They radiated a strong sense of self, and a touch of loneliness. All of this went through my head like a bolt of lightning.

"I'm so glad you're here, Mr. Shepherd. I'm Laura Eskenazi. My mother told me about the mistake she made putting part of our family heritage into the auction. I'm hoping you can sell it back to me. I'll pay cash and give you a reasonable profit."

The smile lit up her face like a summer sunrise, but it was not enough to alter my agenda. "I'm sorry, but I already promised to show it to one of my most loyal clients on Saturday. I don't dare go back on my word. He'd be even happier if I could sell him both halves."

"But it's a family heirloom. It wasn't supposed to be sold."

"Is that the other half you've got in your bag?" I said, hoping to turn things in a different direction.

She nodded.

"I can't promise anything, but if you let me take a look, I might be able to tell you something about it."

Moving with a swift feminine grace, she took it out of the bag and handed it over. For a moment I stood speechlessly staring as I considered what to say. The size and weave were the same as mine, but hers had a startling anomaly in the design—a crown motif in the upper left corner was woven with threads of real gold.

"The golden crown is unusual," I said. "And that raises some interesting questions because royal families normally used their family crest. If you would let me sell the two pieces joined together, a serious collector might pay us some serious money."

Her face tightened, and her eyes blazed. "Nonono! No way am I going to give up the part I have. What I want is the whole rug and the inscription."

"I'm sorry, but the inscription is also of interest to my client. Please, let me take some pictures so I can do more research and I'll let you know what I find out."

She nodded, but her lips were tight.

Anxious to grab some photos, I almost stumbled as I maneuvered around, shooting rapid-fire shots. The crown motif made it all too obvious that selling the panels joined together would be far more profitable than selling just a half.

I breathed in a fragrance like orange blossoms when I handed the panel back to her, and I was desperately trying to think of some way to keep the joining option open on both fronts—the lovely lady, and the ever more astounding table cover.

Hoping my charm wasn't wearing too thin, I offered a grin. "There must be a way you and I can work something out."

She eyed me suspiciously. "What's that supposed to mean?"

"Well, if my client doesn't buy my half, I could contact your parents and try to come up with something that would be good for all of us."

She didn't take it the way I hoped. A sizzling glint burned in her sky-blue eyes. "But that's not fair. You're taking advantage of my mother's mistake."

"I'm sorry it turned out this way," I said, and I meant it. "But once I offer something to a client, I've got a professional obligation to follow through."

An icy look raked me over me from head to toe as she put the panel back in her bag. "Professional isn't the label I'd be giving you."

"I know how you feel, but I bought it fair and square."
Her eyes frosted. "Nobody knows how anybody *feels*."
"Where did you learn that?"
"What difference does it make?"
Sure, I felt bad. I liked this woman. She was straightforward, not afraid to assert herself, and looked at me like she was looking into my soul. But there are times when you can't help disappointing people, and this was one of them.
She walked out without another word—and she looked good doing it.

That golden crown had me more than puzzled. A crown is not only a symbol of power: they can represent honor, glory, righteousness, and immortality. Hoping to find something similar, I spent the rest of the day going through all my books on European rugs, and twenty years of auction catalogues.

After hours of searching, I had gained nothing but a throbbing headache. All I'd found was a Greek mosaic with a design that vaguely resembled the seashell border, and a repeating star design on some thousand-year-old wall tiles inside the Alhambra.

Coming up with nothing is a form of information, but it's still nothing. When I closed the last book, I considered what I had. It wasn't much. It was less than that. I was stuck, and I had only a few days to come up with a price.

On top of that, I was having second thoughts about having promised the panel to Doctor Paterson.

The dream I had that night was strange and unsettling. I was sitting at a table covered by a rumpled rug in a room illuminated by a spectral blue light. Wooden doors went all around the walls, and people outside were twisting at the knobs, clamoring to get in.

Suddenly, the patterns began to glow, the colors pulsated, and a spooky thing resembling rubbery lips began whispering to me in a gibberish language. To say it was horrifying would be putting it mildly. But, for some reason, I was drawn to the voice and repelled by it at the same time.

Then an electrical jolt shot through me, followed by bells ringing, and my eyes popped open to the raucous insistence of my bedside phone. The numbers on the digital clock said 2:59 in pale green and a man's voice was telling me the burglar alarm had just gone off at my gallery.

Alarms always seem to go off after the bars close, and it had reset like it did when some drunk banged on the window, but I needed to check it out. Throwing on some clothes, I rushed out with a powerful steel-cased Maglite in one hand and my keys in the other.

Driving way too fast, I made a rubber shredding turn onto Fremont, and lurched to a stop in front of my gallery. In the eerie glow of the streetlights, everything looked normal, but I got out anyway to scan the street for suspicious-looking characters. I was the only one.

Swinging the flash to and fro, I followed my shadow into the blackness of the alley. There was an ominous silence as I beamed my light into the tree-lined parking area behind the building, seeing everything that should be there and nothing else.

Then I heard it. A soft sound like my own footsteps. Suddenly I was aware of everything: a cool breeze stirring the air, dark shapes beneath the trees, and my own ragged breathing. I stopped to listen. Heard it again. A sound like someone trying not to make a sound. Then it stopped, like a kind of echo. But it wasn't an echo. My pulse quickened when I made out a human form. An unknown presence was walking beyond the trees, pacing me.

Or had it been a shadow? When I tried to focus, it vanished. I listened again. Hearing nothing but the sound of distant traffic, I turned back to the comfort of the streetlights.

A blue and white police car cruised by and stopped abruptly when I emerged from the shadows. Holding my hands away from my body so they could see them, I moved farther into the light. "This is my store. My security company notified me that the alarm had gone off. I live close by, so I came to check it out."

"We had a report that someone was walking around the apartment building next to you, trying all the doors."

"I thought I saw someone walking around back there."

"We'll circle the area. You might want to check inside."

"I'll do that."

I was digging out my keys when I remembered my dream about people trying to open doors.

Security is always an issue in any business that is a magnet for thieves, so my entry was secured by bulletproof locks similar to padlocks, but stronger and more complicated. I also had the alarm, motion detectors, and decorative bars behind the windows.

It took some fumbling to get all three locks open, then I hurried inside to deactivate the alarm and flip on the lights. Everything was fine, so I re-set the alarm, turned off the lights, and left thinking that the sensitive motion detectors must have registered a false alarm.

The police drove by again while I was replacing the locks. I gave them a thumbs up. As they drove off, I noticed fresh gouges in the wood, like someone had tried to pry one of the locks off with a steel bar. That would be difficult to do, but violent shaking could have triggered the alarm.

So, someone had tried to break in, but bailed when they discovered my security was no pushover. Hoping the gouges might reveal some deeper secrets I studied them from a couple different angles, but nothing was revealed.

When I got home, I was too tired to read, but not tired enough to sleep. After pouring myself a stiff shot of sour mash salvation, I sat in my wicker rocker thinking about stealthy footsteps, catlike women, and golden crowns.

Maybe it was two or three stiff shots.

Old bourbon whiskey tasted pretty good at four in the morning.

10

A Los Angeles art dealer who sold to the highest concentration of wealthy Iranians outside Iran was coming to see a section of a Qajar dynasty hunting tent. Artifacts from the days of Persian glory were often made in an opulent fashion. Delicate woolen piecework in the form of birds, blossoms, and flowers was pieced together and then decorated with sumptuous chain-stitch silk embroidery.

I was draping it over a display rack when a white Toyota Camry rental car pulled to the curb and a portly dark-haired man in his sixties came in wearing a blue Corneliani suit, a creamy white shirt, and a silk tie with flowers.

"It's always a pleasure to see you, Mr. Shepherd," he said, smiling like a politician and gripping my hand so tightly I thought he might not give it back.

"Nice to see you too, Joseph. How are things in LA?"

Releasing his grip, he sighed and gazed down at the floor. "Not so good. Prices are lower than they used to be, and only the best pieces are selling."

I refrained from asking why he was on a buying trip if things were so terrible in LA, while he prowled around my gallery, glancing briefly at everything before condescending to look at the dazzling gem I had laid out for him.

"How much is it?" he said, without looking at me.

"Ten thousand."

"Ten thousand?" he said, raising his hands in supplication to the Almighty. "You are always too hard with me."

41

"It's similar in style to a well-known Persian hunting tent in the Cleveland Museum of Art."

"Yes, but that's a complete tent, with woven lace windows and all its interior walls and hallways."

"They're also not likely to sell you any pieces of it," I said.

He gave a sorrowful look and spread his arms apart. "I bought a similar panel at auction for only forty-five hundred."

"That just means there wasn't much competition," I said back.

He couldn't argue. Everybody knew dealers form rings. One does the bidding, so they get it cheaply. Afterwards the team split the amount they would have paid. But he had not disputed it was Qajar Dynasty, so maybe I should have asked fifteen-grand.

Still putting on a show, he pulled out a tiny tape measure, and measured the sides and ends with theatrical care. "Your tent panel is crooked," he said, shaking his head sadly. "That makes it less valuable."

Hand-woven textiles are never exact, but why argue? "All I can do is give you a dealer discount and knock off five hundred."

Taking a step back, he raised his hands palm out in a gesture of rejection. "Just give me your best price. Then I'll either buy it or I'll pass."

It sounds sensible, but the ancient ritual of hammering out a deal has one eternal element—the buyer always offers less. Instead of lowering my price, I called his move by draping the Qajar panel over a chair, like it was out of play.

Now it was his turn to make a move, and I was surprised when he didn't. Instead, he turned away to examine the Spanish piece that was spread across my desk. "What have you got here? Have I seen this before?"

"I just got it, so nobody's seen it before."

"Somebody sent me a photo of something very similar."

"Did it have a design like this?"

"I believe it did, except theirs had an unusual crown motif at one end."

For a moment I was too stunned to speak. "What were they trying to find out?"

"The usual stuff. They wanted to know what it was, and what it was worth."

"What did you tell them?"

"I don't handle that sort of thing, so I referred them to the Textile Museum in Washington D.C."

"The Textile Museum never does valuations."

"No, but they would like to have a piece like that in their collection."

Twenty minutes later, I was mulling over who might have been sending out photos of Laura's half when another white Toyota Camry pulled up and another out-of-town dealer came strutting in.

Benjamin, from New York, didn't spend a single second looking around. He flew straight to the Qajar tent panel behind my desk. Without pausing to examine it, he spread his arms wide and said, "Mr. Shepherd, this is not a Qajar Dynasty piece."

A piercing jolt of clarity ran through me. I'd never even talked to Benjamin about it, let alone told him it was Qajar Dynasty. He must be working the town with Joseph.

Born into families that had been in the rug business for generations, they had a hard time believing a guy like me could know as much as them. They got away with these little cons when I started out, but I had seen it all too often and knew how to give it back.

"And look," he said. "It's crooked. I prefer to buy them when they're not so crooked. How much is it?"

The only thing crooked around here was these two buyers, so I decided to jam him. "I'm sorry to have to tell you this, but I offered it on the phone to a client a few minutes before you came in. You'll have to check back in a couple days."

His shoulders slumped, and he raised his hands in defeat. Then he looked upward as if he was gazing into the heavens. His timing was so effective, I almost looked up there myself. If they ever award an Olympic gold medal for gestures, these guys could win it every time, hands down.

Benjamin didn't have another move, so I tried to pick his brain. "You read Persian and Arabic. Maybe you can tell me what the inscription says on this old Spanish piece."

He puzzled over it for a while. "The writing looks like the Hebrew we studied at synagogue. That word there," he pointed. "That's the Hebrew word for temple."

"Hebrew!" Danny had said the same thing. I had to sit down. "That's unheard of."

"It's not entirely unheard of. They used Hebrew on Ottoman era rugs that were made to cover the entrance to the synagogues. But this is way too small for that."

If this was Hebrew writing, I'd been missing something important. After flipping over my *Closed* sign, I hurried out to pick up my 8 x 10 glossy photos that would show both panels.

I was shuffling through them on my desk when a curious kind of thrill began coursing through me. If photos of both panels were placed side-by-side to make a complete image, a three-dimensional vision materialized.

The brighter yellow stars formed an ovoid shape, like a constellation, and the crown in one corner and the cartouche in the opposite floated within that field of stars like oddly shaped UFO's.

It was dimly perceived, but definitely there. Then it was gone, and I could no longer make out what it was.

A peculiar sensation was still tickling my brain after I folded the panels into the safe and slid the locking bolts into place. The pictures had been telling me something that I could not see.

11

The snow-white cone of Mount Rainier towered in the distance as I drove to the south part of town and parked behind an old model Mercedes with a flat tire. The brother of a friend had called about an oriental carpet he wanted to sell. Calls like this could be a waste of time, but Howard had given the right answers to my list of screening questions.

After climbing the wobbly wooden steps to the front porch, I stood waiting for someone to answer my knock on a rusted screen door. I was about to give up when I caught a flicker of movement behind the grimy curtains. I knocked again, and the door opened just far enough to reveal the gaunt face of a forty-year-old man.

He studied me with suspicion before realizing who I was. "Sorry, Tony. This neighborhood's gotten so I don't want to open the door. If it ain't someone wanting me to donate money, it's bums with backpacks trying to rip off my stuff."

He pushed open the screen door. "C'mon in. The rug's in back."

It took a few seconds for my eyes to adjust to the darkness. All the shades were drawn, and the place was a mess. Overflowing ashtrays and greasy pizza boxes were wherever somebody had forgotten them last.

I caught a whiff of decay when he led me through the cluttered dining room and past the kitchen. A swarm of houseflies was buzzing above a sink full of dirty dishes.

It crossed my mind that I might want to find myself another line of work when he led me into a musty-smelling hallway, but

45

my spirits rose when I saw an antique Persian carpet through the doorway to a lighted room.

My spirits rose even higher when I realized it was made of silk, but they sank like a rock when I saw it was ripped and torn like it had been mutilated by an ax-wielding madman.

Sucking in breath, I let him have it. "This was a museum piece before it got wrecked. What the hell happened to it?"

He was slow to answer, like he hadn't expected this question to come up on the final. "I rented the place to some buddies of mine, and they used it outside under the patio table. You sure you can't get it fixed?"

"This is so finely-woven that the tiniest repair would cost a fortune. Now it's worthless, except to cut up for pillows. I can't pay more than a hundred bucks for a mess like this."

He picked a moth off the pile and crushed it between his fingers. "I'd sell it for a hundred."

"I'd have paid you sixty-grand before your friends destroyed it."

Cruel, but I wanted him to feel some pain.

Someone hammered on the ceiling from the room above, and a shrill voice called out. "Howard? Is that you, Howard?"

"Yes, Mom. It's me."

"Who are you talking to?"

"I've got company, Mom. You don't need to yell so loud."

"When are you going to bring my breakfast?"

"You had your breakfast. Take one of those red pills and go back to sleep."

After a moment of silence, he turned to me with a faint smile. "Are you interested in seeing some old guns?"

I shrugged. "I know a little about Colts and Winchesters."

He chuckled. "You'll like these."

He led me further down the hallway into another bedroom reeking of gun oil and cheap perfume. Dozens of rifles stood against the walls, and a *Shotgun News* magazine was propped open on a bedside table with a black handled Nazi dagger.

I stifled a grin when he bent to toss a frilly pink slip into a closetful of flashy women's clothes. Talk about a Freudian slip. No way did those disco dresses belong to his elderly mother.

"Check these out," he said, reaching into a jumble of vintage pistols spread across the unmade bed.

He handed me an ivory-gripped Colt Peacemaker, an old-time cowboy gun, a Colt automatic straight out of a Bogart movie, and a sinister looking German officer's Luger.

I enjoy examining these classic weapons, but I was beginning to feel uneasy in a room full of guns with this guy.

"Are you selling these, too?" I said.

"No, but I sold a crate of fully-auto AK-47s to a cocky little jerk who's buying for that Swami group over by Walla Walla. Calls himself Prim Noron, or Moron, some shit like that. Didn't know squat about guns. Said they've got a fifty-man squad trained in commando tactics and are looking for silencers."

Silencers. That was shocking news. "Why would they want silencers? Are they planning to assassinate someone?"

"So long as I get paid, what they do with this stuff's none of my business. The guy asked if I knew anything about using explosives with airplanes. Hell," he smirked, "I've got ideas for bombs nobody's even thought of."

He picked up a pistol with a long barrel. "Take a look at this baby. It's an old German machine pistol called a Broom Handle."

Seeing that my hands were full, he tossed the gun on the bed and lifted a glass water pipe from the bedside table. The pipe gurgled when he held a match to it but didn't smell like pot when he exhaled. He caught my questioning look.

"I crushed up some Oxycontin pills I got from the guy buying the AK-47s. Said he could get anything I want through the Swami medical clinic. Uppers, downers, Ludes. What a set-up. You want a hit?"

"No thanks."

"Go ahead," he said, holding the pipe just inches from my face. "It will help you relax."

Howard didn't look relaxed. His eyes were dancing, and a smudge of lipstick was showing on one of his teeth. Suddenly the room felt way too cramped, and I wanted out.

Okay, I admit it—being alone in a room full of guns with an armed and loaded, cross-dressing dope-head can have that effect on me.

"Sorry Howard. I'm on the job. In fact, I'd better be on my way. Tell you what," I said, reaching for my wallet. "I'll give you a hundred cash for the rug."

After wrapping my arms around the unwieldly bundle, I eased my way out his door, and drove away as fast as I legally could.

When I got home, I turned on the evening news to catch up on the latest doom and disaster. BREAKING NEWS flashed across the bottom of the screen while a breathless presenter recapped the story of a massive salmonella outbreak in Walla Walla, the largest city close to the Swami ranch.

"A shattered community is struggling to come to terms with a horror that visited this once peaceful city. Hospitals and clinics are overflowing with people who have been poisoned. First reports say that eight-hundred victims are experiencing severe headaches, diarrhea, vomiting, and chills. We now pass you to our correspondent who is on the scene in Walla Walla."

The image changed to another reporter standing outside a Taco Time surrounded by flashing lights and the sound of sirens wailing in the background.

"Questions are being asked, but answers are eluding everyone. Some are calling it the largest case of bioterrorism in American history. Nobody has died yet, but ages of the victims range from a six-month-old baby to an eighty-nine-year-old grandmother."

The camera zoomed in on a stretcher bearing a fragile white-haired lady with tubes in her arms, then back to the reporter.

"Public health investigators have traced the source of the poisoning to contaminated salad dressings in ten of the city's most popular restaurants. More on this story now, direct from a news conference taking place live at the Swami commune."

Portentous music played as the screen switched to a string of green SUVs escorting a pink Cadillac with huge tailfins across a desert landscape.

Then to a dark-haired, olive-skinned woman in her thirties wearing an emerald-green robe. Men in lime green police uniforms stood stiffly on either side of her with rifles across their chests as a fluffy-haired reporter shouted out a question.

"As Swami's second in command, do you have anything to say in response to allegations that the poisoning of an entire town might be traced back to your group as retaliation for the county not allowing the homeless people you bussed in to vote in the upcoming election?"

Glaring imperiously, Sheena stared into the camera. "It won't be my hand those liars can kiss," she said, smirking to let the meaning sink in.

"Won't that sound heartless to those who are praying for their loved ones as we speak?"

"We're here to stay," she sneered, baring her white teeth. "If that means blood will be spilled, then that's the price we're prepared to pay."

The microphones moved an inch closer. "Are you suggesting there might be violence?"

Contempt filled her face. "If those bigoted pigs touch even one of our people, I'll take twenty of their ugly heads."

Spiritual endeavors were rapidly becoming less transcendental at the Swami ranch.

12

I was staring into the gloom of a lose-lose kind of situation when the day for showing the panel had arrived. Since buying it, the mystery of it had grown and expanded until it had become far more beguiling than any money I might earn. But I couldn't go back on my word. Dealers live and die by their reputations, so the only option I had left was to price it as high as I could.

Doctor Paterson was late, so I rummaged in my safe hoping to find something else to tempt him with. I was removing an 18th-century Caucasian embroidery when he came in carrying a leather shoulder bag. "Sorry I'm late, Tony, but traffic is a mess."

"Not a problem," I said, unfolding the Caucasian embroidery. "It gave me a chance to dig something out that you might like even better."

I was holding it high to catch a few rays of sunlight, when a white van, suspiciously short of windows, pulled in and blocked the light. I noticed vaguely that nobody got out.

Doctor Paterson took a quick look at the embroidery, checked his watch, and went straight to the touchy topic. "That's a nice one, Tony, but you called me about a medieval Spanish piece."

"After washing it, I realized it shows more wear than you usually like, and I need to get twenty-five-grand for it. This Caucasian piece is less expensive and might be better suited for your collection."

"I appreciate knowing that, but I'll never convince my wife if I come home with something different than what I told her about."

Controlling my emotions, I took the table cover out of the safe and pointed with my finger at several inconsequential low spots. My attempt at subtlety didn't work.

"Even with a bit of wear, it is most unusual. But I'll have to show it to Claire before I can make a final decision."

I closed my eyes and opened them again. "Can I carry it to the car for you."

"No thanks. It will fit in my bag."

"You sure?"

"Absolutely. I parked around the corner."

That was the deal I'd agreed to, but I was dying inside after he left. All I could hope for was that Claire might not like it, or that my price would be more than he could afford.

Twenty seconds later, I was jolted out of my gloom by the heart-stopping sound of screeching brakes, and people screaming. Rushing out the door, I was almost run down by some skateboard-riding nitwit.

Then I got hit by the sight of Doctor Paterson stretched out on the pavement behind his blue Mercedes. The bag with the Spanish piece was nowhere to be seen. A woman took my arm to steady me. "I've already called for an aid car."

I had knelt to examine a bloody cut that was oozing from Doctor Paterson's forehead when a local character known as Bicycle Man skidded to a stop. Dressed in a brown woolen jumpsuit he must have knit himself, the thing that bothered people was not what he wore. People shied away from Bicycle Man because he was always smiling. He wasn't smiling now.

"I saw it all," he said. "Two women came out of the laundromat and crossed the street real quick. One of them grabbed that guy's bag while the other hit him from behind. Before he hit the ground, a white delivery van came tearing around the corner, and sped off as soon as they climbed in."

"Did you catch the plate number?"

"I was too far away."

I glanced at the laundromat across the street. With people coming and going, it was an ideal cover for watching my shop. Bicycle Man turned away to talk to someone else, and I bent to pick up a gold hoop earring that was sparkling in the gutter. Where had I seen that before?

After the aid car took Jim away, I went inside to gather myself, and had just sat down behind my desk when a champagne-colored Bentley glided slowly into the parking space just vacated by the white delivery van.

I knew I was in for a difficult day when the driver's door swung open and the same broad-shouldered tough guy who had been prowling around my store got out and looked my way.

Then the passenger door swung open, and a man in his sixties climbed out wearing an ankle-length vicuna overcoat. Pausing to gaze up at my sign, he showed a helmet of wavy black hair, and a handsome face that could have played the lead in any movie.

The big man led the way, taking long strides, until they halted side-by-side in front of my desk like a firing squad. "I want to introduce a friend of mine," he said, smiling down at me. "Harrison Woodhouse. You might have heard of him?"

Of course, I'd heard of Woodhouse. A man with deep pockets who has made a name for himself by reenacting historic Medieval battles at his English manor house and appearing on TV talk shows.

"Nice to meet you," I said, standing. "What brings you to Seattle?"

We shook hands, each keeping our distance. "I flew in to buy some French tapestries," he said, in a voice with a crisp British accent. "The owner wouldn't sell them until he sold the house, so I bought the house. You don't need a house, do you?"

"Not at the moment," I said, wondering why the wrong people always seem to be the ones with all the money.

"I suppose you'd like to know why Vincent and I came to see you."

I waited, letting my silence do the talking.

"We came to congratulate you," he said, smiling with his face, while the deep-set eyes hung back and watched.

"What for?"

"You got to the Spanish piece before I did." "

I didn't feel like admitting that my panel had just been snatched in a drive-by mugging, so I dug deep for a response. "Sometimes I get lucky."

"Then this must be your lucky day," he said, posturing with self-importance. "That little piece of history belongs in my collection."

I remembered that comment later and wondered why I hadn't asked what he meant by piece of history.

"You own so many great pieces, why would you need that one?"

"It's sort of like with women," he said, unleashing a toothpaste-commercial smile. "I always want one more."

His pretentious arrogance justified my little white lie. "I'm sorry to have to tell you this, but it went out on approval earlier today. If it comes back, I'll be sure to give you a call."

The smile slid off his face, and he turned to gaze at a Flemish tapestry hanging on the wall.

There was an awkward silence until he spoke with his back to me. "You disappoint me, Mr. Shepherd. If you know where it is, then you must know how to get it back."

Vincent nodded. Then something caught his attention, and he moved closer to eyeball the sleeve of my shirt. "That looks like blood. You gotta get that out before it sets. Lemon juice with a bit of baking soda usually works for me."

"Thanks for sharing," I said, seeing a smear of Jim's blood on my sleeve. "Maybe we can get together sometime and exchange ideas for creative living."

Vincent moved his shoulders. The deep-set eyes didn't change.

Woodhouse checked his watch and reached inside his overcoat. "Let me leave my card. Now that you know I have a special interest, and there's money in it for you, I trust you will endeavor to get it back. Otherwise, we'll have to act accordingly."

The room had gone quiet. The way he capitalized *accordingly* you could almost see that word floating in the air.

"That sounds like a threat," I said, taking the card without looking at it.

Vincent made a quick, calming gesture with the fingers of his left hand. "Harrison just wants to help you make a good business decision."

"That's right," Woodhouse said, fingering his vicuna overcoat. "One adapts to money much more easily than to poverty."

I felt my face stiffen. No matter how much money he had, it wasn't a result of his charm.

"You must be watching too much TV," I said.

He narrowed his eyes. "Why do you say that?"

"What else could make you think you can waltz in here and make me dance to this sorry little tune."

His face did a little jump. "You don't like me much, do you?"

"I'm a businessman, I don't have to like you."

He frowned. "I appreciate a man who speaks his mind, but I don't care much for your manners."

"Sorry about that. They're the only ones I've got."

He paused, eyeing me shrewdly. "You've probably heard the old adage that one should never bite off more than one can chew."

"By the look of things, you'd know more about that topic than I do."

His eyes darkened. "I'm only trying to appeal to your more sophisticated sensibilities."

"My sensibilities aren't very sophisticated. You'll just have to wait for my phone call."

He tightened his lips like he was tasting something unpleasant. "When might we expect you to make such a call?"

Now it was my turn to look at my watch. "You'll know that when your phone rings."

He smiled thinly. "Is there anything else you'd like to add?"

54

"Canned laughter."

Still angry after watching them file out the door, I hung my 'Back in 20 Minutes' sign and walked up to the Marketime deli while trying to chess things out in my mind.

It was no surprise that Woodhouse wanted the Spanish piece for his collection, but what did he mean by calling it that little piece of history. What did he know that I didn't know?

And why was he working with somebody like Vincent to put the screws to me? That wasn't his usual game. It was a troubling coincidence that the panel had been stolen just minutes before they showed up, but the sloppy rip-off was a sign that those two weren't playing on the same team that mugged Doctor Paterson.

I could have asked why the Spanish panel was so important to him, but that would give him a chance to shovel a load of lies. Sure, he might sell it for a lot more than others might get, but now I was wondering if I was missing something.

One thing was certain. I don't like to be pushed around. *The moving finger writes, and having writ, stands erect.*

"Sir?"

"Huh?"

"That'll be twelve ninety-eight."

"Oh yeah." The cashier had just rung up my purchases while my mind had been somewhere else.

I handed her a twenty and held out my hand for the change.

13

The only thing I had to work with now were the photos I had taken, so I stopped on my way home to order some 8 x 10 enlargements of the ones I'd taken of Laura's piece. I was cooking myself dinner when Doctor Paterson called.

"I'm home now. I feel terrible about losing your little treasure."

"Don't worry about it. Are you okay?"

"I have bump on my head, but I'm doing fine."

"How did it happen? What did they do?"

"I was putting my bag in the trunk when I had the odd sensation of smelling sandalwood. Then a woman pressed up behind me, pinned me against the car, and grabbed the bag."

"Did she say anything?"

"Not a word. I remember thinking how strong she was after I managed to reach around and grab it back. Then she yelled the word Rati, and the next thing I remember was waking up on the pavement."

"Rati? That's a woman's name in Sanskrit. She must have been the one who hit you. The important thing is you're all right and you survived with just a bump on your head."

After hanging up, I tried to picture all that in my mind and found myself fingering the gold hoop earring I had picked up from the gutter. Something about it had rung my doorbell and now it was playing hide-and-seek, tugging at my memory. Then it hit me. The girl at the Buckaroo Bar had been wearing gold hoop earrings.

I felt like punching myself in the head. What a fool I'd been, not being more careful after my car was broken into. And telling Laura Eskenazi my client was coming to pick up the panel was an airhead move, even though I had no reason to believe she was in on the theft. A more likely scenario was that she mentioned it to someone without knowing it would help set things up so they could steal it.

Of course, none of this explained why they wanted the panel in the first place, but it was a near certainty that my piece was three hundred miles away at the tightly guarded ranch and an alliance with Laura was the only path for getting it back. It was a longshot, but I told her I would contact her mother if I didn't sell my piece, and I hadn't sold it. Maybe that would open a door for me.

Her mother picked up on the first ring.

"Mrs. Eskenazi? This is Tony Shepherd. We talked the other day about the table cover."

"Oh, yes," she said, sounding distracted. "What can I do for you?"

"I was hoping you could get a message to your daughter." I paused. "Are you all right?"

"I'm sorry, I've been better. I thought this call would be from Laura. I've been leaving messages, but I'm wondering if she even gets them. After all the news about salmonella poisoning in Walla Walla, I'm afraid to imagine what's going on over there."

"Everything I hear about that group is pretty strange."

"Strange is the least of it," she said.

"What do you mean?"

"First, they brought in hundreds of foreigners and married them to Americans so they could stay in the country. Now they've brought in busloads of homeless people. Six thousand people are crowded together on a farm that's zoned for no more than fifty workers. The latest reports say they've blocked the road into the ranch with bulldozers to keep out the county inspectors."

It was the same story Bradley the Bum had told me. "How did Laura ever get involved with a group like that?"

"She went to teach, not to join. That was before all the trouble started. She was going through a rough patch after her divorce, and they offered her a job teaching classes on comparative religions, one of her favorite topics. At the time, it looked like a good opportunity."

"We got off on the wrong foot, but I'd like to talk to her some more about the family history of the table cover."

"I can try to get a message to her. She might be busy with group activities. They're always having group activities."

"Then I should free your line for Laura's call. I bet she'll be in touch before long and will have a perfectly good reason for not having called sooner."

"I certainly hope so."

"There's one other thing. If she can't come home, would it be possible for me to visit her at the ranch?"

She sighed. "They used to have special days for visitors, but it takes more than a smile to get inside now. We don't even know if Laura is free to come and go anymore. Men with guns are guarding the gate, and outside contact is being discouraged because of the conflict they've stirred up.

That was discouraging news, but from talking with Bradley I knew there might be alternative ways to get in, and some unguarded ways to get out if things got dicey.

It crossed my mind that some of the people over there might recognize me, like the two women that had been following me, or the gal at the Buckaroo Bar.

Maybe it was time to let my beard grow. Before going to bed, I showered, but left the two-day stubble that was darkening my face.

14

I was sorting through my photos the next morning when Mrs. Eskenazi called me back. She sounded excited.

"Laura's coming home. I'll call you when she gets here."

"That's great. Will she be bringing her half of the table cover?"

"She will if she can. The people who run the ranch took it for their art expert to evaluate."

"Oh my god. How did that happen?"

"She didn't say. She was worried someone might overhear her talking on the phone."

That confirmed that someone at the ranch had their hands on both panels. The news about an art expert coming to evaluate them was even more troubling.

After hanging up, I got out my dad's old magnifying glass with the mother-of-pearl handle and went over my pictures of the Eskenazi piece. Enlargement had sharpened the details, and I spotted a couple things I had not noticed when Laura brought it to my store.

A small white circle, only an inch in diameter, centered on the top of the crown contained a red X. Directly beneath it, on the lower rim, a similar white circle enclosed a red cross. Both were the same size as the circle I had found in the cartouche on my panel containing a fat T shape.

The three little circles outlined in blue looked the same at first glance, but each had a different symbol in the center. That prompted me to go over every inch of the photos of my own panel and I discovered another anomaly. One of the scallop shells had an upside-down crescent shape attached to its base. This made the scallop shell resemble the sail above a boat. So, in addition to three little circles, a sailboat was cleverly hidden among the white shells.

Then, my eyes were drawn to the mysterious inscription. It was almost screaming it had something to tell me. For this, I needed some expert help, so I picked up the phone and called a friend who teaches at the University of Washington.

I heard the tail end of a muted conversation, followed by, "Languages Department."

"Larry, it's Tony. I have a foreign language puzzle on my hands. I wonder if you can spare me a few minutes?"

"I'm done with my classes. You can come over now."

After sliding my photos into a secure pocket of my book-like check register, I took 45th to the University District and parked close to the campus.

Students hauling books flooded the tree-lined lanes as I searched for Denny Hall, the oldest building on campus. Built from blocks of gray sandstone, it was designed to resemble a French chateau. When I spotted the cone-roofed towers poking through the evergreen trees, I crossed a grassy quadrangle surrounded by redbrick buildings and followed a paved path up the hill.

The Language Center filled the entire basement level of Denny Hall. I wandered through a maze of scuffed-up hallways before finding Larry Mintz's name hand-printed on a three by five card pinned to a door. After knocking twice, I stepped into a shoebox-sized cubicle. Stacks of files were everywhere and Larry, a bookish man with receding, curly brown hair, sat behind a wooden desk covered with papers.

"Hey, Larry," I said, as he stood and extended his hand.

"Tony, you haven't been around here in ages. What are you working on this time?"

"I brought some photos of a Medieval Spanish table cover. It has some unusual writing. I'm not sure if it's a real language or some kind of a code."

I sat in one of the straight-backed chairs facing his desk and handed him an 8 x 10 closeup of the inscription.

He studied it closely for a few seconds. "The Middle Ages was when the art of secret writing became popular, but these letters are squared. It could be Rashi script. That's a form of Hebrew that a Spaniard named Rashi used in the fifteenth century to transcribe the Hebrew Bible. Hebrew's not my specialty, but we've got someone here who could probably tell us what it says."

"Can he do the translation from these photos?"

"Sure, why not? Do you have any other information that might be helpful?"

I slid across the rest of my photos. "The scallop shell border makes me think it might relate to the Way of Saint James, the old pilgrimage route."

Larry shuffled through them and nodded. "My sister walked the Camino a couple years ago. She wore out two pairs of expensive hiking boots."

He reached for a jeweler's loupe and squinted again at the inscription. "This is strange. Your cartouche is shaped like the floor plan of a medieval church, and all the writing appears to be some form of Hebrew, except for that one little thing."

Turning the photo in my direction he pointed his finger at the blue circle with the fat red T form.

"I saw that," I said. "I wonder what it is."

"It's the Greek letter *Tau*."

"The Greek letter Tau? That makes no sense. Why would a Greek letter be woven into a Spanish table rug?"

"I have no idea, but my sister was studying Greek when she walked that route and was surprised to find a *Tau* on one of the castle entries she passed."

"What would a Greek letter be doing on a Spanish castle?"

61

"The Greeks traded all over. They used their port in Marseille as a base for doing business along the Spanish coast and up the Rhone River into the middle of France."

He examined another photo. "What have we got here? It looks like a constellation."

"The brighter yellow stars seem to form a shape," I said.

"They certainly do, they form the shape of a sail. It's the constellation Vela. Vela is part of a larger constellation called Argo Navis which was named after the Argo."

He saw the puzzlement in my eyes. "The Argo was the ship Jason and the Argonauts sailed on when they went searching for the Golden Fleece."

He shuffled through the photos again and held up a close-up of the crown while tapping a pencil eraser against the table. "Is that a tribal symbol in the middle of the crown? Or is it what it appears to be?"

I leaned forward. "What does it appear to be?"

"A Maltese Cross. See how it flares at the ends? Variations of that form were used by several of the Catholic military orders sent in to guard the pilgrimage routes."

I was so used to seeing all kinds of tribal symbols that it never crossed my mind that it might be a Maltese cross.

"Why would there be Hebrew writing on something Spanish from the Middle Ages? And why would it have an insignia used by the same Catholic Knights who were persecuting the Jews?"

"I can't answer any of that. But, if this was made during the time Jews were being forced to leave Spain, or convert to Christianity, there were many educated Jews still living in Spain who could read and write old Hebrew."

A pan of garlicky spaghetti sauce was steaming up my kitchen window when Larry Mintz called that evening. "Tony, I'm with my colleague at the Language Department. He translated the inscription. Can I put him on?"

"By all means."

"Hi, I'm David. That's an intriguing bit of text you've got there."

"Were you able to figure out what language it is?"

"That was the easy part because of the shape of the letters. It's written from right to left in an old form of Hebrew script that's associated with Spain in the late Middle Ages."

"Why was that the easy part?"

"The fuzziness of the nap made the inscription almost impossible to read from the front. To get around that, I worked off your picture of the back by using a mirror."

"That sounds kind of complicated."

"It was complicated, but what I came up with makes literary sense. Are you ready to write it down?"

I grabbed a pad and a pen. "Okay, I'm ready. Please go slowly."

"Reading from right to left, this is what I get:

Midway on the journey of life, the path we walk has brought us strife. To protect our souls, and our bounty save, we set forth upon the savage waves. A sternward wind carried us far, to the sovereign crown above the field of stars. Here we sleep in peace and pray, beneath the tower that guards the way.

"Wow," I said. "That's almost poetic."

"It is, isn't it? Sort of like a medieval canto. I have no idea what any of it means, but I'm certain that's what it says."

"I have no idea what it means either. Tell Larry I owe him one."

No wonder it was hard to figure out. The inscription was done in an extinct language that was written backwards.

As I puzzled over those curious words, my eyes kept going back to *the Field of Stars.*

15

My mind was darting around like a hamster in a cage thinking about constellations, Greek letters, Maltese crosses, and Hebrew writing. Pieces of paper with notes and scribbles were scattered across my desk, as if they were a reflection of my unsettled thoughts.

I was getting nowhere on my own, so I opened my laptop and searched for experts on symbolism. I discovered A.R.A.S. The Archive for Research in Archetypical Symbols was a Swiss organization that had developed out of the studies of Carl Jung.

Jung believed that certain symbols were common to all mankind and could be construed as references to an invisible reality that resides in our unconscious.

Since their online data base was only accessible to members, I called their San Francisco office. They gave me the number of one of their people in Seattle, and a pleasant-sounding female voice picked up on the second ring.

"Hello, my name is Tony Shepherd. The Archive for Research in Archetypical Symbols gave me your number. I'm a local artifact dealer, and I've been trying to research some motifs on a medieval textile. I wonder if you might be willing to look at some photos."

"I'd be glad to, but I'm flying out of town tomorrow. Could you come today? I live in a houseboat just off Eastlake."

"I'll come right away."

"Now?"

"That knocking on your door will be me."

Flashes of sunlight beckoned me across the metal grillwork of University Bridge and brought me to the eastern shore of Lake Union where houseboats were still allowed.

After parking in the shade of a huge willow tree, I followed wooden steps to a softly shifting dock flanked on either side by whimsically structured houses built on floating platforms of fat cedar logs. Most were decorated with brightly colored flags, little windmills, and other fanciful ornamentation.

The one I was looking for was at the end of the dock, almost covered with plants and vines. A blue and white sailboat that looked like it had not been tended to in a while was tethered beside it.

I tapped twice on with a brass door knocker shaped like a mermaid. Seconds later, a woman wearing a loose-fitting paisley print dress opened the door. She might have been eighty years old, but she had shoulder-length blondish hair and youthfully alert eyes. The wrinkles lining her face had not altered the lingering beauty of her features.

"Hello, I'm the one who called about some symbols."

Holding my eye, she offered her hand. "I'm Diane Finley."

"You've got a great place here. Is that your boat out there?"

"Yes, it is. When my husband was alive, we used to sail Puget Sound, but it hasn't been used since he died. It's another thing I'll have to sell."

"How long ago did he die?"

She brushed some hair out of her eyes "Oh, it's been four months now, but I miss him terribly. Please come in. I'm still struggling to get things in order."

The house was basically one large room with skylights. A tiny kitchen filled one corner, a cozy living room/dining room occupied the middle, and a narrow hallway led to a bedroom and bathroom. Windows everywhere gave her a sweeping view across the lake to Queen Ann Hill in the west, and south to the gleaming towers of downtown Seattle.

"You've got quite a view," I said, following her past a small aquarium where red fish with big eyes gazed out at me.

"I find it very peaceful."

"We can sit here," she said, gesturing at a circular table where a Screen Actors' Guild publication was lying open "Would you care for some coffee?"

"No thanks," I said, sliding the photos out of my check register. "I'd like you look at the symbols on an old Spanish table cover. You might see something that relates to your studies with the ARAS organization."

She studied them for a drawn-out moment, then beamed a smile. "One of these stands out, and it brings back some pleasant memories."

Seeing my questioning look, she reached into a display case, carefully removed a silver framed photo, and handed it to me. The image was of a beautiful young woman wearing a white peasant dress and standing beside the actor Anthony Quinn.

"You knew Anthony Quinn?"

"I was on contract with MGM and worked with him on *Zorba the Greek*. I had small parts in a lot of movies. Sometimes I was a stand-in for Bette Davis."

"How was she to work with?"

A slight smile. "Bette was meaner than cat shit, but Anthony was a sweetheart."

Reaching into the case again, she took out an enameled amulet on a silver chain and handed it to me. "Anthony gave me this after weeks of difficult shooting on a remote part of Crete. It was an affectionate gesture."

The amulet depicted a squat red T form inside a white circle with a blue border exactly like the one woven into the cartouche on my panel. For a moment, I was at a loss for words.

"It's beautiful," I said. "Can you tell me the significance of this symbol?"

"The Tau Cross was a symbol for three major deities who died and were resurrected. The Sumerian Sun god, the Roman god Mithras, and the Greek god Attis. It was also used in ancient Egypt as a symbol for resurrection."

"Can you think of any reason a symbol for resurrection might have been woven into a medieval Spanish table cover?" I said, handing the amulet back.

She smiled as she took it. "Symbols are ways of expressing the unknown. They have multiple levels of meaning that depend on your ability to perceive them."

"Multiple levels?"

"That's right. Resurrection is not only about the return to life. In mythology, the higher purpose of resurrection is our own personal transformation. Seeing the world around us with new eyes."

She watched the gears turn in my mind as a low-flying seaplane splashed in for a landing outside her windows. "If you're interested in artifacts, maybe you could tell me something about my embroideries."

"I'd be happy to," I said.

She disappeared down the hallway and returned with an armful of 18th-century Greek textiles displaying festive bouquets of tulips, people, horses, cypress trees, and birds.

"Did you get these when you were filming in Crete?"

"No, I bought them from an antiques dealer when we visited the island of Rhodes during a break in shooting."

"What you've got here is a complete dowry set," I said. "Greek women of marriageable age were expected to embroider their own bridal costume, bed tents, and pillow covers. It's rare to find a whole set. If you want to sell them, I can pay five thousand dollars, cash if you like."

"Another dealer offered me ten thousand."

I was stunned. "That's as much as they can be sold for. You'll never get a better offer. You should call right now and accept it."

She lifted a business card from a bowl on the table. "That offer was from Abraham Tehrani. He has a store in Pioneer Square."

I couldn't believe Abraham would pay that much. "Go ahead, call him. But don't tell him I'm here, or what my offer was."

I watched as she punched in the number.

"Mr. Tehrani? This is Mrs. Finley. I've decided to accept your offer of ten thousand dollars for my embroideries."

Confusion showed on her face as muffled staccato sounds came from the phone. "No, I don't want to give you a price. I want you to tell me what you can pay."

Her eyes remained downcast as she endured another drawn-out response. "Let me think about it and I'll get back to you," she said, putting down the phone, and turning to me with a bewildered expression. "I can't believe it. He said his offer was only for yesterday and he can't pay that much today. He said he'll pay me five thousand, the same as you."

"I'll top that and pay you seven thousand."

All the tension evaporated from her face. "That's very kind of you. If my daughter doesn't want them, I'll accept your offer."

Abraham had tried an old trick. He knew the seller would be getting other offers, so he made his so high she would have to come back to him. What he did not anticipate was that I would be standing there with money in my hand.

I was on my way to the door when her fingertips curled across my wrist. "Wait," she said, turning to the display case. "There's something I want you to have."

"That wouldn't be right," I said, as she removed the amulet and pressed it firmly into my palm. "It was a very personal gift to you."

"It was," she said, "But it may have more significance for your life than it does now for mine."

Her generosity touched me so deeply that I walked away suffused with a glow of warmth, but before I reached the end of the dock, my thoughts had wrapped themselves around the amulet I was holding in my hand.

I ran across all kinds of curious things in my business, but I had never come across anything that appeared to be sending such a powerful message about resurrection, reappearance, and transformation.

16

Mozart's overture to The Magic Flute was playing when I opened the door to The Bookworm, a second-hand bookstore near the Fremont Bridge.

Tall bookcases filled the high-ceilinged room and books were piled everywhere. A fresh stack stood on the checkout counter where Steve Arnold, a thin man in his fifties, was writing out a check to Danny Shine.

"Hey, Steve. I need to pick your brain."

He studied me coolly through wire-rimmed glasses. "What are you after this time?"

"Anything you can tell me about the Catholic military orders that were sent to guard the pilgrimage routes in the Middle Ages?"

"Why do you need to know about that?"

"I turned up an old textile with symbols related to that era."

"Did you happen to notice my sign?"

"Sure, what about it?"

"It says bookstore. If you weren't so cheap, you might learn something by reading."

"C'mon, Steve. You do a blog on French history. I've told you plenty of stuff about old textiles whenever you've asked."

"You should find everything you'd need on that topic over in the French history section."

I followed the direction his thumb was pointing, took the biggest book from the French History section, and started reading about The Camino.

The Way of Saint James was drawing so many people in the Middle Ages that it became overrun with predatory bandits and con men. Christian military orders were sent from France to protect the pilgrims. The Knights of Tau were the first ones sent, and their symbol was a white Greek Cross on a black background. That was interesting, but I needed to know more about the Maltese Cross.

The emblems of the other military orders sent in were displayed on the following page. The Knights Hospitalier wore a white Maltese Cross on a black background, and a red cross on white, like the cross in the table rug, was worn by the Poor Knights of the Temple of Solomon. I had never heard of either of these groups, so I carried the book to a table by the window so I could read while sitting.

I could hardly believe what I was seeing. The Poor Knights of the Temple of Solomon were also known by a more familiar name. A full-page picture showing gallant knights in white mantles with a red Maltese Cross on their chest was captioned *The Knights Templar.*

The Templars took all the standard religious vows of pious knights, poverty, chastity, and obedience, but ended up becoming obscenely rich and powerful. Before their downfall, they had the world's largest army, owned thousands of castles, and the city of La Rochelle in France was their private port.

How they acquired all that wealth and power was not such a pretty story. They raked in wealth by going to war as a private army that was accountable only to the Pope. They were so good with handling money that they became the biggest money lenders in the world, and it was the loaning of money that eventually caused their downfall.

The king of France was not so good with money. After squandering his treasury on long and costly wars with the British, Philippe IV became the Templar's biggest customer.

But all the money he borrowed was not enough to get him out of trouble. Desperate to stave off impending bankruptcy,

Philippe devised a plan that would allow him to go after the assets of the very bankers he had been borrowing from.

Secret warrants authorizing seizure of Templar assets on grounds of heresy were delivered throughout France to a newly installed system of royal bailiffs. On the dawn of October 13, 1307, the orders were opened, and soldiers loyal to the King arrested all the Templars they could get their hands on and confiscated their property.

It was an incredible story, but I still had no idea why those cross symbols were on the Spanish table cover. Hoping Steve could tell me, I carried the book to the checkout counter.

Steve adjusted his glasses. "Are you going to buy it now that you've got it all dog-eared?"

"It's not dog-eared. I know how to treat a book. I just need you to explain a few things."

He glanced at Danny. "What do you need to know?"

"It looks like Philippe, the King of France, wiped out the Templars in 1307 and ended up with their treasure."

"No. But that was how Friday the thirteenth got to be an unlucky day."

He smiled at my stupefaction. "The warrants got leaked, and Templar vaults all over France were quietly emptied. By the time King Philippe's men broke into the Paris Repository, everything was gone except for the mice."

"Okay, but what happened to the loot?"

"Lots of people would love to know the answer to that question," he said, turning away to write something in a ledger.

Danny folded the check into his wallet. "Steve skipped over few things."

"He'd learn something from reading if he wasn't such a cheapskate," Steve said. "But go ahead and tell him."

"What he left out is that a flotilla of ships loaded with the most legendary treasure in human history sailed out of La Rochelle in the dark of night and vanished into thin air. People are still trying to figure out where they went."

"Where could they have gone?"

71

"They didn't leave behind any clues, or anyone to tell the secret. The most popular theory is that they sailed up to Scotland."

"With a treasure like that, how come all we ever hear about is that Da Vinci Code holy grail nonsense?"

"Fantasy is what Hollywood does best."

"So, it is a fantasy?"

"Who knows? But it's a fantasy to believe that such a thing could ever be properly identified."

"Why is that?"

"Graal is a medieval word meaning cup. In biblical days, everyone was using plain old terra cotta pottery, the red stuff. If the Holy Grail did exist, it would most likely be nothing more than common catering-grade tableware from the first century."

Steve was watching with amusement. "You can have the grail if I can have the treasure."

I must have looked perplexed.

"People expect something magical that glows in the dark. Not something utterly ordinary."

"So?"

"So, none of the big auction houses would dare sell something like that unless it was magical."

Danny grinned. "You could put it up on eBay."

"They might even invent a new category for Holy Ghost Memorabilia," Steve said, with a sharp edge of sarcasm.

"Any idea what that treasure could be worth today?" I said.

"It would be worth billions," Danny said.

"Billions?"

"Think about it. Not a single piece of the treasure has ever been recovered. If the tiniest part of it ever turned up, the news media would go bonkers, twenty-four-seven."

I slept late the next day and was brewing up coffee when Mrs. Eskenazi called to say Laura was home and invited me over. A strange feeling was growing inside me as I donned my camel hair sports coat. Everything was riding on this meeting, not just getting the panels back, but making amends with Laura. I didn't know exactly what it was, but something in her eyes still burned inside of me.

Blue Ridge, an upscale neighborhood of rambling houses with lush green lawns, had west facing views of Puget Sound and the Olympic Mountains. When I spotted the right number, I pulled in behind a blue Lexus and a white Mercedes parked side by side in the driveway, climbed concrete steps flanked by huge rhododendron bushes, and pushed a brass doorbell.

A slight, graying man wearing a cardigan sweater opened the door, and extended his hand. "You must be Tony. I'm Sol, Laura's father."

I nodded as I took his hand. "I bet you never get tired of that view."

He smiled with the same blue eyes as Laura as he beckoned me inside. "We can thank Bill Boeing for that. Back in the fifties he developed our neighborhood as a residential park for his top executives."

The cozy scent of cookies baking filled the air as I followed him down a carpeted hallway to a wide-windowed living room.

Laura was seated on a white sofa beside a pleasant-faced woman in gray slacks and a loose-fitting yellow blouse.

"Tony, this is my wife, Thelma," Sol said. "I understand you've already met our daughter, Laura."

Laura looked fetching in a purple and gold University of Washington sweatshirt, but her reluctant smile without really looking at me told me she was still thinking of the day we had butted heads.

Mrs. Eskenazi offered me her hand. "I'm so pleased to meet you after our little talks on the phone. Would you like some tea?"

"I'd love some," I said, lowering myself into an upholstered chair opposite them.

A spicy smell hit my nose as she poured me a cup. "It smells good," I said. "What is it?"

"Just Earl Gray. Would you care for a ginger cookie? Laura made them."

I took a cookie and turned to Laura. "I'm sorry that we got started off the way we did. I hope it's not too late to find a way to work things out."

She exchanged a look with her mother and sighed. "Well, that's gotten more complicated than ever."

"What do you mean? What happened?"

"Sheena's having my panel evaluated by her art expert, and I don't know if I can get it back."

"Why did she show it to an art expert?"

"I'm not sure, but it all began because Swami used a scallop shell as the cover for his most recent book."

"A scallop shell? Why did he use that?"

"Because it goes with the title of his book, 'All Paths Lead to Me'."

"You mean the only reason she took it was because of the scallop shell border?"

"Not exactly. It was all so silly I can hardly believe it. My roommate told Sheena about the shell motif and Sheena showed it to Swami. When he saw the stars and the crown on a green field, he got excited because his spiritual name, Taja-Sutara, signifies a crown on top of a holy star."

"That is an unusual coincidence," I said.

"It was enough of a coincidence that he wanted to use the table cover as the image for his new book. His books are a major source of money for the ashram. When Sheena found out you bought the other half, she started having you watched and told me that it was my spiritual duty to get the panel back."

"Was that why you tried to buy my piece?"

"Not at all. It's always been part of our family history. It was after I came back from meeting you that Sheena's art appraiser told her it might be historically valuable because he'd seen something similar in a fifteenth-century painting."

My mind took a leap, and I almost spilled my tea.

"Did he say where he saw the painting?" I said, almost choking on the words.

"Not that I know of."

"Did you ask for yours back?"

"Of course, I did. They said it was locked up and only Sheena had the key. That was the last straw for me. Things have been getting crazy at the ranch, and I'm not the only one who thinks that. My roommate, Indira, is thinking of leaving too. Swami's teachings are okay, but the people who run things seem to be mostly after money and power."

"Do you have any idea how long the table cover has been in your family?"

Mrs. Eskenazi jumped in. "It's been in our family forever. One of our Spanish ancestors moved to France after the French Revolution and that's when we think the panels were separated. The ones who stayed in Spain kept one panel and the other was carried off to France. We never knew why they took apart a perfectly good heirloom, unless it was some symbolic promise to reunite. Those were difficult times."

"How did the pieces end up here in Seattle?"

"That's the incredible part," Sol said. "They came to us through Laura's grandparents when the two branches of our family came together again in Chicago during the nineteen-twenties."

"Can you imagine?" Mrs. Eskenazi laughed. "It was like the panels had somehow attracted each other. My mother's side, the Alhadeff's, had one half, and Sol's family had the other. My grandmother used her piece to cover the back of her sofa, so I never thought of them as being valuable in a monetary sense, just a reminder of our heritage."

My heart beat faster as I sat for a moment trying to gather my thoughts. Finding something with historical value is the cardinal passion of my profession. Finding the same table cover that was depicted in a Renaissance painting might not be as grandiose a discovery as Howard Carter stumbling on King Tut's tomb, but it could be the ultimate achievement of any career.

On top of that, such a story could lead to scholarly papers, book tours, and talk show appearances.

I decided to tell them a bit more.

"Your family heirloom has some curious features. The scallop shell border and the field of stars appear to be references to the Camino, the pilgrimage route to Santiago de Compostela."

They exchanged glances as I turned to Laura. "We should try to get it back before they do something, like sell it. You know the lay of the land over there. How about letting me take you to dinner so we can figure out a plan?"

She blinked. "What did you have in mind?"

"How about tomorrow night at a good Italian place?"

She glanced at her mother.

I smiled. "I'm not going to take a bite out of you."

Thelma gave Laura a slight nod, and a smile crept across her face when she looked at me. "I like Italian food. What time do you want to pick me up?"

I was walking on air when I left. I liked everything about this woman—her quietly determined physical presence, the way she carried herself, her subtle gestures. Above all, the beauty of her soul was even brighter than the beauty of her person.

Since the death of my wife, I had never dated with much enthusiasm. Now a series of unforeseen events had me champing at the bit to share a simple meal with a woman I barely knew. Like any guy, I began imagining other pleasures we might share, and before long, I was parked in front of my house.

Then a barrage of thoughts hit me—Sheena was working with an art expert, so I had to move fast, and would need some help with the thievery end.

Fortunately, I knew just the guy.

18

Sammy Tracks was only seventeen when I met him years ago at a summer music festival. On this murderously hot day, he was strolling among the multitudes hawking tofu hotdogs and orange juice from a tray hung around his neck. His jubilant sales pitch, corona of golden curls, and the heavy cast on his leg caught my attention.

I bought one of Sammy's tofu hotdogs and learned that he had been living entirely on his wits since being orphaned at fourteen. By necessity, he had become a jack of all trades. He never finished high school, but just by looking into your eyes he would know more about you than any psychiatrist ever would.

There wasn't a thing Sammy didn't know how to do. He had washed dishes, done farm work, plumbing, and construction. He was a hard worker who could swing a hammer all day, but he was never afraid to engage in less than legal activities if it was necessary to support his wife and children.

During the years that passed, I had seen him working the weekend swap meets wearing a straw hat and bib overalls. He would sell whatever he could get his hands on, but sometimes salted in modern reproductions of old cast iron toys and Edward Curtis photographs amongst the usual bric-à-brac.

Sammy never claimed his were the highly prized originals. He just offered them for sale after leaving cast iron toys in the damp outdoors for a few weeks and putting the repro photos into old looking frames. Buyers walked away with sly grins on their faces, taking it for granted that they had just outfoxed some dim-witted rube who was selling his family heirlooms for half their real value.

Now, all I needed to do was find him, and hope this wasn't one of those times when Sammy didn't want to be found. I had no idea where he could be living, but I knew places he might pass through, like Belltown, a trendy waterfront neighborhood that was always buzzing on a Friday night.

Along the way, I stopped at FedEx to pick up the book I had ordered about the Vizcaya Carpet. I was eager to see what it looked like, so I tore open the box on my way out the door. The design had no relationship at all to the table cover, but the colors were so similar they might have been made by the same hands. I slid it back in the box for later study.

My first stop was the 5 Point Café near the Seattle Center. 'The Best Dive Bar in Seattle' wasn't trendy, but they served strong drinks and were open twenty-four hours a day. Lance, an old buddy of mine who was tight with Sammy, used to spend a lot of his drinking time there.

After parking beneath the Monorail near the statue of Chief Seattle, I pushed open a door with a sign reading *Alcoholics serving alcoholics since* 1929 and took a stool at a horseshoe-shaped bar across from two grizzled guys who looked like they might have been sitting there since the place opened.

Red-headed Mary, the full-figured bartender, was wiping the far end of the bar with a rag as I pondered what to order. Let's see, a vodka martini, shaken not stirred?

I decided to settle for what the other barstool patrons appeared to be drinking. When Mary caught my eye, I called out, "Double vodka rocks." Seconds later, my drink slid down the bar and stopped directly in front of me.

I was crunching on tiny pieces of watery ice and admiring the long dead hula hoop-sized Alaskan King Crabs trying to crawl free of dusty old fishnets decorating the walls when Mary wandered over to collect the money.

"You're looking good," I said. "You've lost a few pounds."

She laughed. "I've even got a new boyfriend."

"He's just after your mind."

"God, I hope not."

"I'm looking for an old buddy, guy named named Lance."

"That must be the one we call Lance Romance. A skinny fellow always going on about Mayan glyphs and Tarot cards?"

"That's him."

"He used to come in every day, but I haven't seen him for months. I heard he moved back to Spokane."

It looked like I'd be hitting more bars, so I stopped in the men's room on the way out. Standing at the urinal, a small window with a tilted mirror reflected another mirror higher up and gave a telescopic view of people silently eating in the revolving restaurant on top of the Space Needle six blocks away. You don't get that sort of thing in the classier joints.

Another popular watering hole, The Two Bells, was a short walk away. I could hear the boisterous crowd of half-hammered smokers that were gathered outside from two blocks away. After pushing my way through them, not a single familiar face was in sight, so I pushed my way back out and drove to a small park behind the Pike Place Market.

Rumpled men sat on a bench sharing a bottle in a paper bag and soft jazz music was coming from The Virginia Inn where they've been pouring drinks since the 1800s. Back then, First Avenue was the original 'Skid Road' for sliding logs down to the waterfront and the customers were sailors, fishermen, and loggers. Tonight, the narrow room with rough, redbrick walls was humming with a hip-looking fashionable crowd.

Scanning the booths, I spotted Elena, whose bloodline blends Native American, African, and European. Wearing an apricot scarf wrapped turban-like around her head, she was holding court over a covey of acolytes from the ballet class she teaches. The short, muscular man sitting next to her, looking like a buddha with a hangover, was Sammy Tracks.

Elena gestured for people to scoot over, and I slid in. When the barman came, I turned to Elena's man, Frank, a Scotsman who knew his beer. "What do you like, Frank?"

"I'm drinking Manny's Ale, but the Ballard Bitter's pretty good."

Ready for something to wash down the double vodka rocks, I ordered a pint of Manny's and then turned my attention to Sammy. Looking fit and trim in a sweater matching his sandy brown hair, he had not said a word. He just gazed at me with a bemused expression in his intelligent eyes.

Something in the air between us had lingered from the last time we worked together. He had shorted me in the pay off on some low-end rugs I'd fronted him to sell at the Sausalito swap meet. But there is one solid advantage of working again with a guy like Sammy. You know enough to count your fingers after shaking hands with him.

"It's been a while," I said.

"A few years. You still doing the old stuff?"

"Yeah, still doing that. Are you still living in Seattle?"

"I'm mostly in LA now, but I'm up here helping my brother with some construction work."

"Are you here long enough to do something with me?"

Several moments passed as Sammy stared across the room like he was lost in thought. But Sammy was never lost in thought. He was figuring.

"How long is long enough?"

I was giving that some thought when the waiter placed a foam-topped pint in front of me. I took a taste, then a slow, yeasty swallow.

"Maybe a week," I said. "But it would be better to talk at my place. That is, if you've got time to drop by."

"You still on Fremont?"

"Still on Fremont."

"My brother lives near the Ballard Locks, not far from you."

"How about noon tomorrow?"

81

"I'll be there."

Sammy's attention drifted back to amusing a young woman, so I took another sip and turned to Elena.

"You used to come here more often," she said. "What keeps you away?"

"Business. It takes most of my time. I'm usually worn out by the end of the day."

She gave me a penetrating look. "Your aura is energized. Something important must be on your mind. Is there a new woman in your life?"

I wondered how the heck did she did that. "Actually, there is. A mysterious old weaving has led me to a beautiful lady."

"What's she like?"

"Young, intelligent, and uncharted territory."

She held my gaze. "Do you believe in dreams?"

"That's one of those questions I never know how to answer."

She tipped her head closer. "Dreams must be woven into reality by our actions. The things we learn in life only make sense if we apply them to what we do."

It sounded almost biblical, and I had to agree, but when it came time for a refill I passed. I needed an early start on an estate sale where I might make some money.

The plaza behind the Pike Place Market was silent and empty. The bench where the drinkers had been sitting was occupied by two seagulls, and a determined looking crow. They tilted their heads and eyed me as I went past.

I got a terrible sinking feeling when I saw a light shining from inside my car. When I looked inside, it was coming from the glove box where my check register containing the photos of the Spanish piece and the translation of the inscription had been.

I glanced at the back seat. The book about the Vizcaya carpet was gone. My first thought was people from the ranch, but they would never bother stealing something like that.

19

I was circling the car, searching for clues, when a man and a woman walked up loaded down with shopping bags. "We saw two guys break into your car about an hour ago," the man said.

"Did you get a good look at them?"

"Not really. They were moving pretty fast. One was wearing a short blue jacket, and the other had red tennis shoes. Maybe they didn't get very far."

"Thanks for the tip," I said. "They took some things that would be hard to replace."

So, drugged-up-street punks had ripped me off, but the couple had given some useful clues that might help catch the bastards. I hopped in my car and drove along Alaskan Way to go looking for them.

The smell of frying fish hung in the air from the joints along the waterfront as I slowed to scan the line of people waiting to get on the cross-Sound ferry. Figuring they hadn't gone too far, I swung a left on Yesler to go past Pioneer Square, the historic part of town. When I saw the sidewalks teeming with Friday night revelry, I gave up any hope of spotting the guys.

I was stopped for a red light with a panhandler tapping on my window when I sensed a flash of blue in the corner of my eye. A mid-twenties guy in a blue nylon jacket had just come out of a pawn shop, and he was carrying my book on the Vizcaya Carpet.

I must have scared the hell out of the panhandler when I gunned it through the red light and bounced to a stop on the sidewalk in front of the blue jacket. Next thing I knew, I was pointing my finger across the roof of my car and doing my best Dirty Harry imitation. "Freeze or die!"

He froze.

"Where's the checkbook?" I snarled.

His eyes got round, and he glanced to the left. I shifted to the left. He glanced to the right. I shifted to the right. The intensity in my eyes must have registered because he threw down the book and ran.

A police car came roaring by as I bent to pick up the book — blue lights flashing and sirens wailing. Seconds later, another one screamed past. Pumped with adrenalin, I leaped into my car and followed them up the street to look for the red shoes.

After parking illegally in a loading zone, I stalked like a hungry lion along a stretch of First Avenue lined with pawnshops and seedy bars. I was so busy scanning feet on both sides of the street that all the gaudy neon, shabby drunks, and puffy-faced hookers giving me the eye barely registered. A herd of elephants could have marched by, and I would never have noticed unless they were wearing red shoes.

A guy in a black leather jacket whispered something as I came to a narrow alley between building. I stopped walking. "Are you talking to me?"

The air from the alley smelled of sour food, and he seemed to be grinning. "You're out walking all alone," he said, with pink neon reflecting off his teeth.

"Yeah. So what?"

His eyes seemed to sparkle as he moved closer. "What would you do if someone tried to mug you?"

"The way I feel right now, I'd kick him in the face until his teeth fell out. Then I'd make him eat them."

He looked slightly confused and backed slowly into the shadows.

Two blocks later, all I'd come up with was a headache and a wad of chewing gum stuck to my shoe. I stopped to rub the gum off on the curb when I spotted a pair of red shoes with white bottoms coming down the opposite sidewalk. The shoes were attached to another skinny, mid-twenties guy.

Keeping my eyes glued on Red Shoes, I jaywalked across First Avenue, watching as he stopped a heavyset dude and patted something under his jacket about the size of my check register. The heavyset guy shook his head, walked on, and Red Shoes continued towards me, closer and closer.

As he was passing, I grabbed him by the shoulders and slammed his body against the brick wall so hard his head bounced.

"You've got something that belongs to me," I said, pinning him with one hand on his chest and yanking my check register from under his jacket with the other.

A dozen lies formed and dissipated behind his eyes before he could make his mouth move. "It wasn't me who took it."

I pulled back my fist but stifled an urge to punch him when I saw the mala beads around his neck. "Where the hell did you get that?" I said, pointing at the picture of the Swami.

"They gave it to me when they bussed me over to that commune."

"Why aren't you still there?"

"They caught me shooting up."

"Get the hell out of here while you can still walk." I said, poking him hard in the chest.

He took off like a frightened squid, and I flipped open my check register. I felt like I was floating above the sidewalk when I saw the photos and the translation were still safely tucked inside.

It was past my usual sack time when I got home, but I could no more sleep than flap my arms and fly. I tried to unwind by reading a book with Tyson on my lap and a half-full bottle of bourbon on the table next to me.

The book claimed to be a thriller, but it wasn't half as exciting as what I'd just been through. I stuck with it until the bottle was empty. Then I went to sleep.

20

Morning came all too soon for the busy day I had arranged for myself. An early estate sale, a mid-day meet with Sammy, and a decisive dinner date with Laura.

What was dragging me out of bed at the yawning rays of dawn was a hot tip. An appraiser had told me there was "a pile of worn-out oriental rugs" at a Mercer Island estate sale. Those words set my bells ringing because age can be far more important than condition.

Mercer Island sits in the middle of wind-whipped Lake Washington but connects to Seattle on the west and Bellevue on the east with six lane floating bridges made of concrete pontoons.

I made a mental note to stop at Map House Antiques on my way back as I exited into a small village known for its antique stores. Their collection of historical maps, old globes, and cartophilia might have information about the original routes of the Camino.

The sale was in a low, 1950s-style waterfront house with a panoramic view of Seattle. I was the first to arrive, so I took a seat on the cold concrete steps to hold my place for the nine o'clock opening. If there's anything good in these sales, the late bird ends up looking down an empty worm hole.

I wasn't alone for long. Two men I took to be art dealers arrived ten minutes later, a chubby one with round red glasses, and a thin one with quick eyes. Both wore jackets with ties and were talking about a Caravaggio that had been stolen out of a church in Palermo, Italy.

"What would a painting like that be worth?" I said.

"Over twenty million," the chubby one said. "Of course, they'd get far less on the black market."

"It's a tragedy," the thin one said. "The churches can't afford alarms. That same church got hit again and they made off with the sixteenth-century choir stalls."

"Churches are even losing their bells," the first one said. "The artistic heritage of Europe is leaving as easily as rich tourists."

"Don't they ever catch the thieves?"

"Stolen art is difficult to trace. It gets hidden away. It's become an eight-billion dollar a year industry, the third-largest illegal enterprise behind illicit drugs and weapons."

"Where could it all be going?"

"A lot of it ends up in Paris because that's one of the best art markets."

"Who could be doing it?"

"Nobody knows for sure, but they're not stealing for ransom. Criminal organizations are supplying wealthy people with whatever they want."

The chubby man adjusted his glasses. "Criminals aren't the only players. Men in high position and terrorist groups have entered the market. It's so lucrative that a family of trapeze artists is suspected of scaling the walls of a castle and stealing Old Master paintings valued at over fifty million dollars."

"What kind of person would buy something they knew was stolen?"

Chubby shrugged. "People who want something nobody else has. The demand for art is huge. Forgeries of certain famous artists have become so common that buyers are wary of purchasing their works."

Twenty-five people were standing in line behind me when a fresh-faced man in his twenties opened the door. I stood blocking the entrance until he told me where the rugs were, then hurried down the steps into a finished basement.

Five small rugs were rolled up on a sofa and the prices were so low that I didn't bother to open them. I just wrapped my arms around the bundle and hurried back upstairs to the checkout. I examined the bundle more closely when I was putting them in my trunk. I wouldn't make much on the beat up kelims, but the *sofre*, a small rug to serve food on, and a ceremonial saddle cover would make some collectors happy.

I almost gasped when I unrolled the last one. Lotto rugs acquired that name because a Venetian painter named Mario Lotto depicted them in his paintings This one was such a ghost of its former self that most people would consider it worthless, but its age and design made it highly saleable.

I was locking my trunk when an elderly couple known as Bonnie and Clyde wheeled up in a white Cadillac. Nobody knew their real names, but they worked as a team to steal jewelry and watches. Silver-haired Clyde wore a tweed suit with a gray felt hat. Bonnie was equally stylish in a long fur coat with a white scarf over her currently red hair. That coat was known to have deep pockets.

Hurrying back inside, I alerted the couple running the sale to move small valuables closer to the check-out table. A familiar looking woman bumped into me as I was leaving. She was carrying a small weaving with a triangular flap. I thought it was her purse until a price tag from the sale tipped me it was a south Persian jewelry bag from the 19th century.

The woman was a veteran dealer I had seen at other sales, so I followed her around pretending to study other things. When she set the bag on a table to examine some glassware, I reached across and took it. I was dropping a hundred-dollar bill at the check-out when she realized what had happened.

"I was going to buy that," she shouted. "You had no right to take it"

"But you didn't buy it," I said, turning to face her. "You put it down. You go to a lot of these sales. You know everything's for sale until it's paid for."

That brought me a dirty look, but she knew I was right.

Map House Antiques occupied a small country house on the edge of the central village. When I opened the door, a little dog barked a couple times and came to sniff at my ankles. I reached down and patted its head. He licked my hand, did a little dance, and pressed his body against my leg.

"That's a cute little dog," I said to the dour-faced lady who sat in a spindly rocking chair doing a crossword puzzle.

She lowered the puzzle a few inches and adjusted her glasses. "He keeps me company."

"I came to see your collection of old maps."

"That was my husband's specialty. I sold most of them after he passed away. The oldest ones are displayed on the wall, but I'm keeping those."

One of these was a map of the Camino hand-drawn on heavy brown paper and dated 1648. A spider web of red lines marking the traditional routes across France all came together at one point. From there, the remaining four hundred miles was a solid black line across the top of Spain marked 'El Camino Primitivo.'

"Do you know why this black line is called The Camino Primitivo?" I said.

"That's the oldest route. The Spanish King Alfredo was the first pilgrim to walk it in the ninth century."

Those connecting lines on a four-hundred-year-old map had a strange effect. Like the end of a thread had been placed in my hand. A thread that might lead me to the right path.

The woman went back to her crossword puzzle while I examined the other maps. I was heading for the exit, when I saw the little dog was curled up on a section of an old Chinese monastery rug that once graced the benches the monks sat on.

"That little fragment your dog gets to sleep on is the kind of thing I'm looking for," I said, interrupting her look of concentration.

She looked up, alert now. "I've got the rest in back. I cut that piece off because it's so worn."

"I'd like to see what's left."

Following her down a crowded hallway lined with dark paintings and tarnished mirrors, I paused to study an etching of La Rochelle in the Middle Ages. A ring of forty-foot-tall stone walls encircled the city, and a massive chain stretched between two cannon-filled towers that controlled the traffic in and out of the port entry.

She came to stand beside me. "That belonged to my late husband. He loved medieval history."

"Wasn't La Rochelle where the Knights Templar berthed their main fleet in the thirteen-hundreds?" I said.

Her face lit up. "Oh, how he loved that story. Especially the part about sailing away at night in ships filled with treasure greater than that of any king."

"Did he ever talk about where those ships could have gone?"

She sniffed. "He never believed the story about them sailing up to Scotland. He was always partial to another legend that said they sailed to Spain and hid the treasure there under the protection of the Spanish king."

"Why did he think that?"

"Those boats weren't just carrying treasure, they were carrying thousands of knights, along with their wives and children. It makes much more sense when you look at a map. A boat leaving La Rochelle could easily hug the coast of Spain. That would be far safer sailing than trying to go up to Scotland through waters patrolled by warships loyal to the king of France."

That bit of information was something Steve and Danny had left out. Maybe I should have bought one of Steve's books.

At the end of the hallway, the tattered remains of a Ningxia temple runner were heaped on the floor. Eight panels featured a cloud pattern on a pale-yellow background. All the panels were slightly worn, but collectors would buy these in almost any condition.

"How much do you want," I said. "Including the doggie's piece?"

A bird-like gleam flashed in her eyes. "How much would you pay?"

I needed to offer enough to tempt her, but not so much she might get second thoughts. "How about three hundred dollars?"

A smile glided across her wrinkled face. "I thought I'd never sell that mess."

I thumbed through my book on the Vizcaya Carpet while waiting for Sammy to arrive. Commissioned by Spanish royalty in the fifteenth century and woven by Sephardic weavers during the dark days of the Inquisition, it was described as the only medieval carpet known to contain Talmudic symbols.

What intrigued me even more were the colors. Medieval textiles are so scarce that it's almost impossible to find reliable comparisons. But style is like a signature, although more subtle. The stylistic hallmark of the Vizcaya Carpet was the colors, and they were remarkably similar to those in the table cover.

The book also pictured an Egyptian tomb painting that showed Jewish women weaving on vertical looms. That was proof of an early weaving tradition but told me nothing about its continuity into the Middle Ages.

Sammy showed up outside my store wearing a black beret tilted at a cocky angle, and an attractive young woman on his arm. The woman covered him with kisses before continuing on her way. When he came through the door, he was still limping from the broken leg he got while saving his brother from drowning in a raging river many years ago.

"You got a new girlfriend?" I said.

He grinned. "She's an X-ray technician."

"I suppose she sees things in you that nobody else does?"

"You better believe it."

"I thought you were married."

He nodded. "Most of the time."

I let that drop when a viper-eyed teenager with a shaved head came through the door, seemed to recognize Sammy, and left without saying a word.

We watched in silence as he crossed the street and stood there talking to a fat man in baggy denims while taking quick puffs on his cigarette.

"Those are the kind of guys you don't want anywhere near your store," Sammy said, when they walked away.

"You know them?"

"I've seen them around. The fat one's goes by the name Dog Food. His buddy is Puppy Chow."

"How'd they get those names?"

"Do you really want to know?"

Deciding I didn't, I began outlining what I had in mind. "The people who run that Swami place took a rare rug from a lady friend of mine and I want to help her get it back. Things could get dicey, but I've got a plan for getting in, and some ideas about getting out."

Sammy frowned. "I've been in places like that, and they usually have people watching everything. This caper could be a risky one, so what's in it for me, and how long will it take?"

"Maybe you could straighten me out on something?"

"Be glad to."

"How come you always seem to be singing that same tune?"

He squinted. "What same tune?"

"Mi, mi, mi, with a little do thrown in."

"How can you say a thing like that?" he said, raising his voice.

"I say it because you're the one who knows the answer."

He folded his arms. "You're offering me a job that could get me two years for breaking and entering. Unless you can come up with something better, I'll stick with money."

"Okay," I said. "You can put away the violin. I'll cover costs. We'll drive over, spend a couple days, and drive back. You pay me what you owe me from that last deal, then I'll pay you five hundred, plus a kickback if I end up making some money?"

He uncrossed his arms. "Look at me. Do I look like I've got money?" He pulled at his beret. "I'm an artist now. A gallery sells the mandalas I draw, but that's barely enough to live on."

"Everybody knows you work less often than Santa Claus. Anyway, why should I believe anything you say after you took me for two grand worth of my stuff?"

"I was going to send you a check, but a problem came up."

"No ink in your pen?"

"Don't give me that look. My daughter needed some dental work. I'm not a bad guy. I try to be honest. I really do, but maybe I don't always look it."

"Trust me. You don't."

"You're usually a more reasonable kind of guy."

"I'm trying to break myself of that."

"I'll never be able to pay you back, so why not just cancel it?"

He was right, but a basic rule of business was involved. "I won't cancel it, but I might stop squeezing you. If this works out, I'll pay you the five hundred plus a kickback."

"You never pay me what I'm really worth."

"Careful," I said. "You might be negotiating in the wrong direction. And you better ditch that beret and scarf."

"Are you saying you don't trust me to know how to dress for a job?"

"Would you trust you?"

"Clever. When do we do this?"

"We need to get into the ranch this the weekend, so consider it set and be ready to roll in two days."

"I'll be ready, but if you're thinking of black stocking caps, black turtlenecks, and one of those long flashlights, that's not how it's done these days."

21

It had been too long since I dated a woman who felt so right on so many levels. Laura and I hadn't hit it off very well, but now we had a common goal, getting back the things that had been stolen from us.

I felt like a sophomore on his first date when I knocked on the door. Laura's mother opened it, greeted me with a gentle smile, and led me down a carpeted hallway to the living room. After calling her 'Mrs. Eskenazi' for the third or fifth time, she sensed my unease.

"Just call me Thelma," she said, patting me on the arm.

Then Laura came in looking stunning in black linen trousers and a vanilla-colored blouse. I was struggling for something clever to say as we climbed into my car, but all that came out was, "You look like a different person in those slacks."

A smile filled her face. "Lime-green has never been my favorite color."

I relaxed a bit at her sense of humor. "So, what made you get involved with a group who wear it all the time?"

"It's a complicated story. I was finishing up a degree in Classical Studies when I married a doctor. He was doing his internship, and it didn't take long to see that his career wasn't going to harmonize with my interests in mythology and religion. I stuck with it for a while, but we drifted apart. The divorce left me feeling like I needed to take a step on my own to create a future for myself."

"You can learn something from breaking your heart."

"Has that ever happened to you?"

"I never quite thought of it that way," I said, slowing for some children in a crosswalk.

She gave me a questioning look

"My wife was running an errand for me and died in a car crash."

"Yours was far more tragic than mine."

"I'm learning to live with it."

"What was her name?"

I didn't answer until the children had passed. "Gina."

"It must still be difficult for you."

"I should have been with her."

"There are aches we can live with, and others that never seem to fade away. Which is yours?"

"It's a day-by-day thing. Sometimes it's hard to move on."

"I took the first opportunity that came along. Friends from school told me about people coming together around a spiritual leader. I went to see what it was all about, and they offered me a job teaching classes on my favorite subjects, oriental philosophy and the mythology teachings of Joseph Campbell."

"I can see how that would be a tempting proposition."

"It was. In the beginning, it seemed like we shared a common purpose. They weren't trying to escape the world. They just wanted to change the way people live."

"That's never been an easy thing to do."

"No, it isn't. My confidence started to fade when I realized we never had any real privacy, and the leadership was always pressuring people to give more money. After a while, I started taking walks in the hills instead of attending meetings, but I kept teaching because I felt an obligation to my students."

"It was actually pretty daring to do all that."

She half-laughed. "I wish my parents could see it that way."

"It can be hard for parents to let their children make their own life."

She was quiet for a moment. "Enough about me. How did you ever get into this relic business?"

"That's a long story, too. My father authenticated relics for collectors, so I grew up in a house stuffed with what seemed like King Tut's treasures. After my mother died, he turned it into a full-time business. One day he told me and my sister he had found an Inverted Jenny, a stamp that sold for a fortune because they had printed some with the airplane upside down. We thought he was kidding until we learned a trusted colleague had tricked him and stole it."

"What a cruel thing to do."

"He never got over it. I think it shortened his life."

"Things like that can stay with us a long time."

"He died when I was getting my degree in Fine Arts. The long process of researching and selling his collection baptized me in his world of art dealing. I suffered some losses, but I learned. One name that kept showing up in his files suggested a French collector might have been the one who stole the stamp. After hearing through the grapevine about a stamp that had passed down through his estate to a grandson, I devoted an entire summer to chasing down the grandson."

"Why did it take so long?"

"He was wandering around Europe. In the end, I found him strung-out on drugs at a beachfront villa on the Côte d'Azur. He had squandered his family fortune and laughed when he told me that the valuable stamp had vanished forever when one of his drug-addled friends used it to mail a postcard."

"That sounds horrible."

"It was horrible. I felt like my quest had been a failure. But that wasn't entirely true. It blessed me with some remarkable experiences and propelled me into a new calling."

"How did all that cause you to specialize in textile arts?"

"When I tried to sell my dad's oriental rugs and tapestries, none of the antique dealers seemed to know much about them. I began studying on my own, found magic and beauty, and it drew me like a flame."

A faint smile hovered on her lips. "Magic and beauty, along with money to be made? That sounds like serendipity to me."

"Or dumb luck. A neighborhood store was going out of business, and I signed a lease even though I had no money, no customers, and barely enough merchandise to make it look like a gallery."

"That was more daring than what I did."

"You learn fast what it's like to be self-employed. You put in twenty-four hours a day and your time is never your own. You're the buyer, the seller, the bookkeeper, and the guy who sweeps up at night. People think you must be doing great because you have a store, but the bills don't stop just because you have lousy months. On top of that, your income goes straight back into stock and there's no pension when you're done."

"So, what's the payoff?"

I had to think about that. "There are times when you run across something so beautiful that it cracks your heart open, changes the way you think and see. Once that happens, it becomes more than just a business. It's an unending process of discovery, as well as what's left of my social life."

"It sounds like you've been a loner for most of your life."

"I suppose so, but something about the thrill of the hunt and the chance to land a priceless treasure keeps it interesting."

"All I've ever hunted for are bargains."

"Finding diamonds in the rubbish is the same sort of thing."

"Does that happen to you?"

"Not often enough. It happens mostly with old oriental carpets because nobody understands what the patterns represent."

"What do they represent?"

"If I tell you, you might become my competitor."

"I promise I won't."

She grinned when I gave her a questioning look.

"The patterns are a visual language that evolved out of thousands of years of human consciousness. The earliest versions turn up in cave paintings and petroglyphs. They represent a view of the cosmos, a view of the heavens."

"The heavens?"

"The weavers call it the eternal flow of creation."

"That's incredible. Like a window to another world?"

"They saw it as a way of viewing the truth of this world that was passed down from mother to daughter."

"Why do you say from mother to daughter?"

"Making things out of fiber and thread is as old as Adam and Eve. There's even a story about Eve spinning their hair into yarn so she could weave a cloth to cover their naked bodies. We know from history that it was always the women who made the clothing, blankets, and baskets while the men were out hunting, fishing, or fighting. Archeologists think that knotted pile weaving got started when some Neolithic woman discovered it was an improvement over animal pelts and started tying her own patterns."

I was babbling a bit, but I kept at it because she was listening so intently.

"The earliest examples are the most sought-after because the weavers of earlier centuries were more skillful at creating that magical window. Sometimes I think that's where the legend of the flying carpet comes from."

"How could that be?"

"The flying's not so much on the carpet, as into it."

She smiled. "Have you ever found a flying carpet?"

"No," I smiled back. "But there's always hope."

22

A friendly waitress and the spicy aroma of Italian cooking greeted us at the door to the Swingside Café. The waitress led us through the packed dining room to a table I had reserved in the more secluded lounge. Red tablecloths and candles in thick, red glass cast the romantic glow I was hoping for, and old jazz music was playing low enough not to get in the way.

We sat and studied the menu. "A good starter is the olives and peppers, with bread and olive oil," I suggested.

She nodded. "Sounds good to me."

"I usually go with the Aglio Olio."

"That's too spicy for me. I'll try the Hazelnut Pesto."

"Maybe a couple green salads, and some red wine?"

"Okay."

Laura leaned forward when the waitress left with our order. "Do you believe in destiny or fate?"

I hesitated. "Those concepts are often misused. I think we forge our own fate. Life doesn't have any remote, you've got to get up and change things yourself."

"You don't have a philosophy of life?"

"I believe in the here and now. That every day is God's day. What are you smiling about?"

"It's nothing."

"Must be something?"

"When we first met, I thought you were some kind of a hardhead."

That made me smile. "Sometimes being hard is the only way not to get eaten."

"I take it that's never happened to you."

"I've been nibbled at often enough, but deep down, I'm just an old softie."

Her lips opened into a wider smile. "I think that remains to be seen."

I waited until our pasta arrived before bringing up the business at hand. I needed to tell her about the theft of my panel without scaring her off. I wanted to avoid talking about the inscription translation and the legend of lost treasure. That was still in the realm of speculation. For now, I wanted to focus on getting the panels back.

"There are a few things I've discovered that make your family heirloom a lot more interesting than I first thought."

She looked up from her food. "What have you found out?"

Her eyes were so wide and beautiful in the soft glow from the candlelight that I had a sudden urge to tell her everything.

"It's what I haven't found out that intrigues me most. It has a highly unusual combination of symbols woven in and probably dates from the Middle Ages."

"You mean symbols like the scallop shell border?"

"The scallop shell border is the most conspicuous. But there's also a Greek letter, a Maltese Cross, and some other odd things."

She sighed. "I don't think I'll ever get my half back. Sheena keeps such an iron grip on everything."

"That brings us to something I haven't told you. Two women from the ranch mugged a client of mine and took my half. Sheena has all of it now."

"Oh, my God."

"I didn't tell you earlier because I didn't want to upset your parents. Besides, it doesn't change what we need to do. We have to get in there and get both halves back before they sell them."

"You mean, steal them back?"

"Sometimes you've got to fight for what's yours."

"But that would be committing a crime."

100

I smiled wolfishly. "It's not a crime to steal back our own stuff."

Amusement flickered in her eyes. "But it could be dangerous."

"We can do dangerous."

She reached for her wine. "Maybe."

"Everything's a maybe until you actually do it."

She took a sip of wine. "That's true."

"I found someone who can help us. We just need to get in for a day or two, take the panels at night, and then get away."

"I don't know. They've tightened up their security after stirring up all that conflict with the county. If they catch us doing this, it will be all over the news as an attack against their religion."

"Being an innocent bystander on the corner of life has never appealed to me."

"Me either," she said decisively. "What would I have to do?"

"Help us get to wherever Sheena might be keeping them."

"Mine was locked in their ashram office, so that's probably where they're keeping yours. Do you trust this person not to tell anybody?"

"I trust him as much as I trust anyone. But he won't be in town much longer, so we should do it this weekend. Can you think of a way to get in?"

She gave a crooked grin. "You mean, be your henchperson?"

"Exactly."

"They will be having a small celebration this weekend. Visitors will be encouraged to come and stay in the dorms. I could show you the office where they keep the valuable things people have contributed."

"We could drive over together."

"We could, but we don't dare be seen coming in together."

"How else can we do it?"

"My parents have friends near there who'd let us stay the night. They could drive me in the next day. Then you two could drive in by yourselves. But you'll have to be careful going through the little town of Dixie. It's been under the ranch's control for almost two years."

"How'd they manage to take over an entire town?"

"It was a small town. All they had to do was buy a few old houses and register their followers as residents. Then they voted in their own people for mayor and city council."

"Why did they want to go to all that trouble?"

"It gave them a police force with access to the national crime database, and total control over the only road in and out of the ranch."

"How does that give them control of the road?"

"The Swami police will run your plates when you get to town, and Sheena will know who you are long before you get to the ranch."

That gave me something to think about while Laura sketched out a floor plan of the ashram office on a paper napkin. I almost smiled when I saw a childish sort of drawing, but with enough detail that even an architect could be proud of it.

"What's the celebration next weekend?" I said.

"Diwali, the Festival of Lights, happens during the new moon near the end of October. It's considered an auspicious time because it's the darkest night of autumn. Mostly all they'll do is burn some candles."

"A dark night's exactly what we want."

Driving home, my rambling stories about characters in my business had us laughing so much it felt like we were old friends. When I parked in her parent's driveway, bouncy music and sounds of celebration leaked from a house across the street. Neither of us wanted our evening to end.

"If you're growing a beard, I kind of like it," she said.

"It'll give me a disguise for our escapade."

"Maybe you need an alias, too. What's your middle name?"

"James, Anthony James."

"That could work."

"What's your middle name?"

"Rebecca. I was named after my grandmother."

"That's a lovely name."

"Did I tell you the name Swami gave me?"

"No, what?"

"Samsaramochan Dasi," she said, touching my arm with a hand that warmed me like electricity.

A current flowed between us when I placed my hand on hers. I repeated the name. "Samsaramochan Dasi?"

She grinned. "I know that's quite a mouthful."

"If you think that's a mouthful, maybe we should try this," I said, leaning over for a kiss.

My body reacted when I caught the hot sweet smell of her. The next thing I knew she was gently pushing me away.

"We're too old to be necking in my parents' driveway."

"I've got a driveway over at my place we could try."

She began straightening her hair.

I pulled her closer.

"If I told you that you've got a beautiful body, would you hold it against me?"

She put her hand on my chest and pushed me away.

"I like you, Tony, but this sort of thing will have to wait."

23

I dug out my USGS topographical map for southeast Washington so I could plot our undercover undertaking into the notorious Swami ranch. That wild country had so few roads that it was easy to spot the one going into the ranch from the tiny town of Dixie. The huge Umatilla National Forest sat right below the ranch, and the only other roads were fire roads and trails the Forest Service installed for easy access in case of forest fires.

If I arrived in a car registered to me, they would know who I was as soon as they ran the plates, so I called in a favor. A few years back I had appraised the antiques at a waterfront property in the San Juan Islands being purchased by the wealthy Whittaker family. They flew me up there in a single engine plane stuffed with real estate agents in suits and ties. The plane bounced around a lot, and the engine coughed from time to time, but it gave us an incredible view of the oddly shaped tree-covered islands bobbing in the frothy blue waters of Puget Sound.

Marshall Whittaker, an energetic man in his thirties, so enjoyed showing me his gun collection that he insisted we go out on the deck and shoot into the bay with a fully automatic Heckler and Koch 416.

The eager faces of the suits and ties filled the plate glass window as we loaded the clips, then vanished in a wink when the staccato rip of gunfire split the air and a fusillade of ejected cartridge casings clattered off the glass inches from their noses.

Nothing comes close to that Fourth of July feeling from firing automatic weapons, so it turned into one of those bonding kinds of moments for Marshall and me. When Marshall realized that my appraisal had saved him a ton of money, he insisted that I give him a call if I ever needed a favor.

Marshal had also shown me his classic car collection and I wanted to borrow one of those for our upcoming caper. If I was driving a car registered to his well-known family, the Swami police would run the plates when we passed through Dixie and pass the news on to the ranch that a wealthy Whittaker was on his way.

Marshall laughed when I explained why I needed one of his cars. "I've got a cherry-red sixty-eight Pontiac Bonneville convertible that should do the job. It's got a four-hundred horsepower engine that can hit seventy while you're still closing the door."

"That's perfect," I said.

"My guys will have it waiting for you in the parking garage beneath my Seattle office building."

Oh boy! I'd landed a flashy, god-awful powerful ride that would give the buggers something to look at when we drove into the ranch.

I called Sammy and Laura and told them to be ready to roll in the morning for a two-hundred-and-fifty-mile drive that would take five hours. We would stay overnight in Waitsburg where friends of Laura's parents lived and arrive at the Swami ranch before noon the next day.

Sammy sounded suspicious when I told him he would be playing the role of a personal assistant to a wealthy businessman, me. "You mean, sort of like your butler? That wasn't part of the deal."

"No, not like a butler. You'll just carry a notepad and take notes."

"More like a secretary?"

"No. More like a companion."

"A companion?" He moaned. "I don't want people getting funny ideas about me."

"Heaven forbid."

The keys were waiting in the ignition when we parked next to the boat-like Bonneville in the Whittaker Building garage, and I drove out praying that I would never have to do any parallel parking.

Skies were overcast and gray as I took Mercer Street to I-5 and headed east on I-90 against the incoming tide of morning commuter traffic. Snoqualmie Pass is an hour's uphill climb from Seattle and would take us through the breathtakingly beautiful Cascade Mountain range.

Crossing the Cascades is like entering a different world. The mountains, dominated by the menacing violence of a string of snowcapped volcanoes, cut the State of Washington in two, holding the wet sea air on the Seattle side, and leaving the east an arid sprawl of open space and sky that looks like the Old West—a landscape of rocky steppes and deserts forged during millions of years of lava flows that were later carved up by glaciers and massive floods.

Sammy stretched out and dozed in the cushy back seat as we ascended the steep switchbacks. Outside was icy cold, but our powerful heater made the inside feel so warm and cozy that Sammy had begun to snore.

We were driving between sheer rock pine-topped cliffs when I rolled down my window and a rush of cold air blasted us with the heady smell of pine resin. "Smell those trees!" I said.

Sammy bolted upright, half asleep. "If you like the cold so much, why don't you put the top down?"

"I'm getting goose bumps," Laura said.

I was getting them too, so I rolled it up as we approached the summit. Snowplows were sitting idle, and the ski lifts were empty, but that would all change when the heavy snow arrived.

I had to use the brakes when we began coasting down the other side of the pass beneath a pale blue sky that seemed to go on forever. The landscape opened wide as we descended into the foothills. Gray rocky peaks and forests of Douglas fir gave way to rolling hills covered with smaller Ponderosa pines and plants in earthy tones of tan, brown, and pale yellow.

Sammy stretched and yawned as he squinted out the window at herds of elk grazing peacefully in grassy fields. "This car rides so nice I could almost live back here."

"Maybe you could hire on as a chauffeur," Laura said. "You'd look cute in a suit with a bow tie and one of those little hats."

There was a prolonged moment while Sammy mulled that one over. "Some people think I'm cute just as I am. Maybe Tony's the one who needs the outfit."

Laura patted my knee. "Tony doesn't need a hat to look cute."

Sammy leaned his head between us. "That reminds me of what the hat said to the tie."

"Okay," I volunteered. "What did the hat say to the tie?"

"You can hang around while I go on ahead."

Laura and I groaned as road signs announced a turnoff for Roslyn. "It's too bad we can't stop there," Sammy said. "That place had some real wild west action about a hundred years ago."

"What happened in Roslyn?" I said.

"Butch Cassidy and his gang robbed the bank for the mine payroll and galloped off into the mountains with saddlebags full of gold."

"I suppose he's one of your heroes?" Laura said.

"No, but he got away. That's a good thing to keep in mind now that we're about to do something similar."

We drove in thoughtful silence until we left I-90 at the Ellensburg turnoff and began a steep climb into the sagebrush-covered hills of the Saddle Mountains. A strong wind was blowing, and I had to constantly hit the brakes to avoid tumbleweeds that were bounding across the highway.

"You can blame those tumbleweeds on the Russians," Sammy said.

"Why the Russians?" Laura asked.

"Russian immigrants were the ones who brought in flax seed contaminated with Russian Thistle, otherwise known as tumbleweeds."

The wind diminished when we cleared the Manastash Ridge summit and began our descent into the Yakima Valley. Thanks to irrigation, the fields surrounding the city of Yakima are filled with seemingly endless orchards and vineyards that draw thousands of seasonal field workers.

"It's getting to be lunchtime," Sammy said. "Why don't we find a Mexican place?"

The highway circled the city and brought us to the tiny town of Union Gap where I pulled into a graveled lot next to a run-down gas station and parked outside Los Hernandez, a family run restaurant.

After stuffing ourselves with asparagus tamales and chili rellenos ladled up with eye-watering tomatillo salsa verde, we followed the twisting Yakima River through Zillah, Granger, Sunnyside, and Prosser. Crossing the wide Columbia River put us onto narrower roads through sleepy farm towns named Eureka, Lamar, Harsha, and Prescott.

"My dad came from a town near here," Sammy said wistfully.

"Which one was it?" Laura said.

"I never knew, but my mom always kidded him about it. Said it was too small to have a town drunk, but everybody was more than willing to take turns."

The dry, dusty hills gave way to rippling fields of ripe grain and wooden farmhouses with huge red barns sitting back from the highway. When we passed the Waitsburg Grange, I took my foot off the gas and followed Preston Avenue down the middle of a western-style town boasting three traffic lights and seven blocks of redbrick shopfronts. Laura dug in her purse for directions.

A left at Cooper Feed and Grain brought us to a blue house with white trim. Two people rose from a porch swing to greet us when we pulled into the driveway. They took turns hugging Laura before she introduced us to Margaret, a gray-haired lady who was a retired schoolteacher, and Phil, a ranch worker before he retired.

"That's a pretty fancy car you're driving," Phil said.

"It's a loaner so we can look good when we roll into the Swami ranch," I explained.

Margaret glanced at the three of us. "We've only got one guest bedroom, but you're welcome to use the trailer next to the house."

"The trailer will be fine for Sammy and me," I said.

Margaret served up a hearty country dinner and we turned in by 10 p.m. so we could get an early start. The Hills would drive Laura to the ranch in the morning, and Sammy and I would leave a bit later.

The twenty-minute drive to Dixie would give us a chance to find out how the Swami Peace Force handled two friendly guys driving a cherry-red Bonneville convertible.

24

Margaret's breakfast of scrambled eggs and buttery pancakes disappeared fast. She was brewing up a second pot of coffee when I asked a question that had been on my mind. "How'd they ever turn a dusty old cattle ranch zoned for fifty people into a small city?"

She wiped her hands on her apron and turned to face me. "They were stupid enough to think they could bribe the local officials like they did in India. They spent millions before they realized they couldn't bribe anybody. Then they had to block the road with bulldozers to keep the county inspectors out. Two inspectors who did get in had to be airlifted to a hospital after being poisoned with something in their drinking water."

Sammy and I exchanged a glance. We hadn't heard about that.

"How did a town in this part of the country get to be called Dixie?" Sammy said.

"That's a great story," she said. "Back when immigrants were crossing the prairies by train, three brothers who entertained people with their catchy rendition of "Dixie" became known as the Dixie Boys. The creek they settled at was called the Dixie Crossing and that became the name of the town as more people arrived. It's a shame they changed the name of such an historic town."

"What did they change it to?"

Her eyes narrowed. "They changed it to Anahata, their name for the heart chakra. They say they wear green because it's the color of the heart chakra. I think they wear green because it's the color of money."

"Maybe they need a chakra transplant," Sammy said, grinning. "You ever hear the one about the doctor who tells a guy the only heart available for transplant is a sheep heart?"

We all shook our heads.

"The man agrees, and the doctor transplants the sheep heart into the man. When the man comes in for a checkup the doctor says, 'How are you feeling?' The man says 'Not BAAAD!'"

We all groaned.

Phil tapped his car keys on the table and stood. "Maybe we'd better get on our way with Laura. We wouldn't want to have to drive too FAAST."

Thirty minutes later we filled the gas-guzzling Bonneville with super unleaded, put the top down, and began rolling across black asphalt with the wind blowing through our hair.

"There's a clipboard in the glove box," I said. "When you're playing my assistant, it will be more convincing if you carry it around and act like you're making notes."

"Sure thing, boss." Sammy's tone of mock sincerity made it perfectly clear he didn't really mean it. Truth is, nobody has ever been Sammy's boss.

He pulled out the clipboard along with two black baseball caps. Both had the Whittaker Corporation logo stitched in white on the front.

"Check out the hats," he said, holding them up. "These will make us look even more convincing."

We were putting them on our heads when a concrete grain elevator signaled the outskirts of the town formerly known as Dixie, an oasis surrounded by hills of wheat.

I slowed to a law-abiding twenty-five as we passed a freshly painted sign reading *Entering Anahata.* Just beyond the sign, a lime-green, four-wheel drive pickup was parked facing our way. It had a police logo on the door and a rack of lights across the roof. Two stone-faced cops with neatly trimmed beards were

111

sitting inside wearing mirrored sunglasses and green police-style uniforms. An ominous looking pair of black military assault rifles hung from the gun rack behind their heads.

"Those guns are the only things inside the truck that aren't green," Sammy said, as we drove by.

"I wonder if they use green bullets?"

"I'm not so sure we want to find out."

It had taken twenty minutes to reach Anahata, but less than twenty seconds to drive through. There wasn't much—just an old county road running through four blocks of small store fronts surrounded by clapboard houses.

A few people in western style clothing stood talking beneath the faded awning of the Dixie Grocery Store, but the scattered empty storefronts and soaped-up windows suggested business wasn't exactly booming in Anahata.

When we came to a sign reading *Swami's Mommy's Café*, I pulled to the curb and killed the engine. I was closing my door when a second cop truck came creeping by. Two pairs of mirrored sunglasses reflected silvery light back at us from inside the cab.

We were climbing the wooden stairs to the cafe when the door flew open, and a boisterous group of green-garbed followers came filing out. They stopped talking and studied our clothing as we let them pass.

All the lime-green vinyl-covered stools facing the green Formica counter were empty, but we went for a table near the entrance. The pleasing drone of recorded Indian music gave the place a timeless feel and the waiter dressed in green had a tempo to match. Eventually, he wandered over, poured us some water, and handed us a couple light green menus.

After studying their creatively named vegetarian dishes, we ordered cappuccinos and sat listening to the haunting sadness of a well-played raga. My tranquil train of thought left me in the station when the waiter was setting our coffee on the table.

The sudden scraping of chairs had drawn my eyes to a dimly lit back room. Sheena and broad-shouldered Vincent were seating themselves in the shadows across from a ghostly pale bald man wearing a clerical collar. The bald man grinned cadaverously as Sheena slid a fat manila envelope across the table.

Tipping Sammy to them with a glance, we tossed back our coffee, left some money for the waiter, and headed for the door. When I pushed it open, two Swami police trucks were parked in the street with their motors running.

The cop with a cell phone to his ear glanced our way. He must have been telling Ranch management that a wealthy Whittaker was on the way.

With Dixie shrinking fast in our rear-view mirror, my mind was galloping in different directions with half-formed ideas, and too many coincidences. I had a flood of questions and no answers.

Criminal types seemed to be involved at both ends, with Sheena and Woodhouse. Vincent may have been working with Woodhouse, but now he could be buying or selling for anybody. Maybe the pale-faced man was the ultimate client all along? Except that didn't explain why he'd tipped me off about the Vizcaya Carpet. Maybe he was trying to cut his own deal with me?

But everything could have changed if they knew about a painting in a museum that might depict the same table cover.

When there are so many overlapping coincidences, they should start fitting together sooner or later. But I kept moving the pieces around in my mind and couldn't make anything out of them. There were too many variables and too many unknowns. I didn't have a clue whose side anybody was on.

The only thing certain was that the bald guy was doing a deal with the Swami crowd, and we had to move fast. I began filling Sammy in about Vincent, Woodhouse, and the pale-faced man visiting my gallery.

"It's hard to figure what the guy dressed like a priest is doing with Vincent and Sheena," I said.

"That Friar Tuck dude's no priest," Sammy said. "I knew a guy who'd dress like that to go shoplifting."

"I have a feeling this one's up to something way bigger than shoplifting. Now that we're close to the ranch, I better tell you my plan. We'll pretend to be interested in joining up so we can scope out their buildings and steal back the panels. And we've got to be careful about what we say in our room. It's probably bugged."

"You may have that part figured out, but have you come up with a plan for getting us out of there after we're done?"

"We'll just have to see how it goes. If we can snatch the panels without anybody knowing, then we'll drive out the same way we drove in."

"Any idea where the panels are hidden?"

"Laura thinks they're in a padlocked metal cabinet."

"I can do padlocks."

Sammy opened his duffel bag so I could see his packet of tools: screwdrivers, jimmies, masking tape, gloves, tiny flashlights, paperclips, a small bolt cutter, odd-shaped whistles, a spray can of WD-40, and a corkscrew.

"What's with the whistles?"

"They're bird whistles for the lookout to signal if someone's coming. One's an owl, other's a blackbird. When people hear bird sounds, they think it's something natural."

"What about the paperclips?"

"If you cut and bend one of them just right, you can pick almost any cheap lock."

"And the WD-40?"

"It silences squeaky doors."

"What about the corkscrew?"

"You never know when you might run across a good bottle of wine."

114

25

A left onto Biscuit Ridge Road had us bouncing in and out of ruts with dust and stones rattling off the underside. It was hard to imagine anything living in that wilderness of brush except snakes and scorpions. Then we rounded a bend and I had to hit the brakes for two yellow bulldozers that were blocking the road beneath a wooden observation tower.

Furtive green shapes manning the tower aimed binoculars at us as I slowed to guide the Bonneville into the narrow space between the bulldozers. I hadn't counted on this, but it was too late to turn back.

"They sure don't make it very easy to get in," Sammy said, as we crept between the huge machines.

"I'm more worried about getting out," I said, accelerating away from the prying eyes.

After winding through parched gullies and over dusty cow-paths, we topped a ridge and looked down on an oasis of green surrounded by steep, barren hills. Two more observation towers were positioned at opposite ends of a complex of structures flanking a small airport where a Lear jet was parked beside a black military type helicopter.

Along one side of the valley, newly built wooden buildings were laid out in a grid pattern. On the other side, rows of A-frames were under construction next to irrigated fields. The flat land in between was packed with rows of aluminum house trailers surrounding a cluster of one-story buildings resembling a shopping mall.

The entry to the compound, a guard shack with a *Welcome to Rancho Sutara* sign, and a heavy metal bar blocking the road, was at the base of the hill.

"I hope you know what you're getting us into," Sammy said.

Two men in green uniforms stepped out of the shack as we pulled to a stop. Both had neatly trimmed beards and wore mala beads with a picture of the smiling Swami.

One guard was writing down our plate number. The other came to my window. "How can we help you on this beautiful morning?" he said, one hand resting on the butt of his pistol.

"I was told we could visit for the weekend and participate in some of your social activities."

He bent to scrutinize the interior, and the cherry-red reflection of the Bonneville flared from his mirrored lenses. "Seekers of truth are always welcome in our temple," he said, gesturing for the other guard to raise the bar. "Just continue to visitor parking and the Reception Center will take care of you."

"I wonder how they'd feel about seekers of loot," Sammy said, as the iron bar clanged shut behind us.

After parking in front of a low wooden building, we climbed the steps to a small office smelling of sandalwood. A pair of green-garbed women were waiting behind the counter, a redhead and a blonde. Both had thin lips, watchful eyes, and wore mala beads. On the wall behind them, the Swami gazed down on us with a caption reading: *You are Safe at the Feet of the Master.*

For some reason I didn't feel so safe.

I smiled as earnestly as I could. "We've been listening to Swami's tapes in our yoga class. Now we'd like to stay a couple days and see what things are like in the ashram."

The blonde spoke her lines with the assurance of someone who has found the one and only true path. "Our life of sharing is open to all people who are striving to regenerate their true spiritual nature."

My heart skipped a beat when I heard her voice. She was same woman who had set me up at the Buckaroo Bar.

I stopped breathing while she opened a register book. "I can offer you a double room for two hundred dollars a day that will include vegetarian meals designed to facilitate bio-spirituality and inner harmony."

Struggling to keep my cool, I pulled out a money clip, and fanned four one hundred-dollar bills onto the counter. Darting glances showed a strong interest in my beard as she swept them into a drawer and slid a pen and a piece of paper across to me.

"You must sign our consent-to-search form. Visitors to the ashram are not allowed to bring in any illegal drugs or excessive alcohol."

Keenly aware of being watched, I signed the form in a sloppy hand, hoping I had spelled Whittaker correctly.

She was studying my face when I handed back her pen. "You seem kind of familiar," she said. "Have we met before?"

"I don't think so. I'm sure I'd remember a pretty face like yours."

I could feel her eyes flick over me with the cold sweep of a camera. "What name shall I write on the receipt?"

"Whittaker Corporation," I heard myself say.

She knew how to spell Whittaker without even asking.

Then a buzzer sounded, and a man who had no facial expression came through the curtains leading a black dog. The dog sniffed at our luggage, while the man patted us down top to bottom without saying a single word.

When he nodded approval, the blonde handed me a room key, a map of the place with meal hours, and said we could join a tour if we came back at four o'clock.

I had the constant impression of heads turning as the expressionless man led us down a busy street. For a moment, I felt uneasy, like someone wandering naked in a dream. Then it dawned on me. We stood out like clowns at a funeral among all these people wearing green.

Nobody said anything, but you didn't have to listen very hard to know what they were thinking. Foreign bodies were among their swarm.

A paved walkway brought us to a long structure resembling a two-story motel and a sign reading *Special Accommodations Center*. It was a no-frills kind of room. Just a pair of metal-frame beds, a cheap nightstand with a flimsy chair, and a bathroom with two stiff towels.

The only effort at decoration was a poster showing a big white scallop shell above the words *All Paths Lead to Me*—maybe it was true. After all, look where we were.

After the man left, I put a conspiratorial finger to my lips to remind Sammy that the room was probably bugged. Then I stretched out on the bed to study the map while Sammy wandered around, checking things out. Catching my eye with a silent gesture, Sammy slid the nightstand chair against the wall and beckoned me to come look. A small camera lens was barely visible in the electrical outlet.

We started out to join the tour, but Sammy turned back, unzipped his bag, and tore a piece of tape off his roll. After closing the door, he pressed the tape across the opening near the bottom and smoothed it with his finger.

Using our map, we followed a walkway to the *Ashram Guidance Center,* a solid looking building across from a cluster of pay phones. Its front door was made of steel and iron bars protected all the windows.

"That's probably the one we want," I said. "Too bad it's buttoned up so tight."

Sammy squinted and gazed at the building. "These are all built on post and pier construction."

"What's that mean?"

"Instead of a concrete foundation, the buildings are supported by posts set on concrete blocks, called piers. They don't have a basement, but they have a crawl space."

"Is that good for us?"

"They should have a trap door to access things like pipes, valves, and drains from inside the building. A trap door would be an easy way in and out."

118

"How does that help us if the crawl space is all boarded up?"

"Take a closer look along the base of the building. The side vents are simple metal screens held on with screws. If I can get in through a vent, I can scope it out."

The tour group had already assembled when we arrived at the Reception Center. Four women and two men were listening intently while the blonde delivered her pitch.

"Devotees have given up their worldly lives to serve our Master, an Advanced Being who teaches us how to fulfill all our needs on both the material and spiritual planes. During the tour, we must avoid interfering with anybody's devotional activities, and you are not allowed to leave the group for any reason."

Holding up a stick with a triangular green banner, she led us down the main street and stopped in front of a cluster of buildings teeming with activity.

"Chakra Mall is where we house some of the commercial activities of our *Taja-Sutara Investment Corporation*. We have a bookshop selling Swami's books, CD's, and DVD's. A boutique selling his special incense, mugs, and clothing. And a post office where letters can be postmarked with Swami's face."

Further down the street, she stopped again in front of a row of buildings with signs reading: *Creative Awakening Center, Purification Center, Serenity Studies Workshop, ESP Workshop*, and *Hall of Joy*. Rhythmic chanting was coming from inside one of the buildings.

"Here is where we offer classes that teach devotees how to plug into the universal energy source."

One of the women in the tour group raised her hand. "What is the chanting about?"

The blonde smiled benevolently. "Our Group Leaders are skilled instructors in all forms of consciousness raising meditation. The chanting of the Rig Veda is designed to pierce the sensual levels of existence and raise the spinal energy."

Sammy made a show of scribbling notes onto his clipboard.

Our next stop was an open-sided building with a high ceiling that was larger than a football field. "This is our spiritual center. Swami Hall is where we gather here for morning meditation and our Master's weekly discourse on Awakening."

Gesturing down the street with her banner, she directed our eyes toward endless rows of white tents on wooden platforms filling the rest of the valley. "We have housing with showers and toilets for up to six thousand visitors who attend our week-long Spiritual Cleansing Festivals."

Sammy whispered to me as we continued on. "If the price of our crummy room is any guide, this set-up must be a real money-maker."

The blonde was leading us through a grove of newly planted fruit trees when we passed a dirt path with a sign reading *Staff Only*. Sammy had darted thirty feet down the path before our guide turned to admonish him. He rejoined our group with an apologetic look and whispered again. "They've got a shooting range. The human-shaped targets are all full of bullet holes."

For a fraction of a second, I felt a definite heightening of my senses.

Back in the Reception Center, our guide was fielding questions when the piercing notes of flute music from outside loudspeakers startled everyone in the group.

She smiled at our surprise. "Group Leaders are calling us to assemble for a Swami drive-by. You can't imagine the bliss and harmony he generates, even at twenty miles an hour."

Hundreds of people had lined both sides of the street, and Peace Officers with automatic weapons had positioned themselves twenty yards apart. The guards stiffened when people started chanting and a pink 1950s Cadillac convertible came into view with the top down. A small man with a white beard and long white hair was steering with one hand and waving to people with the other.

The hypnotic chanting rose to a fever pitch as the Cadillac drew closer, then ebbed as its tailfins passed, leaving behind weeping, hugging people. When the driver came to a bend in the road, he was so busy waving that people had to scatter to avoid being hit.

"Good thing he isn't driving something speedy like a Lamborghini," Sammy whispered, as the crowd started flowing towards the Annapurna Dining Hall, an arena-sized room.

Hoping to spot Laura, we went with the flow and joined one of the slow-moving lines queuing up at serving stations.

People wearing emerald-green robes were positioned along the walls watching everybody as we served ourselves spaghetti, green beans, and fruit. We ate near the exit, and were putting away our trays, when I spotted Laura walking out with a woman wearing a green sari. She wore gold bracelets on her arms and her thick blue-black hair was worn long down her back.

We followed behind until they did a quick embrace and the other woman headed off. Then I spoke to Laura in a low voice like I was just talking to Sammy. "Take us to the building we're after, then run your fingers through your hair when we get there."

She led us past the pay phones to the same Ashram Guidance Center we had seen earlier, ran her fingers through her hair, and turned the corner at the next intersection.

"These phones could be perfect for our lookout," I said to Sammy.

"What's so perfect about phone booths?"

"It won't look suspicious to be hanging around here at night."

"You and I will look suspicious wherever we are in this place."

Sammy took me by the arm to stop me when I started to open the door to our room. The tape he had attached to the bottom was hanging loose. We looked at each other for a moment, then Sammy cautiously opened the door. The light we had turned off was on, and the travel bags we had left open were zipped tightly shut. This must have been what we had agreed to when we signed their consent-to-search form.

Night came at its usual pace with Sammy calm as moonlight, and me jumping up every few minutes to peek through the curtains. According to Bradley, most of the outside lights would shut down at midnight. Fifteen minutes before that, two Peace Officers passed by on their routine patrol. When they were on their way back, I poked Sammy.

He yawned, stretched, and rummaged in his duffel bag.

"Which whistle should I use on lookout?" I said.

"The owl," he said, handing me a wooden whistle. "There aren't many blackbirds around this time of year."

Sammy took a small flashlight and a screwdriver for himself, and we slipped outside to the smell of cooling earth and sagebrush baked by the sun. Pearl gray moonlight cast sharp shadows behind the buildings as we followed a paved path to the cluster of phone booths.

Feeling conspicuous, I huddled in a booth with the receiver pressed to my ear as Sammy strolled calmly toward the Guidance Center and vanished into the shadows like a trout darting out of sunlight. The cop kiosk was out of sight around a bend. If the cops returned, I would spot them from a hundred yards off and signal Sammy with two owl hoots.

The stillness of the night was punctuated by brief laughter, a door slamming, and the faint hum of electrical motors going on and off. We had calculated ten to fifteen minutes, but time was crawling, and a feeling of agitation was growing inside me with each passing minute.

I tensed when I heard voices and a laughing couple emerged from the shadows. They stopped laughing as they walked past me. Forcing myself to calm down, I took a deep breath and checked my watch. Thirty minutes had passed. What could have gone wrong?

I had started to mutter a curse when I sensed something moving behind me, and powerful hands gripped my shoulders. Startled out of my wits, I spun around and raised my fists to defend myself. Sammy was smiling his head off.

"What took you so damn long?" I hissed. "You scared me half to death."

He couldn't stop smiling. "The hatch goes up into a storage room filled with wigs and clothing they use as disguises. I took a quick peek at the office. Those cabinets use cheap padlocks that should be easy to pick. It'll go faster next time."

Back in the relative safety of our room, I closed the door just as the building trembled and shook. A helicopter had thundered past, its bright searchlights sweeping the darkness along the distant hilltops.

"What the hell was that?" Sammy said.

"It must be their night patrol."

26

Flute music from loudspeakers, followed by a short burst of rhythmic chanting, jolted us awake for a breakfast that would be followed by the eight o'clock assembly with the Swami. After joining the slow-moving line filing into Annapurna Dining Hall, we served ourselves cereal, yogurt, and juice, along with some disappointing coffee.

Seconds after sitting near the exit, a bearded man wearing a worried look and thick glasses sat at the other end of our table. I looked his way a couple times, but he blinked owlishly and looked away.

After putting away our trays, we left the dining hall to join the long line of people filing into Swami Hall. We were shuffling forward a few steps at a time when Sammy stopped to look at the posters on a kiosk, I thought he was thinking about taking one of the classes being offered until he whispered, "Don't turn your head, we're being followed."

Sure enough, the owl-eyed man sat down behind us when we picked a place to sit on the concrete floor.

Joss sticks filled the air with a sandalwood fragrance, and soothing Indian music played on the overhead sound system. The music livened up when a yellow 60's Eldorado Town Car oozed past. Sheena was at the wheel, and the Swami sat in back with his arms around two young women wearing emerald-green robes.

Everyone stood as the Cadillac came to a stop, and the passengers disappeared into a side entrance. Then the stage lights brightened, and two guards with rifles positioned themselves on opposite sides of the stage.

A moment of silence was followed by a woman singing a Hindu chant. The audience repeated the chant in English, "I go to the feet of the Awakened One." Then the curtains parted, and the silver threads in Swami's white robe sparkled as the two women escorted him to a throne-like chair. He seated himself. They went offstage, and everybody sat.

Swami gazed over his audience for a long moment, then spoke in a high-pitched, sing-song inflection.

"Truth and knowledge are beautiful to behold, but that which is good is even more beautiful. Truth and knowledge are thought of as being like the good, but they are not equal to that which is good. That which is good must be honored even more than truth and knowledge. In our world, light and sight are considered to be sun-like, but it is wrong to think of them as being the sun."

Pausing, he raised a hand as if to shield his eyes from the stage lights. The audience erupted in joy. He grinned benevolently until the commotion died down, then he continued.

"Like anyone who has suddenly arisen from a deep sleep, the awakening soul cannot look at bright objects. Before the soul can look at bright objects it must be persuaded to look at beautiful habits, and at works of beauty produced by men who are known for their goodness. Even then, it is only the mind's eye that can perceive this mighty beauty. The ambition of every ascending soul is to see with their mind's eye and arrive at the realm where this mighty beauty dwells."

A flute played as he bowed his head. Then a voice from the loudspeakers read a religious text, Faster music brought everybody to their feet, chanting and swaying while the Swami waved his arms in a clumsy rhythm. As the music slowed, the two women came out to lead him off stage. The lights dimmed when they disappeared through the curtains.

The whole room remained standing in silence while the yellow Cadillac slowly circled the building. Then it zoomed off.

Sammy nudged me with his elbow as we headed for the exit. The blonde from Reception was waiting outside the doorway. My toes began to curl when she took me by the arm and guided us away from the crowd.

"Have you sensed any changes to your level of consciousness during your stay in the ashram?" she said.

I glanced at Sammy. He gave an almost imperceptible nod "We're both feeling more alert and sensitive to the things that are going on around us."

Her eyes brightened. "We always feel a sense of awakening whenever the Master is near."

"That's got to be it," I said, watching the wheels turning as she studied my face and struggled to remember where she had seen me before.

"Our group leaders have invited you to a ceremony of Spiritual Transition. Swami will be initiating his new devotees in Buddha House at three o'clock."

I glanced at Sammy again. "We'd sure hate to miss something like that."

Buddha House was a small auditorium in Jesus Grove, the luxurious living quarters for the Swami. When I saw the blonde waiting outside to greet us, I pulled the Whittaker hat down more tightly on my head.

We followed her to an upstairs room furnished with leather club chairs arranged in a circle. Sandalwood incense filled the air, and a wide window made of thick glass overlooked the auditorium. I felt like a heretic sneaking into the promised land when she invited us to sit in the circle of chairs.

Her eyes were fixed on my face when she brought us far better coffee than was served in the dining hall. "I think I'm remembering where I saw you," she said, after leaning over to pour it.

"Maybe it was someone who looks like me."

The pupils of her eyes narrowed as she thought it over. "No, it was you."

"People can look alike from a distance," I said, trying to sound cheerful.

"It wasn't from a distance. It was up close."

"Up close?" I said, suppressing a tremor of panic.

"Face to face."

Sammy's cup stopped halfway to his lips.

"It's your most distinctive feature," she said, pointing an accusatory finger straight at my face.

"What are you talking about?"

"The hat."

"The hat?"

"You were wearing it yesterday when I was coming out of Swami's Mommy's Café."

Sammy raised the cup to his lips and drank.

"Oh yeah," I said, letting out air. "That was us."

Seconds later, a dozen green-garbed initiates came in and seated themselves around us. The blonde ignored Sammy and me as she went around filling cognac snifters from a bottle of Remy Martin.

Snippets of small talk drifted over while everybody tasted their cognac. A couple sitting close to us introduced themselves to everyone as Peter and Suzie Atwood. He said he was a Hollywood film producer and named a couple movies that sounded familiar.

When there was a lull in their conversation, I turned to Peter. "How does being initiated change your life?"

"It's a huge change. We'll renounce all material attachments and declare absolute surrender to our Master's teachings."

Suzie leaned forward. "Part of today's ceremony is receiving our new spiritual names."

"What does that signify?" I said.

"It means we've become part of Swami's spirited family. Oh my. I mean spiritual family. Maybe I've had enough of this cognac."

Peter checked the time on his diamond encrusted Patek Philippe watch and drew a sleeve across his forehead. "That's enough for me, too. I'm feeling kind of hot."

Suzie gave her husband a clumsy hug, and spilled cognac down his chest. Sammy lifted an eyebrow at me.

I lowered an eyebrow back as the blond came to announce it was time for the initiates to go to the auditorium.

After they all filed out, Sammy walked over to the Remy Martin bottle she had left on the table, poured himself a shot, and raised the bottle in my direction.

"I'm a devotee," I said.

Sammy poured me a generous shot, and we took seats in front of the window as the stage lights brightened below us, and the Swami was escorted to another throne-like chair.

We watched as a line of initiates passed before him, bowing as he tapped their foreheads with his finger and hanging a mala around each neck. When the ceremony was over, Sammy got up to refill his glass.

He was pouring another shot into his cup when the blonde brought Peter and Suzie back to our room. At first, she looked startled, then she grabbed the bottle out of his hand.

"That's only for the initiates," she said. "I hope you understand."

The blonde went to lock the bottle in the cabinet as two women wearing emerald-green robes came through the door and introduced themselves as Savita and Rati. Savita was a graceful blue-eyed brunette Rati was an unattractive dark-haired woman with expressionless eyes that lingered on my face, scanning it like a page.

"Swami is so pleased that you have chosen to become one with our spiritual family," Savita said, using the kind of voice you would expect her to use.

"I feel so good I can hardly believe it." Suzie said, her fingertips fluttering like butterflies on acid.

It was then I saw her face was flushed and she was sweating bullets.

Savita saw it too and moved quickly, placing a reassuring arm across Suzie's shoulders. "We all feel a surge of spirit when Swami is near," she said. "It also pleases him that you have been blessed with worldly wealth from your husband's work in the movies."

"We have been blessed," Suzie said, stroking the walnut-sized emerald hanging around her neck. "But money has never brought the wealth of spirit we're feeling today."

Rati moved closer to touch Peter on the arm, and spoke in a flat, mechanical voice. "One of Swami's most important teachings is that no one can return to the Atman if they are encumbered by earthly possessions."

Peter wiped a few beads of sweat from his forehead, glanced at his wrist, then at his wife. "All I can offer today is my watch. It would be a small token for all the love we are feeling."

When Suzie saw her husband unhooking his Patek Philippe watch, her eyes filled with tears. "Oh yes," she said, reaching to unclasp her emerald pendant. "Please, let me contribute my Castafiori emerald."

Rati's pupils narrowed as she accepted the gifts, and I realized what made her so unattractive wasn't so much her physical appearance. It was her attitude. She peered out at the world with a malevolence she wore like mascara.

Sammy nudged me with his elbow, signaling it was time to leave, and we stood to say our goodbyes. When the door closed behind us, I felt a lightness in my head, and a sense of relief.

"That watch is worth over forty grand," I said. "And a genuine Castafiori emerald could be worth a small fortune. Not a bad haul for just a few minutes work."

"How can you tell if the emerald is real?"

"Hell if I know."

"Have you noticed? Something funny's going on.

"What do you mean?"

"I think we've been dosed."

Then I felt it. Colors were brighter, and a tingling euphoria was rushing through my veins.

"They must have put something in that cognac we drank," I said.

"That's how they get money out of the initiates. They make them think it was caused by Swami tapping them on the forehead."

"Then it's a good thing we know better."

"No kidding," Sammy said. "We might have given them the big red Bonneville."

We burst out laughing.

"I hope this drug doesn't have any weird side effects," I said as a kaleidoscope of colors melted Sammy's face.

"You mean we might start saying things like far out, and groovy?"

"It's been known to happen."

"We need to pull a heist tonight, and I'm getting way too much lime-green in my reception."

"I believe you've opened my heart chakra."

"Not to mention the goodness and the good."

"But you did."

"Did what?"

"Mention it."

Suddenly I felt wobbly, and nearly stumbled. Sammy gripped my arm, pulling me toward the trees as my eyes were drawn to the minutiae of living things we were passing.

An iridescent butterfly appeared and fluttered around in front of my face. Then it was lifted by the breeze and carried away. It was as though I was seeing everything in precise detail for the very first time. Dew drenched spider webs hugging the grass. Graceful tendrils reaching for light. Blossoms in the form of delicate white fountains opening in time lapse. Insects hopping, crawling, flitting about. All of it bathed in a great vividness and flourishing as if they had minds of their own.

Beneath the shelter of the trees, I collapsed on a carpet of pine needles and closed my eyes while scintillating patterns and radiant colors exploded across my eyelids.

"Thanks for helping me back there," I said, startled at hearing my voice come out in a slow monotone.

Sammy answered from light-years away in a voice that mocked my slow monotone. "You...are...welcome."

We had another outbreak of laughter.

I was thinking how incredible it was that we could communicate over such a long distance when the drug carried me farther away, humming and surging through my entire body. Trying to cling to reality, I laughed out loud as I imagined trying to crawl under a building when I was ten feet tall.

I had completely lost track of time when piercing flute music and distant chanting jerked me back to the earthy smell of the forest. Cautiously opening my eyes to the mesmerizing chanting, I saw Sammy stretched out flat on the ground beside me.

"That means dinnertime," I said, as softly as I could. "Are you ready to join the living color crowd?"

Sammy answered without opening his eyes. "I never like to commit burglary on an empty stomach. It would be uncivilized."

Barely able to stand, we gathered what was left of our wits, and headed back to brush the forest out of our hair before showing up at the dining hall.

27

Laura walked by when we were putting away our food trays and we followed her outside. "Midnight at the phones," I said softly from several steps behind.

She nodded once, quickened her pace towards her living quarters, and hadn't gone ten feet when three Peace Officers stepped from the shadows and blocked her way.

I murmured, "Oh shit," but we kept on walking.

My mind was churning. Doing cartwheels.

"Maybe we should we change our plans," Sammy said.

"We'll never get another shot. We don't even know why they stopped her. It could be nothing."

"Or it could mean we're walking straight into a trap."

I stood behind our window curtain waiting for the guards to pass while Sammy bent paperclips into L-shapes with a small pliers. When the guards returned from their routine patrol out to the main gate, I signaled Sammy, and we slipped outside.

Gray-blue clouds moved slowly across a black sky filled with twinkling stars as we approached the phone booths. The distant whinny of a horse was followed by the soft footsteps of Laura. She was wearing a look so tense I thought her face might crack.

"What was that about with the security guys?" I said.

"Questions about my loyalty. They wanted to know why I left the ranch and went to Seattle."

"What did you tell them?"

"I told them I needed to pick up some reference materials."

"So they let it go?"

"They seemed to, but I hated having to lie to my roommate about leaving to make a phone call. Maybe I should just ask Swami for the rug back."

"Wouldn't that be risky?" Sammy said.

"I could probably outtalk him."

"Yeah, but could you outrun him?"

She sighed, and then whispered, "One of those cabinets has a sticky door. You'll have to pull hard to get it open."

I put a comforting hand on her shoulder. "Don't worry. Everything will be fine with you as our lookout."

Sammy handed her the owl whistle. "All you have to do, is toot twice if someone comes. You do know how to blow a whistle, don't you?"

"I just put my lips together and blow," she said, blowing on it softly, and grinning.

"You better blow a whole lot louder if it's for real," Sammy said. "Any mistake now could be dangerous."

Sammy quickly unscrewed the vent screen, and we crawled across dry dirt with small flashlights gripped between our teeth. I was still getting visual effects from the drug as I followed the soles of his shoes through a cramped space with spider webs and wooden beams inches above our heads.

I had a chilling thought when I heard rustling sounds that I took to be scattering rodents. "I hope there aren't any rattlesnakes in here," I whispered.

"Rattlers always rattle first. It's the Black Widow spiders I'm worried about."

"Now you tell me!" I groaned, tensing up and whacking my head on a floor joist. "How come you never mentioned the spiders?"

"You're the man with the plan, boss. I'm just your personal assistant, remember?"

Thirty feet in, Sammy brushed away cobwebs, and pushed up at the plumbing hatch. It snapped back down with a sharp crack.

"What's the matter?" I said.

"It wasn't like this before. Something heavy must be on it."

Moving in closer, I helped him push, and something hit the floor so hard it sent dust into our eyes. When the dust cleared, Sammy stood in the opening, flashed his light around, and we took turns climbing into a small storage room stuffed with Styrofoam mannequins wearing coats, scarves, and wigs.

Sammy grabbed me by the arm when I started to kick aside the metal-box we had tipped off the hatch. "We better leave that where it is."

Fluorescent markings in orange read *PETN*. Smaller ones in yellow said *Pentaerythritol Tetranitrate*.

"What the heck is it?"

"It's an explosive more powerful than nitroglycerine."

Stepping carefully over the box, I aimed my light at the far end of the closet. Red, green, and yellow lights were blinking from shelves lined with recording equipment. Beneath the shelves, metallic blue canisters marked *Nitrous Oxide* stood erect beside a horizonal stack of wooden boxes with *AK-47-Automat-Kalashnikova* stenciled on their sides.

"I wonder what they're planning to do with all this stuff," I said.

"I'm guessing we don't want to find out," Sammy said, cautiously opening the door to a larger room set up as an office. Following him to the locked cabinets, I held my flashlight steady while he worked the left padlock with one of his paperclips.

"Damn, it bent," he said, digging in his pocket for another one.

"I thought you said you've done this before."

"I never said I'd done it. I just said it could be done."

"What are we going to do if you can't get it open?"

"We don't give up that easily," Sammy said, switching to a different paperclip.

After a few more twists, the lock clicked, and the door opened to a compact medical dispensary: big bottles of white pills with labels reading *Diazepam, Percodan, Demerol, Viagra*, and *MDMA*. Below the pills and powders, sliding drawers were filled with tiny microphones, pinhole cameras, and UHF voice transmitters.

"What's all this?" I said.

"It looks like equipment to spy on people and enough mind drugs to keep everyone here doped up for months."

"Viagra's not a mind drug."

"No, that must help the old guy fulfill his spiritual potential. But MDMA's another name for Ecstasy. Diazepam is a popular tranquilizer known as Valium, and all the rest are narcotics."

Closing that cabinet, Sammy turned to the other lock. The first paperclip bent, but the second one opened it almost immediately.

I patted him on the shoulder. "Way to go. This is turning out to be easier than I thought."

Suddenly, the stillness of the room was pierced by the distant toot of an owl whistle, followed by the sound of a door slamming shut. Footsteps could be heard approaching as we scuttled back into the shelter of the storage room.

Sammy snicked that door shut just as the office door opened and bright light flowed across our feet. The footsteps came closer and closer, until they stopped outside our door, and the voice of Sheena penetrated our hiding spot from inches away. "We will lose millions of dollars if the inspectors shut down our festival. We could even lose the Ranch."

A brief silence was followed by the flat voice of Rati. "Don't we have ways to defend ourselves?"

"We have all kinds of things, but people are too timid to use them."

"The accounting people told me we're short of money after bussing in all those street bums."

"They're right. Our only ticket out of this mess might be that table cover with the scallop shells."

"What could make a rag like that so valuable?"

"My art appraiser says he saw something like it in a museum painting."

"Why would that be important?"

"If it's the same one, it could be worth a fortune. It's also got something to do with the inscription. Now that we've got both pieces, he's bringing in a professor of medieval history to take photos, translate the inscription, and make us an offer."

"That little bald guy makes my skin crawl. He's white as death and never smiles."

"He is creepy. But he pays cash, and never asks questions. He may even have a buyer for the Castafiori emerald. If Swami ever gets his hands on that little gem, we'll never see it again."

"How did we ever get involved with someone like that?"

"We needed some forged passports and he got them in no time at all. I've been using him ever since for all sorts of things."

The closet was getting warm and stuffy. I was doing my best to ignore the beads of sweat running down my ribcage, but I couldn't stop thinking about the powerful explosives at my feet.

I stiffened at the sound of metal on metal when they opened one of the cabinets. "How much serenity medicine is Borgia using for the daily beer ration?"

"She's serving four thousand a day and it takes two milligrams apiece to do the job. You better take one of the big bottles."

"We need to keep an eye on Borgia," Rati said.

"Why do you say that?"

"She's been dipping into the serenity medicine."

"Why the hell do I always have to put up with crap like this?"

"That's not the worst of it. She's supposed to persuade Swami to cut down on his happy gas."

"Fat chance of that. He'll do his raging midget routine if we don't bring him another canister of nitrous oxide."

"They're heavy. I'll call security for some help."

We shrank farther back into the closet at the sound of someone pushing buttons on a land line.

"This is Rati over at the Guidance Center. Sheena and I need a couple men to give us a hand." A pause. "Let me ask. He says they can be here in half an hour."

"That's too long, we'll do it ourselves."

136

We flattened ourselves behind layers of clothing as light filled our hiding place, and four arms reached in to muscle out a canister of laughing gas.

"What do you think of those two who came in the flashy red convertible?" Rati said.

"Our watchers are paying close attention. Those types usually think they can waltz in here and pick up some girls. But the tall one inherited a fortune. We'll take good care of him in case he wants to make a contribution."

"Some of our magical potion might loosen up his wallet."

"I've got my lab people working on something even better."

We stood in frozen silence listening to them giggle like catty schoolgirls until an outside door slammed shut. Then we pushed our door open and went back to the second cabinet.

"Dammit," Sammy said, struggling with the lock.

"What's the matter?"

"That was the last one."

"The last what?"

"The last paperclip.

"You've got to be kidding."

"Do I look like I'm kidding?"

"Don't you have anything else you could use?"

He gave me a pained look. "A key might come in handy."

"We're in an office," I said. "They must use paperclips."

Flashing my light around, I saw that all their papers were held together with staples. I was about to give up when my beam of light fell on a small box of paperclips in the back of a desk drawer.

After struggling to bend one into a useable shape, Sammy slipped it in, twisted it around, and the padlock clicked open.

"Something's wrong," he said, pulling at the handle. "I can't get it open."

"Pull harder."

Sammy put his weight into it and fell backwards into me when it popped open.

I hid my grin. "Laura said it would take a little jerk to open it."

He pushed himself away from me. "Next time we'll let the big jerk open it."

The interior of the cabinet danced and glittered in our combined beams of light. Silver and gold jewelry, fancy watches, and wads of cash filled the top two shelves. Paintings, and other artwork were stacked below.

"Maybe we're in the wrong business," Sammy said, rummaging in the jewelry.

"You want to start a religion?"

"I'll let you be the god-man if I can handle the finances."

Sammy was still poking around in the jewelry when I found our two panels folded together on the bottom shelf. "Knock it off, Sammy. Leave that stuff alone."

He said, "OK," but his light lingered a moment before he closed and locked the cabinet.

Wasting no time, we crawled out the way we had come, secured the vent screen, and strolled as coolly as we could to where Laura was waiting by the phones. The strain that tightened her face softened when I patted the sack.

"I was terrified when Rati and Sheena showed up. I blew the whistle as hard as I could."

"We heard you just in time to hide. You better be extra careful going back to your room."

"I'll be careful, but I'll feel better once we're away from this place. Sheena has people working for her who will do just about anything."

A disturbing thought occurred to me after she left. Maybe it had been a mistake to get Laura involved in something so full of risk.

28

We left before the call to breakfast so we could get away before anyone looked inside the cabinets. Sammy was itching to drive the Bonneville after we hid the panels in the trunk, and his face lit up when I handed him the keys.

We were rolling slowly toward the guard shack when a guard stepped out and held his hands palm out in the universal symbol to halt.

Sammy slowed to a stop and rolled down his window. "Is something the matter?"

"I need to look in your trunk."

"Aren't you supposed to have a warrant for things like that?"

Another guard stepped out, one hand on his pistol.

"The consent-to-search form applies as long as you're on our property."

"Then go ahead and look."

"This could be big trouble," I whispered, as both guards walked to the rear of the car.

"I already thought of it."

"You thought of what?"

"I thought of this."

We could hear them talking to each other as they fumbled with the handle. Then one of them called out, "We can't get it open."

Sammy leaned his head out, shouted, "Okay, see you later," and stepped on the gas.

For a second, I was too shocked to speak. Behind our cloud of dust, both guards watched us drive away with their hands on their guns.

"Are you out of your mind?" I said.

Sammy chuckled. "The bird that's eaten flies away."

"Have you forgotten? That same bird has to fly past another guard tower up ahead."

"You worry too much. It kept them from looking in the trunk."

"Maybe so, but that little maneuver could have gotten us shot at."

"Shooting at departing guests would put a big dent in their recruitment. They aren't even following us."

"They don't have to follow us," I said. "They can radio ahead to the cops in the guard tower and tell them to look inside our trunk. What if they've already discovered the rug is missing?"

A crooked smile was playing around his lips. "Can I level with you?"

"Don't strain yourself."

"That's not all that's missing," he said, wiggling something that was sparkling on his wrist.

It was the diamond encrusted Patek Philippe watch.

"Shit, Sammy! Stealing their stuff wasn't part of our deal. You should have told me."

"I didn't want you to think I was a bad person."

"It's too late for that."

There was a tense silence as we cleared the top of the hill. The guard tower loomed ahead of us, and the two massive bulldozers were still blocking the road.

"Getting back our own stuff was one thing. Now they can arrest us for felony theft."

"Okay, I should have told you."

"But you didn't. You said you put everything back. It amazes me how you can lie so effortlessly."

"It's hard to be an honest man in a dishonest world."

There was sudden movement on the tower. Green garbed figures had moved to the upper railing. One was training

140

binoculars on us. Another held a phone to his ear. Three more were hurrying down the wooden steps.

"If they see that watch, both of us are going straight to jail."

"I couldn't help myself," Sammy said, slowing to squeeze the Bonneville into the narrow space between the bulldozers.

"I'll never understand your way of thinking."

"You don't have to understand me."

"You've probably never felt remorse for anything," I said, holding my breath as we crept between the huge machines with only inches to spare.

"Should I feel bad about that?"

"Some people would consider it to be a character defect."

"You mean like I ought to do something about it?"

"Yeah."

"Maybe I will."

"But not today?"

"Not today, because it wasn't really like stealing."

"How can you say it's not like stealing?" I said, as the nose of the Bonneville began clearing the cramped space.

"Because the watch wasn't really theirs. It was a gift to a higher power. Like a gift to God. Things that belong to God belong to everyone."

"I love how you can say that without smiling."

"Think about it," he said, grinning at me as three figures wearing sidearms came racing towards us across the rough ground. "If those people are serious about dropping attachments, then I'm helping them to practice it."

"Then the watch is your full payment for the job."

"It's a deal," Sammy said, spinning gravel and accelerating away from the frantic hands that were clawing at my door.

Sammy was driving way too fast through rough spots in the road when a jack rabbit darted out of the brush. He hit the brakes and swerved, saving the rabbit but slamming me forward.

"Take it easy. You can't go so fast on a road like this."

"That was suicide by impulse."

"What are you talking about?"

"The rabbit was trying to kill itself."

I shook my head in disbelief. "Why would a jack rabbit try to kill itself?"

"Out here in the middle of nowhere? Boredom."

"If you're getting bored, we still have to drive through Dixie. It's a no-brainer that the Swami cops have been told to watch for us."

When the Dixie grain tower came into view, I gave our map a quick scan. No road bypassed the town, but we could avoid most of the main drag by circling through side streets. The problem we faced was that those would eventually bring us back onto the road we wanted to steer clear of.

Sammy pulled over just before we came to an intersection with the main drag, and I got out to look around the corner. As expected, one cop pickup was parked where it had been when we first came through, pointed out of town next to the *Welcome to Anahata* sign. Another was positioned at the opposite end of town where they expected us to be coming from.

"It's a good thing we didn't try to go straight through," I said. "They've got both ends of the street covered."

"Then we'll just pop out here while they're looking the other way. Maybe we'll get to see how fast this baby can go."

The eight-cylinder motor made a throaty rumble as Sammy swung a slow left and cruised towards the cops at an even twenty-five. As we passed the Welcome to Anahata sign, he punched it, and the acceleration pressed us back in our seats.

I glanced in the mirror. The cops had remained parked where they were, at the end of their jurisdiction.

29

We waited over an hour for Margaret and Phil to pull into their driveway with Laura. After amusing them with some highlights of our adventure, Sammy glanced at his watch.

"That's quite a timepiece," Margaret said. "I don't remember seeing it when you were here before."

Sammy grinned sheepishly. "I wasn't wearing it then."

A long drive was ahead of us, so we thanked them for their hospitality, and climbed into the Bonneville. When Sammy turned the key, nothing happened. Just a soft clicking noise.

Several tries later, Laura glanced nervously out the window. "This is the worst place to get stuck. Maybe we could get it started by pushing it."

"It's kind of big to push," I said, as Sammy slid out from behind the wheel. After fiddling around under the hood for a few minutes he said, "I need a bottle of water."

Laura got one out of the car, and Sammy poured a few drops of water onto each battery terminal, climbed back inside the car, and turned the key. The engine roared.

"How'd you do that?" Laura said.

"Battery terminals get corroded, but the water created a temporary contact that will get us back home."

We were descending from the sagebrush covered Saddle Mountains into the heart of cattle-raising country outside Ellensburg when Sammy swerved onto a freeway exit.

"Are you trying to get us killed?" Laura said, as we swept past a billboard showing larger than life cowboys dancing with their ladies.

"We can't drive past a place called The Ranch Tavern without stopping to celebrate."

After parking in a graveled lot full of dusty pickup trucks, we followed the muffled twang of country music to a barnlike building. Sammy gave me a quick glance as he pushed the door open to the throbbing pulse of Waylon and Willie singing *Mammas, Don't Let Your Babies Grow up to Be Cowboys.*

Worn-out boots hung above the scarred-up dance floor and lanky men wearing cowboy hats were shaking dice out of a leather cup at a neon-lit bar. The four grizzled men who were playing poker and drinking amber colored whiskey out of short glasses didn't even glance up us as we walked past them and sat at a wooden table on the edge of the dance floor.

Laura leaned forward after the waitress left with our order. "I can hardly believe we really did it."

Sammy smiled. "The best part was getting away."

"If they'd caught you, Rati and Sheena would have paraded you in handcuffs before the media."

"That crossed my mind when they were reaching for the laughing gas," I said.

"People at the Ranch think Rati is more dangerous than Sheena."

Sammy made a face. "Nah. We could have jumped out wearing those wigs and scared the hell out of both of them."

"Then what?" I said, as the waitress served our beers. "Make a run for it in the middle of the night with Sheena and Rati squirming around in the trunk?"

The waitress gave us a questioning look as she turned away.

"That reminds me of two people who encountered a bear in the woods," Sammy said. "One knelt to pray while the other tightened the laces on his boots. The one praying looks up and says, 'You'll never outrun a bear.' The one tightening his boots says, 'I don't have to outrun the bear. I only have to outrun you.'"

"That's a good one," Laura said. "But maybe we should be toasting to our own success."

"I've got one of those, too," Sammy said, raising his glass. "Some ships are wooden ships, and some ships may sink. But the best ships are friendships, and it's to these ships we drink."

The juke box kicked in with Billy Joe Shaver doing *Blue Texas Waltz* as we clinked mugs. Laura tugged at my elbow and gestured at the dance floor.

"Nobody else is dancing," I said.

Sammy smiled as Laura took my hand and pulled me to my feet. "C'mon, cowboy, let's show them how it's done."

Surprised at how warm Laura's body felt against mine, I made a few clumsy moves, but was helped along by her gentle hands and Billy Joe's heartfelt lyrics about waltzing with his sweetheart beneath a star-studded sky.

Sammy was grinning like Christmas morning when I escorted Laura back to the table.

"What's so funny?" I said.

"Nothing is funny, I'm just happy for you."

"I always liked that song."

"Me too."

I took the rear seat when we were leaving so I could examine both panels with a battery-powered black light. Repairs, stains, and differences in materials will show up clearly in the radiance of ultraviolet light. As soon as I turned it on, I spotted things I hadn't noticed before.

"This is unusual," I said, touching Laura's panel with my fingers. "The red X in the crown and the red Maltese Cross were both done with silk."

Moving the light to check my panel, I saw that the red T-form inside the inscription was also made of silk. When I moved the light closer, the scallop shell designed to look like the sail above a boat fluoresced brightly. When I touched it with my fingertips, it was neither silk nor cotton.

"One of the scallop shells in the border is positioned to look like the sail above a boat," I said. "Now I can see it's woven with linen."

Sammy looked at me in the rear-view mirror. "Isn't that what sailcloth used to be made of?"

"That's right. Somebody went to a lot of extra trouble to give these motifs subtle distinctions."

"Something about boats, along with an X, makes me think of a compass," Sammy said.

"My father used to sail," Laura said. "He might have some ideas."

Rain began hitting the windshield when we cleared the summit an hour later. Listening with my eyes closed to the hiss of wet tires as Sammy wheeled us through the downhill turns got me daydreaming about sailboats and treasure maps. I might have even dozed. When I opened my eyes, we were rolling across a floating bridge into the bright lights of Seattle.

After leaving the Bonneville in the Whittaker garage, I drove us out in my old Nissan. I swung by my gallery to pick up the translation of the inscription, then drove Sammy to his brother's house in Ballard.

A blue Ford cargo van with *Track's Construction* printed on the sides was parked in the driveway, and a man that looked like Sammy was unloading boxes of tools.

"That's my brother, Bob," Sammy said as a curly-haired man of about thirty-five came to greet us.

"My god," Laura said. "You guys look like twins."

"That's what people always say," Bob smiled. "But I'm the better looking one who's two years older. I'm glad to see you're keeping Sammy out of trouble."

I was backing out of the driveway when I had to hit the brakes for a blood red Range Rover SUV that had slowed to a crawl.

146

30

Laura's mother welcomed me with a hug that was even warmer than her smile. "You're our conquering hero. We should be throwing roses at your feet."

"We'll all be heroes if we can figure out what the designs in these panels mean. I'm hoping you and Sol might have some ideas."

Thelma pulled the panels tightly together as I opened them side-by-side on the dining room table. "We've never seen the two pieces together like this before."

I nodded. "The designs only make sense when they are viewed together.

Sol leaned closer. "Look at the way those colors shimmer. It's like something from the past is shining through."

"There may be more truth to that than we realize," I said. "The thing to keep in mind is that the designs are part of a story from another era. A time when scallop shells and a field of stars could be seen as subtle references to the Camino."

Heads nodded in agreement.

"One of the peculiar features are the brighter yellow stars. They form a shape that resembles the constellation Vela. In stellar mythology, Vela represents the sail of a boat. Then, there's a second reference to boats hidden in the border."

All eyes followed my hand as I pointed. "You don't notice it at first, but this single scallop shell was cleverly designed to look like a sailboat."

Sol ran his fingers over the form of a boat. "That's incredible."

"It gets even more interesting. At first glance, the two tiny circles in the crown look like jewels. But the one contains a red X, and the other has a red Maltese cross. I haven't figured out the X, but the Maltese cross was worn by the Knights Templar, and there's a legend that they sailed boats full of treasure out of La Rochelle that disappeared and have never been found."

Everyone shifted in their seats.

"The key to the motifs is the inscription. It was written in early Hebrew and placed inside a cartouche shaped like the floor plan of a medieval church. The inscription contains another tiny circle with a red T shaped symbol known as the Greek letter *Tau*. The Tao is an ancient symbol for resurrection and reappearance."

The room went quiet while I unfolded a piece of paper.

"I had the inscription translated at the University of Washington. Listen carefully to what it says. *Midway on the journey of life, the path we walk has brought us strife. To protect our souls, and our bounty save. We set forth upon the savage waves. A sternward wind carried us far, to the sovereign crown above the field of stars. Here we sleep in peace and pray, beneath the tower that guards the way.*

Laura frowned. "How come you kept quiet about all of this until now?"

That was the question I had been dreading, and I hoped my answer would do. "The clues were of no use without both pieces, and some were only detectable by feeling each panel."

There was an uncomfortable silence while Sol leaned in close. "He's right. The crown with its circles is in one panel, and the inscription with a Greek letter is in the other. Whoever made them knew you needed both panels to figure out the puzzle."

Laura was still frowning. "Don't you think the panels were at the ranch long enough for somebody else to spot these things?"

"They may have figured out there's a hidden message, but Sheena said they were waiting to get the inscription translated when Sammy and I were hiding in the closet."

"It sounds like you had quite an adventure over there," Thelma said.

I looked at her and nodded. "It got a little dicey at times."

"If the inscription was written in Hebrew, does that mean it could have been woven by Spanish Jews?" Sol said.

"It is possible. You mentioned that some of your ancestors came from Spain. Do you have any family records that might tell us more about where they came from?"

Sol stood up abruptly and came back rummaging in a battered black and gold metal box. "Most of these letters were written in English after our family came to Chicago, but there's an older one that looks like Spanish. Maybe Laura can read it."

We all watched as Laura carefully unfolded a delicate, yellowed letter. "It does look like Spanish," she said. "Except the spelling is different."

"Spelling wasn't the same hundreds of years ago," Sol said.

Laura held the letter up to the light. "The postmark says it was mailed from La Coruña, España. Corona is the word for crown in contemporary Spanish but spelling it la coruña might have been old Spanish for the same word."

"Corona is also the Latin word for crown," Thelma said, as Sol waved another paper in the air.

"Look at this certificate of marriage. It says my grandmother, Esther, was born in La Coruña, Spain and that Thelma's grandfather, Aaron, was born in Vézelay, France. Let's see where those places are."

Sol got out a map and we watched as he pointed out Vézelay in central France and La Rochelle on the French coast. Then he jabbed the map with his finger. "Look at this. La Coruña is a seaport town just forty miles north of Santiago de Compostela."

"Maybe these puzzle pieces are starting to fit together," Laura said.

"This could be like a treasure map," Sol said, his eyes brightening at the prospect. "If that Greek letter means something reappearing, then that X in the crown could be like a sailor's compass directing us to a place between La Coruña and La Compostela." Then he took a closer look at the crown. "Did you notice? One arm of the X is slightly longer than the other one."

149

How did I miss that? Embarrassed, I pulled out my loupe, and squinted through it. "Sol is right," I said. "The longer arm pointing down to the right has twelve knots compared to the other's eight."

Thelma leaned back and crossed her arms. "All of this is nothing but guesswork."

"But guesswork is exactly what clues like this are calling for," Sol said. "Let's try connecting the dots. If we follow a cross to find a temple, then maybe the X on top of the crown is that cross. And, if we picture the X above La Coruña, then the longer arm is pointing downward at a forty-five-degree angle straight to where the little church shape is positioned on the right side of the rug. Maybe that's the place to go look for the treasure."

"This is all way too mysterious," Thelma said. "What if it's someone's idea of a prank?"

"It's too sophisticated to be a hoax," I said. "The use of complex dyes, along with silk, linen, and wool, suggests a group of people plotted this over several months. Then they took a year tying the knots and weaving in all the weft threads. It's difficult to imagine doing so much work and planning without having a good reason."

"Tony's right," Laura said. "Complex symbols like these wouldn't have been used unless they meant something to whoever put them there."

Sol rubbed his hands together. "This is turning out to be an incredible story. A few years after the Arabs brought rug knotting to Spain, Jewish people wove a rug with a secret message about Christian knights hiding something along the Camino, and it ends up in our family. If I were a few years younger, I'd follow that path just to see what turns up. Even if nothing came of it, it could be the adventure of a lifetime."

Except for the soft ticking of a clock on the mantle, the room had gone quiet. This was no longer merely about rescuing a family heirloom. Now it was about solving one of the world's longest running mysteries and a map to a treasure worth billions of dollars.

Laura spoke in a near whisper. "I could do it. I've studied European history as well as French and Spanish."

Thelma glanced at me. "I don't like the idea of you going all that way by yourself. A young woman shouldn't travel alone in a foreign country."

I jumped right in. "We could go together. It would fit with my annual trip to Paris for the end of the year auctions, and Spain is just a border away. Regardless of what we decide to do about the treasure hunt, we should get the two pieces rejoined, and Europe would be the best place for that."

Everyone liked that idea, but I was dog tired after a long day. I was picking things up to leave when I thought of something. "You should take that old Spanish letter to my friend Larry Mintz at the University of Washington language department. His translation might shed light on how the rug came to be in your family."

Laura took my arm when I was walking down the hallway. "I'm with my dad. A riddle as incredible as this begs answering."

"A friend of mine has an apartment in Paris that's close to all my favorite auctions. I could even get some business done before we head to Spain."

"All my life, I've dreamed of going to Europe."

"You mean you wouldn't come just because I'm brilliant and good looking?"

She laughed. "Who could pass up a chance to begin a treasure hunt in Paris?"

"We could listen to Latin in the Latin Quarter, mount Montmartre, look for cats in the catacombs."

"You're a funny man, Tony."

"Funny ha, ha? Or funny peculiar?"

"I see a little bit of both," she said, and gave me a quick hug.

I tried to make the hug longer, but she gently pushed me away. "Let me talk it over with my parents."

A trip to Europe with Laura was such a great idea that I climbed into my car with a sense of well-being, but my serene self-confidence vanished like a puff of smoke when my headlights swept over a blood red Range Rover SUV parked across from the Eskenazi house. It hadn't been there when we rolled in.

Exhaust was coming out of the tailpipes, and I could see the shapes of two men inside the tinted windows as I drove past. My mind raced, and a sick feeling washed over me, when the Range Rover made a quick U-turn, accelerated, and fell in behind me.

Had the blonde at the ranch finally recognized me? But how could they have gotten here so fast? Even worse, now they know I'm tight with Laura and saw me drop Sammy off at his brother's house.

There was no point trying to lose the tail, so I turned right to head south on Third Avenue. The Range Rover surprised me by going north.

Swinging a quick left into the first driveway I came to, I backed out, and followed, trailing it from a distance. A few minutes later, the brake lights flared, and it turned without signaling into the gated entry for the Highlands, where the big rich live. The guard waved like he knew the driver, raised the barrier quickly, and the Range Rover passed in without stopping.

Seattle's secluded sanctuary for old money is a tightly guarded enclave of stately homes overlooking Puget Sound. It has been a home to the Boeing family, the Nordstrom family, as well as a former head of the CIA.

The Olmstead brothers, who built most of Seattle's parks, developed the Highlands back in 1907 and it operates like a private city. They have their own police force, sewage and water system, roads, and ground keepers.

Buying there requires an application to the Board of Directors and two sponsors who are current residents.

In other words, nobody gets in unless they are already in.

31

Nothing unexpected happened during the next couple days except I was keenly aware of people coming and going. It wasn't like I was hearing noises or jumping at shadows. I just had a gut feeling that you can't kick a hornet's nest without getting some kind of a buzz.

The first buzz came when someone called my private number around two in the morning. My brain was blank with sleep, but I answered the phone like I was wide awake.

"Is this my old buddy, Marshall Whittaker?" a gruff male voice said, in something of a hurry.

I sat up straight in bed. "Sorry, pal. You got the wrong number."

The line went dead, and I had a hard time going back to sleep.

Next morning, the Seattle Times headline announced the death of Marge Tanner, the Grande Dame of the local antique trade for the past fifty years. Her body was found in the living quarters above her store after her personal collection of Fabergé jewelry was stolen during a nighttime burglary.

Only a few trusted friends knew she had such a precious collection, and the thieves were skillful enough to disable the alarm on the safe where she had it stored.

Then Alaydin arrived looking stressed when he came to give a repair estimate on the two sections of the table cover.

"Is something the matter?" I said.

"A white van followed me to your store and nearly hit me when I was getting out of my car. One of them said, say hello to Tony for us. Then they drove off real fast."

"What did they look like?"

"White baseball caps, neatly trimmed beards, and wooden beads."

That was strange. But I didn't want to add to his anxiety, so I steered the conversation into a different channel. "They might be people from the neighborhood. I'm wondering if you'd be able to reweave the edges and rejoin these two Spanish pieces."

He ran his fingers across the surface of the pile. "This Merino wool comes from a special breed of Spanish sheep. It won't look right unless you replace it with the same wool with the same type of spin."

"How do I do that?"

"You have it done in Europe. They would have easy access to the same kind of wool with the same kind of twist. My people could make a good copy though."

"How much would it cost for a copy?" I said, thinking that a copy of such a unique piece might be a good thing to have.

"About a thousand if I have it done in Turkey, but they would use the Turkish knot. The weavers I work with in Spain would cost more, but they would use the Spanish knot so it would be more authentic. Let me send them some pictures and I'll give you a better idea."

"Take all the pictures you need. If it's not too expensive, I'll go for a copy made in Spain. But for now, I want to do a top-notch rejoining."

"There's a woman in Paris who is the absolute best for the dying and matching of yarns." He reached for his wallet. "I'll give you one of her cards."

The first phone call after he left was from a woman with such a pleasant English accent that I forgot the little things that were troubling my mind.

"Are you the gentleman who appraises rare rugs and textiles?"

154

"Valuations are one of my specialties, but the other attribution can be temperamentally challenging."

About three seconds passed. "I have an old prayer rug. What does it cost if I bring it in for an appraisal?"

I shifted to a more scholarly tone. "Is the appraisal for selling, insurance, or estate purposes?"

"What would be the difference?"

"For selling, it's called fair market value and is based on average prices similar pieces have sold for. For insurance, I use replacement value based on the highest sale figures so you could replace it quickly in case of a loss. For estates, the IRS requires me to list comparable sale prices, so it takes more time. I charge a hundred and fifty for an insurance or selling valuation and five hundred and up for an estate valuation."

"I'd like to come in around one for an insurance appraisal."

"I'll write you in, what's your name?"

A rustling sound like she was covering the phone was followed by the muffled voice of a man in the background, and then the posh accent came back. "Hollingsworth. My name is Carla Hollingsworth."

That name sounded familiar. A Hollingsworth family that got filthy rich from selling chemicals lived in The Highlands.

"Okay, I've got you down for one," I said, picturing the brake lights of the red Range Rover from a couple nights before.

An hour later, a silver Mercedes limo glided into the loading zone, and a gray-suited driver got out. He opened the rear door, and a red-haired woman slid out. She looked to be pushing forty, but not in a bad way, and was carrying a rolled-up silk rug.

It was like meeting someone straight out of a society magazine when I stood to greet her. An expensive looking trench coat, shapely legs, and the glorious red hair falling on her shoulders.

"I'm Carla Hollingsworth," she said, smiling coolly. "I brought a rug for an insurance appraisal."

"You can open it right here," I said, keeping my eyes on her.

Appreciating my attention, she unrolled a finely knotted 16th century prayer rug of a type I had never touched because most are in museums.

Kneeling to run my fingers over the silky pile and Islamic calligraphy done in gold threads, I made my biggest understatement ever. "That's a nice one."

I regretted it as soon as it came out of my mouth, but I had never appraised one of these classic rugs made for Persian kings. I pretended to fiddle with my appraisal form while I thought it over.

"What address should I use?"

"Just put Carla Hollingsworth, The Highlands."

Writing as slowly as I could, I filled in details like size and description. Then I bought more time by talking to her while thumbing through old auction catalogues.

"This is what is called a Topkapi prayer rug. They got that name because several were found in the Topkapi Palace in Istanbul. The King of Persia had presented them as gifts to the Ottoman Sultan in the sixteenth century. They are difficult to value because they rarely come on the market."

One catalogue pictured a similar one that had sold for 850,000 euros at a European auction. Since auction prices are often what dealers pay, I ended up writing her a replacement value of one million dollars.

It crossed my mind that she was getting a heck of a deal on my measly $150 appraisal fee. Less scrupulous appraisers have been known to rake in fees by charging a percentage and inflating the values. Maybe I was going about this the wrong way.

She was looking at me, waiting, so I signed the appraisal and handed it to her. "It's best to get a piece like this revalued every year to keep the coverage current. If any others are sold on the open market, the price will likely go up."

She nodded as she studied the form. "I knew it was valuable because my brother gave it to me."

"It was a very generous gift."

"You might have heard of Harrison Woodhouse?"

156

A cement truck roaring by helped to hide my shock. "I believe we've met," I said.

She seemed to pick up what I was thinking. "I married a Hollingsworth, but it didn't work out, so I'm single now."

She said it while running a pink tongue across her upper lip. A simple enough gesture, but with enough sex in it that I could hardly help but notice.

She peered into my eyes as I struggled to keep my thoughts from showing. "Harrison suggested you might help me sell it. I understand you charge a commission for doing that."

"I could probably find you a buyer," I said, as my mind went on fast forward, pondering the log arm of coincidence.

Why was Harrison Woodhouse sending his rich, attractive sister, who just happened to be single now, to ask if I might sell a million-dollar rug on commission? I could make more on that one deal than I make in a year.

"I usually charge twenty-five percent," I said, when I got my mouth to work. "But I'm always flexible about things like that."

"Then maybe we might be able to work something out? she said, doing the thing with the tongue again. "Something that could be beneficial for all of us?"

I nodded, but there were a couple problems with that scenario. When I get something for nothing, that's often exactly what it ends up being worth. And, if her brother had something in mind involving the table cover, I already had plans of my own.

She leaned closer when she handed me the check, and the flowery scent of Chanel No. 5 washed over me as she brushed her manicured fingers across mine. Then she folded the appraisal into her Louis Vuitton handbag, flashed a smile, and headed for the door.

I watched her hips twitch as she walked out the door and climbed back into the limo, but all I could think about was how sharp her teeth had looked.

32

Ray's Boathouse, a seafood restaurant on the end of a pier overlooking Shilshole Bay, was a perfect setting to talk about our trip to Europe. A window table gave us a wide view of the Olympic Mountain darkening to violet and all the small boats bobbing into port with their running lights on.

Laura leaned forward after the waiter brought our grilled Alaskan King Salmon and a bottle of Columbia Valley Riesling. "I can hardly believe we're actually going to Paris. It's like all the stars have aligned."

"I'm not so sure about that star thing," I said, making a little tent out of my fingertips like I was about to turn philosophical.

"You don't believe in astrology?"

"I'm a Taurus."

"So?"

"Tauruses don't believe in astrology."

She smiled at my absurdity, and I took a sip of wine. "Sharing it with someone will be different though. I've always gone there for business."

Her eyes took on a more serious expression. "Maybe it's time you experienced its aura of romance."

"There will be plenty of that."

She nodded. "Their music and films were what first attracted me to French culture."

"I always liked their old black and white gangster movies."

She paused with her fork. "That doesn't surprise me."

I smiled. *Bob le Flambeur* is one of my favorites."

"See, even the name has a romantic sound. It was the beauty of the lyrics in the songs of Gainsbourg and Aznavour that inspired me to study French."

"It's good to know some of the language. Not everybody speaks English."

"I'll have to brush up."

"You should also make a list of things you want to see."

"I've already started. It will be great to see things like the Champs Elysees and the Eiffel Tower, but it's the places where people lived and worked that interest me most. The cabarets, the bistros, the artists' studios on Montmartre."

"There's a lot to see, and Paris is a world unto itself."

"None of this would be happening if you and Sammy hadn't helped to rescue our family heirloom. I hope you let him know how grateful I am."

"I'm sure he knows," I said.

She took a sip of wine. "It's a relief to finally be free of that place."

"It will be an even bigger relief once we get farther away."

"I need to start planning what to bring."

"I'm a one bag traveler, just a carry-on."

"But you're a guy."

"It works best to keep it simple."

"But we're not after simplicity, we're after adventure."

"An adventure with luggage isn't fun until it's over."

"A friend said to take half the clothes and twice the money."

"I'd double that, in both directions."

"*En un largo camino, hasta una paja pesa.*"

"What's that mean?"

"That even a straw can weigh heavily on a long journey."

"That's the number one thing to think about when packing."

Leaving the restaurant, salty air and woodsmoke from scattered campfires drew us arm in arm up a tree-lined path to Golden Gardens Park. Laura pressed against me for warmth as we paused to take in the pale glow of moonlight reflecting off the water. Sensing a perfect moment for a kiss, I pulled her close.

We were walking close to the softly breathing surf when I reached for a skipping rock, fingered it into position, and side-armed it across the waves. "Four skips," I said, counting the radiating ripples.

Laura scoffed. "A ten-year old could do better than that."

"Try to beat it."

"Just watch."

She got six skips.

"Yours was a lucky throw," I said, digging for a rock and flinging it low across the water. This time we counted three, and I gave up.

"Where'd you learn to do that?" I said.

"My dad taught me."

"Does this mean I'll have to subordinate my personality to a more highly-skilled woman?"

"You have no idea what I've got in mind for you," she said, with a grin.

I was trying to think of a way to prolong the romantic mood of the evening when we were climbing into my car. "Do you feel like hearing some live music?"

"Sure, what do you have in mind?"

"We could check out who's playing at the Tractor Tavern."

"Do you feel like dancing?"

"I could give it a try."

We got there in time to catch the last set of the Zydeco Locals, and we danced. Laura was soft and warm as I held her close during several of their slow numbers. By some miracle, my feet stayed out of each other's way when I danced like an arm-waving dervish during one of the fast numbers.

My reverie came to an end when the music ended, and people began filing out the door. Following them into the early morning streets, we topped off the night with long drink cocktails in a cozy booth a few doors down at Hattie's Hat.

We were walking back to my car on a dimly lit street when a peculiar pulsing sound drew our attention.

"What's that noise?" Laura said, slowing her pace.

"It sounds like a radio playing."

"Maybe you left it on."

"No way."

"You sure?"

"I'm sure."

The pulsing sound grew stronger when a human form appeared backlit by a streetlamp. At first, it was just a silhouette darker than the night. Then it disappeared, swallowed by the shadows between the streetlights.

The sound became louder when an oddly gyrating figure wearing what looked like a helmet moved into the bright cone of another streetlight. He was it coming straight at us, bobbing from side-to-side in a jerky shuffle.

Stepping in front of Laura, I protected her with my arm. It was then I saw the black headphones on a white-haired man who was swinging his arms from side to side in syncopated rhythm to Chubby Checker's version of *The Twist*.

Next morning, I was pouring maple syrup on the waffles I had whipped up when a meowing sound came from outside the kitchen door. Laura raised her eyes in silent interrogation.

"It's Tyson," I said, getting up to let him in.

I put out some cat food. He ate it quickly, then looked at me for more. He was purring. "Forget it," I said. The purring stopped, and he walked away to rub against Laura's ankle.

"He's got a clever scam going," I said. "I buy him treats. He eats them. Then he leaves."

"He's huge, she said. "You must be feeding him a lot."

"I don't feed him every day."

"How could he be feeding himself so well?"

"There's a lot fewer cats in the neighborhood."

I smiled at the look on her face. "I was only kidding."

33

Sparrow and Crane, the somber-faced Smithsonian detectives, were peering in my window when I came to open. This time Crane was carrying a briefcase.

"Do you mind if we come in again?" he said.

I smiled. "Did you bring a warrant this time?"

"Oh, no, it hasn't come to that. We just have a few routine questions."

"Routine? Should I be glad for that?"

After settling themselves in my two client chairs, Crane bent to his briefcase and tossed a handful of soumak saddlebags on my desk. "Do you recognize these?"

"They look like the ones Orsini was trying to sell me."

"Look like or are?"

"Are. Where did you get them?"

He smiled a menacing smile. "One of your local antique dealers bought them from a man dressed like a priest a couple days before her store was burglarized."

"I know nothing about that."

Glowering with suspicion, he flipped open a black notebook. "We'd like to know the whole story about your relationship with the man called Orsini."

"I don't have any relationship with Orsini."

"Has anybody else ever mentioned him to you?"

"No."

He slid a black and white surveillance photograph across my desk. It showed a tall man with a shock of white hair and an ankle-length overcoat walking through a museum and taking notes.

"Have you ever seen this man?"

"No. I've never seen him before."

He glanced in his notebook. "Does the name Boris Balakov mean anything to you?"

"Not a thing," I said, feeling all four eyes on me. "What kind of a name is that?"

"We think he's Bulgarian. How about somebody called The Professor?"

"Not since I was in college."

"Marco Passaretti or Tito Cosi?"

"No, they sound like Italian singers."

A cold stare. "How about Vinnie Mingaloni?"

I shifted in my chair. "Never heard of him."

Crane slapped his notepad shut and leaned forward. "If we ever find out you've been holding back on us, it will mean big trouble for you."

"I never go looking for trouble," I said straight to his face. "It always seems to walk in the door uninvited."

They glanced at each other and stood.

"It's not that we don't appreciate your help," Sparrow said. "We're trying to piece together a string of museum robberies. Interpol's stretched to the breaking point, and it's taking a long time to get any information."

Ten minutes after they left, a Bible-black Jeep Wrangler covered with mud splash and wearing Nevada plates slid to a stop in the parking lot across the street. The front was smashed in, and a spider web of cracks ran across the dirty windshield.

Two men got out. Tough Guy Vincent, and a tall man with a shock of white hair wearing a long black overcoat. They started toward me, stopped, appeared to argue, and the man in the long black coat went to lean against the Wrangler.

Vincent strode in, nodded once, and went straight to one of the chairs that was still warm from the Smithsonian detectives. For a moment, he didn't speak.

"We heard someone stole that Spanish rug from the Swami crowd."

"You heard that?"

"Yeah. Some people think you might know something about it."

"Which people are those?"

"If you keep this up, we might start to think you're a bit slow."

"Why would you think that?"

"All this asking and not knowing anything."

"I can't help what people think. Last month a dealer nearly fainted when he saw me at an antique show. Said he'd heard I was dead."

His eyebrows moved up a notch. "Maybe it was one of those fortune-teller tricks, like seeing into your future."

"No trick to that, it's everybody's future."

He pulled a face, like he was unimpressed. "We also heard you got a thing for the girl."

I blinked. "What girl?"

"You heard me."

I leaned back in my chair. "Why all the questions?"

"Just interested."

"What happened to your car? Did a tree jump in front of you?"

His eyes moved, and he seemed to be thinking about it, looking off for a moment. "It was just a little fender bender, except the other guy's future ain't what it used to be.

"Look," he said, adjusting his aviator sunglasses. "Let me explain some things to you. Harrison's a reasonable man and usually gets what he wants. He's prepared to buy the table cover. All you got to do is take your money and put an end to this charade."

But putting an end to it was no longer an option. The game had changed. The Camino was calling, and I needed to stall him. "What's he willing to pay?"

He looked at me without blinking. "You have to come up with a price."

"Why does he want it so badly?"

"He ain't gonna tell you that either."

"They say that desire blinds the soul."

"If the rest of you was as smart as that mouth of yours, we could do some business."

"I'm learning to live with my imperfections."

"Now that you know us a little better, maybe it's time to quit playing cute."

"Remind Harrison I'm a dealer. If I can make money, I'm delighted to do business."

"That's how we've been seeing things so far, but now we're wondering if you're having doubts about our intentions."

"I have doubts about just about everything."

"This thing might be bigger than you've figured out. Like beyond your dreams."

"My dreams are pretty rich."

He made a dismissive flick of his wrist. "It'd be a shame if they got so rich they wrecked your romance with the little lady. You make such a cute couple."

"I didn't know you cared."

"You can cut the tough guy talk. I know people who are really tough."

"Are they shy, like your buddy out there?"

He smiled slightly. "The Professor doesn't speak real good English, but he's never shy." He held my gaze. "All I'm saying is that it might be best to start seeing things Harrison's way."

"Is it Harrison's way to have somebody tailing me around?"

His eyes narrowed. "Harrison doesn't do things like that."

"Then tell your boss I might be game to deal, but to cut the cloak-and-dagger routine."

He gave me his silent hooded look as he stood to leave, but a shadow had passed over his face, and I wondered why.

After starting for the door, he turned. "If you get tired of it, give Harrison a call."

"Tired of what?"

"Tired of jerking us around."

He said it sternly, like there was no room for debate. Then he walked out the door.

I watched as he crossed the street and paused to say something to the white-haired man in the long black coat. The white-haired man turned his angular face in my direction and held my gaze with a steady stillness.

For a moment, I had a fleeting sensation that he had come closer without actually moving.

Then they climbed into the bashed-up Wrangler and drove away.

34

Four people in their mid-twenties bunched up outside my doorway when I was down on my knees trying to figure out the complicated weaving technique in a two-thousand-year-old Peruvian wearing mantle. The two men wore white baseball caps and had neatly trimmed beards. The women wore matching black slacks and tan parkas. They put their heads together for a whispered conversation before filing in silently like a platoon on patrol.

Moving like a drill team, they marched around as if I wasn't even there. After a brief stop in front of my safe, they circled around me for a quick look at what I was examining, and then filed silently out the door.

The lingering stillness had one of those extraterrestrial vibes, so I followed them out in time to see a white van pull away from around the corner. I guess it was to be expected. Sheena's Dirty Tricks Squad had paid me a visit.

I was grinning at their laughable disguises when I parked outside my house at the end of the day, but my flesh began to crawl when I saw a light was on in an upstairs room I rarely use.

A noxious smell assaulted my nose as I climbed the porch steps, and the door was ajar when I stuck the key in. Listening for sounds, I pushed at it gently, and got hit in the face by the rotten egg reek of leaking gas.

Wrinkling my nose, I groped around blindly for the light switch. When my fingers found it, something in my mind screamed out a warning—any electrical contact could blow up the house.

After a quick dash to my car for a flashlight, I filled my lungs with air, followed the hiss of gas to the burners on my stove, and turned them off one by one.

Desperate for another lungful of fresh air, I went to open the back door and stepped on a white baseball cap. Suddenly the air felt colder, and the silence far more menacing.

I hurried to open some windows in the living room, and my beam of light lit up a line of muddy footprints tracking across the carpet to the steps going upstairs.

I stopped to listen, but all I heard was the meowing of Tyson as he came through the back door. Still listening, I eased a fireplace poker out of the stand. Made of iron, and about a yard long, it had a vicious hook at the end. Holding it like a hammer, I went through the house whipping open closets and peering around doorways.

Every room looked like a tornado had passed through. I paused a moment before opening the door to my bedroom. Inside was a scene of devastation: books swept off the shelves, drawers pulled out and upended, clothing strewn across the floor. Moving closer to my bed, I saw that someone had left behind a chillingly personal touch. A partially dissolved green breath mint was carefully positioned in the center of my sleeping pillow.

As my panic ebbed, it was replaced by incandescent fury, and thoughts of what I would have done if I'd only caught the sonsofbitches in the act. For a moment, I considered calling the cops, but a breath mint and a baseball cap wouldn't give them much to go on.

I gave the house another sweep to see if anything was missing. All I found was an empty space on the fireplace mantle where a photo of my wife and I on our wedding day had stood.

After double locking my doors, I made sure my windows were closed and secured, and sat wide awake in my wicker rocker until I got tired of sitting.

Three in the morning. The strident bleating of my phone jerked me away from whatever I was dreaming. Once again, my burglar alarm had gone off, but this time it had not reset.

"Were the interior motion detectors triggered?" I said, still half asleep.

"No. It's your front windows."

Talk about a wake-up call—I was out of bed immediately.

Grabbing a long-handled Maglite, and my vintage Webley five-shot revolver, I raced away in my car. Hearing the jangling of alarm bells, I took a left onto Fremont at about forty, and skidded to a stop in front of my store.

I didn't need the help of Sherlock Holmes to deduce why the sidewalk was twinkling in my headlights. Elementary, I said to myself. That glittering galaxy of broken glass used to be my display windows.

My shoes made crunching sounds as I hurried inside to turn off the strident clamor. I glanced around quickly while dialing 911—it looked like a bomb had gone off. Shards of glass gleamed like crystals of ice in the overhead lights. My two jade trees inside the gaping windows were shattered and torn.

But why? Nothing in the windows was worth stealing and the metal grillwork was a barrier against rushing in to grab something valuable.

Fifteen minutes later, a blue and white police car pulled to the curb. The two cops looked around, took some pictures, and were wandering around outside when one of them called to me from the sidewalk. "Come take a look at this!"

His flashlight lit up a scorched bird's nest of melted plastic and twisted copper wires. "What the hell is that?" I said.

"It looks like an explosive device that didn't completely go off," he said. "Half of it exploded and melted the part that didn't."

The second cop pointed at wafts of smoke coming from joss sticks that had been placed on either side of the windows. "It looks like they left you their calling card."

Even creepier was that they smelled like sandalwood, but that was not something I wanted to try to explain.

The police went on their way after taking the partially exploded device as evidence, and I went to work sweeping up glass. After cleaning up, I sat behind my desk picturing Sheena's vengeful face, and feeling emotionally drained. With the windows gone, I couldn't turn the alarm back on, so I made myself a bed by laying down some tribal rugs like animal pelts and tried to sleep for what was left of the night.

The sleep that finally came was full of shadowy dreams that swarmed around me like schools of fish. When I awoke in the morning, I could only remember one, and it made no sense.

I was chasing two women down an endless hallway with an infinity of doors. The women disappeared into another hallway. It was too dark to see, but I plunged ahead, collided with someone, and spun her around. It was Laura.

The thudding of heavy footsteps came from behind me, and an expression of terror filled Laura's face. I turned to look. It was the pale-faced bald guy.

At first, I was amazed at how fast he could run. Then I saw his lips were moving like he was trying to tell me something.

I couldn't make out what he was saying because I was so horrified by his eyes. They were nothing but empty black holes.

35

Morning came in the guise of an ice-cold lady with a voice like busses and garbage trucks going by. I huddled behind my desk in the frigid air nursing a nagging headache while two overly cheerful workmen took their time replacing the glass in my windows. Too many troublesome things had been happening and they seemed to be spiraling dangerously out of control.

I experienced a refreshing return to normalcy after the workmen left. Jay and Stanley came through the door with a rolled-up rug. It was such a welcome change that I almost smiled.

"We found an old prayer rug," Jay said, unrolling it with a majestic gesture.

It wasn't a prayer rug. It was an *engsi,* a ceremonial door covering from one of the nomadic tribes of Central Asia. People mistake them for prayer rugs because they use an ascending design. This one had the saturated colors collectors love and a masterful rendering of the Wheel of the Universe composition.

"I like it," I said. "How much is it?"

Jay winked at Stanley. "How much would you offer?"

I looked at Jay. "You know how much you want. Why not just tell me? When you had a store, you were famous for saying an offer's a free appraisal and you don't give out free appraisals."

Jay pretended to look hurt, but he knew it was true. "We've got an appraisal from Abraham."

"A written appraisal?"

"No, he just told us."

That told me something too. Dealers are legally responsible for a written appraisal, but a verbal one isn't worth the paper it's written on.

Brushing my fingers across the back, I bent the pile with my thumb to see how it was knotted. The back had the characteristic dryness of an extremely old weaving, and the asymmetrical knot open to the left tagged it as a relic of the nearly extinct Salor Turkmen tribe. Some Salor engsis have sold for over a hundred thousand dollars.

I wanted this rarity and needed to sidestep a bidding war.

"What did Abraham tell you?" I said, focusing on Jay.

"He said it's worth twenty thousand and offered us fifteen."

Stanley shot Jay a hard look for spilling, but this was the break I needed to give things a shove.

"You know Abraham doesn't have high-end collector clients like I do," I said, making a show of checking my watch. "One of my best clients is coming by in an hour. If you sell it to me right now, I'll pay you nineteen thousand."

Abraham had boxed himself in by undervaluing it and they couldn't go back to him with any realistic hope he might offer $19,500. I didn't really have a client coming, but I wanted to convince Jay and Lee they were getting my highest offer.

Jay looked at Stanley, and Stanley nodded.

I was writing out the check when the phone rang. It was Sammy, and he sounded edgy.

"Those swami people are after me. Two women have been watching my brother's house. This morning, that bald guy dressed as a priest came and pounded on the door. He thought my brother was me and bugged him about your rug inscription."

"Oh no. The guy dressed like a priest is bad news. I thought you were going back to LA."

"I'm packing right now."

"Let me know if anything else happens. It's best to avoid that guy."

"If he comes around again, I might need your help."

"Call me if he does. And be careful."

"I am being careful."

Jay was staring at me with a quizzical expression when I put the phone down. "What's this about a man dressed like a priest?"

"Oh, just someone who's giving a friend of mine a hard time," I said.

"Surely you heard about the big Fabergé theft?"

All at once, I was on full alert. "I read about it in the paper."

"A pale man dressed like a priest came by Marge Tanner's shop a day before the burglary. He was missing some fingers and asking about Russian jewelry."

"They didn't mention any of that in the news."

Jay rolled his eyes. "My dear Tony, they also didn't mention she had been tortured, and that they made off with over half a million dollars' worth of jewelry."

"How do they know she was tortured?"

"She had bloody bruises on her fingers. You better warn your friend to be extra careful. It's a good thing we have our guard dog with such brutes around."

I pictured their little pug dog and tried not to smile. "I'll be sure to do that, Jay."

Sammy called again right after they left. This time he sounded terrified. "Those women caught me wearing the watch."

"Stealing that watch was a monumentally stupid idea."

"That's not the worst part."

"What's the worst part?"

"Something I didn't tell you. When I took the watch, I took that big emerald. They're really pissed and want everything back."

"What are you going to do?"

"I'm supposed to meet up with the bald guy to work out an exchange. I need you with me for back-up."

"Jesus, Sammy, you should have told me about the emerald. No way will they let you off the hook for that. Where are you doing the meet?"

"The Ballard Locks are just a couple blocks away, so I set it for there in an hour."

"Okay, but these people are more dangerous than you think. We should meet before they get there."

"I'll be at the entrance to the fish ladder viewing room in thirty minutes," he said. "Don't be late."

"I'm on my way."

Despite his faults, Sammy was always the coolest guy in dangerous situations. Hearing him so frightened had chilled me to the bone.

I regretted not telling him more, and hoped he had enough sense to wait for me if he got there early.

36

I wanted to avoid entering the locks at the busy main entrance, so I headed south on Ballard Bridge, a double-leaf span that opens to allow tall ships to pass. By the time I saw the flashing lights and barriers going down, it was too late to turn back.

Sammy didn't carry a cell phone, so all I could do was wait while the superstructure of a large ship moved glacially past the upright spans. Eventually a horn bleated, the drawbridge closed inch by inch, and traffic began creeping forward.

Taking the first exit off the bridge, I drove as fast as I could past Fisherman's Terminal to Commodore Park overlooking the locks from the south side, left my car, and hurried down a series of railed steps.

The Ballard Locks are massive forms of gray concrete sculpted by the Army Corps of Engineers in 1915 to allow boats to pass between the saltwater of Puget Sound and the twenty-foot higher fresh water of Lake Washington. Fish ladders hundreds of feet long were built alongside the locks so salmon could return to spawn in the rivers where they were born.

One lock is for big ships, and the narrower one is for yachts, sailboats, and cabin cruisers. Both have double gates at each end with steel-railed walkways for people to cross over when the gates are closed.

Sammy was nowhere to be seen when I got to the viewing room entrance, so I stood at a railing breathing the salty scent of Puget Sound and watching the wildlife. Squadrons of seagulls squawked and dove above the torrents pouring from the spillways. A solitary heron stood motionless in the shallow water near the shore. Farther out, gray seals hunted for salmon. Only their rounded heads and intelligent eyes were visible above the dark water.

Remembering that Sammy would be coming from his brother's house, I headed across the noisy spillway toward the locks on the other side. The small one, packed full of pleasure boats waiting to pass out into Puget Sound, had closed both of its gates, and the water was slowly being lowered. I crossed over to the big lock, but it's gates were wide open for a huge fish processor that was gliding slowly in.

It took several more minutes for for the gate to close. When an all-clear signal blared from the control tower, I started across and saw flashes of a familiar shade of green coming from a crowd of people milling around the administration building. Quickening my pace, I hurried over, but if they had been there, they were gone.

After waiting a few more minutes, I retraced my steps to sit on a bench outside the entrance to the fish ladder. The smell of rain was in the air, and dark clouds were massing above my head. When a slow rumble of thunder sounded, I went inside to see if Sammy might be waiting for me there.

The high-ceilinged room resonated with the steady sound of water rushing through the weirs. Along one side, visitors stood on an elevated platform watching the fish through double-height glass windows. Excited children pointed and squealed as salmon surged and leaped, struggling to propel themselves up the steps.

I had walked the length of the chamber and started back when a shrill scream drew my eyes to the viewing windows. Frantic parents were grabbing for their children, pulling them away.

Stern-faced security guards came rushing in as I hurried up the steps for a better look. When I saw what had startled everybody, it was as if someone had punched me in the gut. A pale human corpse was drifting in the current, face-up with its arms outstretched. The eyes, wide-open and staring as if expressing great surprise, were Sammy's eyes, and an open gash on his head showed all the way through to the white bone.

It made no sense. Sammy was in top physical shape and too aware of his surroundings to have somehow accidently fallen over the railing in the opening above. As if in answer to my thought, the corpse slowly turned, raised its left hand to my eye level, and revealed a slight tan line where the Patek Philippe watch used to be.

Sammy didn't trip and fall. Something must have gone dreadfully wrong when he met up with the pale-faced man.

Rigid with shock, I threaded my way through the gathering clutch of gawkers and struggled up the stairs. Outside, birds were singing, children were laughing and playing, but none of it felt real.

Barely aware of distant thunder, I retreated to the shelter of my car. A bolt of lightning flared when I was opening the door. For a second, everything was starkly illuminated by a searing flash of white light. Then a ferocious downpour started hitting the ground, and I collapsed behind the steering wheel listening to the raindrops hammer the roof.

I could feel myself trembling while I drove like a robot through slanting sheets of rain. Suddenly I was parking in front of my store.

I went inside without turning on the lights and sat behind my desk. Tears burned in the back of my eyes, and dark thoughts echoed in my mind: the deadliest webs are the ones we weave for ourselves, everything can turn upside down in a single heartbeat, there's no tearing out the page when your world changes.

A period of time passed before I realized I was staring into space. The phone rang more than once, but I couldn't bring myself to pick it up. I don't know how long I sat there, but it was long enough that I ran out of tears.

Sammy was gone for good, and it called for some kind of justice. I thought of Laura. To tell her or not to tell her. That was the question. If I told her, she might not come to Paris. If I did not

177

tell her, and something bad happened to her, that would be even worse.

A tiny voice inside my head kept telling me I had to do something. No question, it was up to me to get us far away from whatever had gotten to Sammy.

Feeling drained and useless, I got up to wash the tears off my face. When I saw my dismal reflection glowering back at me from the mirror, I gave the counter an angry kick. Something moved enough to expose a tiny piece of paper at my feet. It was the faded business card for Fleet Detective, the prior occupant of my space.

I had a funny feeling, so I stuck it in my wallet. Then I picked up the phone and called my computer-savvy sister, Cinda, to ask for help in finding some quick flights to Paris.

I woke once in the night, sweating buckets with sticky sheets wrapped around me. I'd been having a dismal dream where the images overlapped and changed.

Deep in dark water, I was struggling to rise to the surface. Directly above me, a human corpse, white with death, was blocking my way. In the dimness below, fish with sharp teeth and ugly human faces were nibbling at my feet. Off in the distance, shark-like creatures slowly circled, watching with eyes like gun barrels.

37

Everything was looking resolutely grim. Sammy's death had fallen upon me like an avalanche of icy slush, and the darkening November brought a taste of the chill that would soon be upon us. My mood was as bleak as the weather. Lost in my private thoughts, I didn't feel like doing much of anything. His tragic loss was too great to grasp, but much that had puzzled me was now painfully clear.

The pale-faced man was the prime force behind Sheena's intense interest in the table cover, and he was somehow responsible for Sammy's murder. Part of me said to run. Another part said I needed to find a way to take control of the situation, instead of letting it control me.

Then there was Laura.

We were both surprised by how fast things had developed between us. She had been staying over at my house so often that I was used to her sleeping beside me. Whatever lay ahead, I wanted her with me.

Then there was me.

I had stumbled onto what might be the discovery of a lifetime I couldn't walk away from something like that. The only way forward was to follow the clues all the way to the end. Could I do it? Or had my luck run out?

The day was plodding by like a dreary parade when the mailman appeared outside my door. Something about the ordinary routine of him digging in his sack was a pointed reminder that life goes on for the living.

A small cardboard box landed on top of the usual junk mail and bills when he slid a handful of mail through the slot. The box carried far more stamps than were needed and was taped up like it had been done in a hurry. After tearing off the tape, I ripped open the box.

The Castafiori emerald was nestled inside, gleaming like an Irishman's eye, and wrapped in white cotton. I couldn't tell Laura without letting on that Sammy had been killed, so I slid the emerald into my pocket and tossed the box in the trash.

That evening, my sister called. She had turned up a pair of red-eye tickets on Air France departing a week away on November 15. I snapped them up and phoned Laura. We would spend a week in Paris before following the old pilgrimage route from France into Spain.

Thelma and Sol invited me over for a celebratory going away dinner on the night of our departure. We had all agreed it would be a good idea to have the panels repaired and rejoined in Paris, and Laura's mom shared some encouraging news.

"Your friend, David, at the University of Washington Language Department translated that letter for us. He said it was written in Old Galician, a language that's related to Spanish and Portuguese. It tells about one of our ancestors who was a teacher for an important Spanish family, the Castro family."

"Castro?" I said. "That gives us something to look for once we get there. Did the letter explain how the rug came into your family?"

She nodded. "It told the whole story. Our ancestor tutored the family's only son at a library table that was always covered by the rug. The son entrusted the table cover to his teacher when he was called away to war. The son never returned, and when the teacher died, it went to his children: a brother and a sister. The brother eventually married into a French family. When he was preparing to move to Vézelay, he and his sister separated the panels to share it, pledging that the rug would be rejoined if they were ever reunited."

"What a great story," I said. "They probably had no idea they were separating two pieces of an ancient puzzle."

"There's something else. He confirmed that La Coruña is a corruption of the word for crown in the old Galician language."

"That means we're on the right track. When we get there, we'll begin following the pilgrimage route in Vézelay, where your grandfather came from."

Sol took me aside when we were getting ready to leave and handed me a tiny package. "We know you'll take good care of our daughter, but I want to give you something that might come in handy when you're on the road."

I opened the box and took out a small, black metal flashlight with the words SureFire on the side.

"It feels really solid," I said, hefting in my hand.

"It's military grade."

"What does that mean?"

"It means they're built for combat. Some people use them as a self-defense tool."

"How can this little thing be a self-defense tool?"

Sol grinned. "It has sharp beveled edges and puts out enough light to blind somebody."

I pushed the button. Then I had to blink several times to clear my vision. "I see what you mean."

"You can set it for a flashing strobe if you need to disorient someone."

"I'll keep it handy. Hopefully, we won't be ending up in any dark places."

38

We packed light. Our plan was to vanish in Europe without carrying any computers, phones, or other electronic gear that might give away our location. If necessary, we would use public phones and internet cafes. A few thousand euros were zipped inside my money belt, and we each brought a carry-on with a few changes of sink-washable clothing.

All the world seemed to be going somewhere as we followed the overhead signs through glossy airport halls. Throngs of people were waiting impatiently outside restroom doors, lining up for coffee, and hunched over tables at fast-food eateries.

I saw nothing unusual until the doors were closing on our shuttle out to the international concourse. Two women pushed their way onto the platform. One pointed at our shuttle while the other pulled out a cell phone. It rattled me, but they could have been anybody.

After the shuttle dropped us off in the departure hall, we rode a series of escalators up to our gate where we sat thumbing through boring airport magazines until we were called to board.

When the announcement came to fasten seat belts, I remembered something. "Damn, I forgot my travel clock."

"I left the ranch in such a rush that I did the same thing," Laura said. "Indira, my roommate, mailed it to me."

A distant bell seemed to be sounding deep in my consciousness as I tried to picture the woman with gold bracelets and long black hair. Then I realized I'd never seen her face. I'd only seen her from behind.

"It will be good to get away from all those swami people," I said.

"I wouldn't count on that."

"Why not?"

"They've got a hundred and fifty thousand followers in Europe."

I was running that through my mind until they announced it was time to board. Then the plane moved into position onto the runway, the engines roared, the ground fell away. None of the movies interested me, so I dozed intermittently until I awoke to a cheery stewardess offering a pre-packaged breakfast.

Soon we were descending to land, and I reset my watch nine hours ahead to Paris time. The plane bounced and swayed when it touched down, then taxied around forever before lurching to a stop. There was the rapid un-clicking of seatbelts and a chatter of relief as people stood to gather their carry-ons.

Passport control took forever, then we walked past all the tired-looking travelers standing around luggage carousels, out the *Nothing to Declare* door, and into the noisy bustle of Aeroport Charles de Gaulle.

Forty-five minutes of rumbling along on the RER train got us to the light-filled Gare du Nord where signs for the Metro drew us deeper into the bowels of the earth. Several stops later, we got off at Anvers station near the foot of Montmartre, followed the noisy throng upstairs, and were welcomed to daylight by a rush of pigeons' wings and the clamor of Paris traffic.

From there, it was just a four-block walk to our apartment in the ninth arrondissement. Drained and hardly talking, we plodded along Rue de la Tour D'Auvergne, an oasis of calm lined with venerable apartment buildings and street level businesses. I stopped when we came to number 42, an arched *porte-cochère* carriage entry with a pedestrian door inserted into one of the larger ones. After punching a four-digit code into the keyboard, I led Laura into a quiet flagstone corridor.

I punched another code into the keyboard of a door on the left, and a curving staircase smelling of fresh wax and old wood brought us to a pair of mahogany doors on the second-floor landing. The doors opened to the soft ticking of a tall case clock and a *salle de séjour* furnished with antique furniture and worn Persian rugs still glowing with color.

The parquet floor popped and creaked beneath our feet as we crossed to the master bedroom facing the street. I collapsed on the bed while Laura went to open a window to the courtyard. Soft piano music drifted down from one of the apartments up above.

"Haydn was one of my favorites in music class," Laura said, wistfully.

"You liked to hide?"

"No, silly, Haydn, the composer. I played his sonatas."

"You play piano?"

"I used to take it very seriously."

"So what happened?"

"I got tired of practicing four hours a day and quit thinking about a career. Now I play for the fun of it."

"You continue to surprise me," I said, gazing at the ceiling.

Yielding to an overwhelming fatigue, I sank into a dark calm while Laura explored the nooks and crannies in the three-bedroom apartment. Minutes later, she snuggled up beside me. "I've never seen such a tiny kitchen, but it's got everything you'd need to cook just about any kind of meal."

Cuddling felt so good after the long plane ride that we both drifted off to sleep. I opened my eyes to the chiming of the clock, forced myself to stand, and bent to whisper in Laura's ear. "We need to stay awake so we can adjust to the time difference. It might help to take a walk around the neighborhood."

She yawned and opened her eyes. "The neighborhood I want to see most is Montmartre."

"We're already there. Let's go."

Three blocks up Rue des Martyrs, we crossed the surging traffic on Clichy Boulevard and entered a neighborhood of bistros, cabarets, and theaters. If I so much as glanced into one of the bars, the women inside would smile and wave back.

"Do those women know you?" Laura said.

"I've never seen any of them before."

"Then why are they waving at you?"

"Bars in this neighborhood are different from what we're used to."

We were passing the entry to an orange and black Art Nouveau-styled theater papered with posters of glamorous looking dames when a man came out to pick up the mail. He needed a shave and was wearing a floral print dress. The marquee above him read *Madame Arthur*.

"What's with Madame Arthur?" Laura said.

"Madame Arthur ain't no lady."

"What's that supposed to mean?"

"Drag queens do burlesque routines for a dinner audience."

"Have you seen the show?"

"Not yet," I smiled. "Shall we reserve a table?"

She arched an eyebrow. "A chacun son goût."

When Rue des Martyrs became a series of steep stairs, we turned right onto Rue Yvonne-le-Tac and paused to catch our breath in a small park. Children waved to their parents from a brightly lit carousel, and Sacré Coeur Basilica sat high above them like a bone white crown on top of Montmartre. Now we had to decide whether to climb the steps or ride the funicular.

The train-like vehicle carried us up to a plaza in front of the basilica where we stood gazing in wonder at the variety of Parisian rooftops fanning out at our feet.

"Look," Laura said. "We can see all the way to Notre Dame, the dome of the Pantheon, and the Eiffel Tower."

When the festive sound of an accordion came from the old village square, she took my hand and drew me in that direction. We were passing a silver-painted woman who stood on a pedestal posing as Marie Antoinette when a shabby man separated from the crowd, veered toward us, and we heard a metallic clink.

Quick as a cat, he stooped, snatched up a fat gold ring, and thrust it in my face. "Did you drop this?" he said with a thick Slavic accent.

I took the ring, said "Yes, I did. Thank you," and kept walking.

That got him. He tugged at my elbow saying "Reward, reward" until I dropped the cheap ring in his hand.

"What was that all about?" Laura said.

"It's an old con. I'm supposed to believe he found a valuable gold ring, and we can keep it if I give him some money."

Rounding a corner, we came to a small stone church called Saint Pierre de Montmartre. "This is one of the places I've read about," Laura said, excitedly. "It's one of the two oldest churches in Paris."

It was old enough to have columns from a Roman temple, and the mingled smell of stone and incense made it feel like we had been transported into another era, but what stuck with me most was the floorplan. It was shaped like the cartouche in our table cover.

The sunset was turning the sky a dark purple when we crossed the street to the Place du Tertre where dozens of artists had set up their easels. Some were sketching portraits of visitors; others painting scenes of Montmartre.

Narrow cobbled streets took us out of the old town square, past the piano music coming from old cafes, and down to Place Pigalle, home of the Moulin Rouge. We were passing some live sex shows when a noisy crowd poured out of a tour bus, and we were suddenly surrounded. People speaking an unfamiliar language pushed us from behind, the mob surged past, and Laura and I became separated.

For a frightening moment, I struggled to find her. Then the mob jostled me past a crowded falafel place and into a dimly lit theater lobby where a surly man in a silk suit held out his hand for my ticket.

"I'm looking for my girlfriend," I said.

He sneered. "I've heard that one before."

"I'm not kidding. What do you think I'm looking for?"

"I think you're looking for trouble," he said, as two hard-eyed security types took me by the arms and deposited me outside.

Laura was standing on the sidewalk with a worried frown on her face. "Did you enjoy the show?"

"I was looking for you. What the hell happened?"

"I got pushed into that falafel place."

After climbing the apartment stairs loaded down with groceries we'd picked up on the way, I was almost swallowed up by the accumulated fatigue of more than twenty-four hours without sleep.

"I'm beat," I said. "How about if we just go for some Chinese take-out?"

"That doesn't sound very French. Let me put this kitchen to use and I'll make us something good."

When I came back from washing up, an herb, cheese, and scallion omelet was sizzling in hot butter and Laura was pouring a freshly made sauce vinaigrette over a green salad.

We ate at the long dining room table Laura had set with flickering candles, linen napkins, glasses of wine, and a sliced baguette.

When the tall wooden clock chimed ten times, we drank one more glass of wine, then fell into bed and slept.

Not bad for our first day in Paris.

39

I was awakened by the world outside after ten hours of uninterrupted sleep. Shafts of sunlight were poking through the curtains and the sound of voices and motorbikes were coming from the street below. I got up to make breakfast and was setting coffee and croissants on the dining room table when Laura came in rubbing her eyes.

"Are we getting an early start?"

I nodded. "The auction previews run from eleven to noon. After we eat, I'll grab a quick shower."

I was standing under the hot spray with my eyes closed when Laura pressed up behind me.

"Hey," I said. "What are you doing?"

"You might need a little help," she said, taking the slippery bar from my hand.

She started rubbing me with the soap. "You could use a little more, right about there."

"You could some, too," I said, grappling for the soap until I got it.

If we hadn't run out of hot water, we would have missed the previews.

We started down Rue des Martyrs just past eleven. The historic route to the hilltop village of Montmartre is lined on both sides with bakeries, restaurants, cafes, and shops selling spices, fresh pasta, cheese, and flowers. The fragrances alone were a sensory delight. The sweet aroma of bread baking. The damp-dirt bouquet of freshly watered flowers. The scent of the sea from shiny fish.

The personality of the neighborhood changed after passing Notre Dame de Lorette, and we came into a *quartier* dominated by art galleries, antique stores, and Le Hôtel Drouot, the world's oldest auction house.

"This is where the action is," I said, when an ultramodern building constructed of stone, aluminum, and glass loomed before us.

"It doesn't look very old."

"It was rebuilt in the nineteen-seventies."

"Is this where Sotheby's and Christie's have their sales?"

"They picked a swanky neighborhood near the Elysée Palace, but seventy other Parisian auction companies use these sales rooms every day of the week except Sunday."

After crossing the busy lobby, we took an escalator to the floor below and began working our way up through three floors and sixteen auction showrooms. Some were doing previews for tomorrow's sales; others were setting out chairs for ones that would start this afternoon.

The carpeted hallways flanking the escalators were in constant motion. High-end antique dealers, flea market vendors, and keenly focused collectors of all stripes. Some visitors just came for the show. One of these was a silver-haired man who embodied the word *demeanor* in his dark blue suit, white tie, and cashmere overcoat.

"Did you see that man?" Laura whispered. "He was wearing house slippers with his suit."

"He probably lives in the neighborhood."

Inside the wine-red showrooms, racks of overhead lights illuminated everything on display. One room featured Chinese antiquities and Greek vases. Another offered historic paintings of Paris. Another displayed memorabilia from the estate of Dora Maar, one of Picasso's favorite ladies.

My antennae started to tingle when we began hitting sales containing all kinds of things from Parisian homes and apartments—rugs, paintings, porcelain, books, furniture, you name it.

I stopped in my tracks when we came to a display case holding an Egyptian mummy mask. Next to the mask, a four-inch diameter silk and gold threaded roundel depicted a horseman, a falcon, and a hare in as much detail as an old master painting. The catalogue described it as a 7th century fragment of a finely woven Arab robe that was used to wrap the relics of St. Lazarus when they were removed from Constantinople during the Fourth Crusade.

I was admiring the roundel when I smelled strong cologne and a hand squeezed my arm from behind. Sisko Riloni, a swarthy man in his thirties runs a small store in the *Marché aux Puces de Saint-Ouen.*

"Mr. Tony, I didn't know you were interested in pieces like that."

"I always enjoy examining the old ones, even if I'm not going to buy them."

He gave Laura the old up and down look. "You should bring your charming lady to my store."

"Have you turned up something?"

"I can show her far better pieces than these."

He rarely told the truth.

"We'll come see you the first chance we get," I said, lying to him with a certain pleasure.

Laura took my hand on the way out. "Who was that man?"

"He runs an antique rug store in the Marché aux Puce."

"He seemed nice enough."

"He's not."

"He said he had some good things to show us."

"Even when he's lying, he's lying."

"Well, now that your business is out of the way, maybe we can do something fun."

A number 85 bus was pulling into a stop. "I know just the thing," I said. "We'll see Paris the way Parisians see it."

From our window seat near the back, Les Halles, the Bourse, and other Paris monuments flicked by like a newsreel. A left at the Louvre took us past the *bouquinistes* lining the banks of the Seine. When the Tour Saint-Jacques loomed on our left, the bus turned right and crossed a bridge onto the Ile de la Cité.

The doors hissed open for a quick stop in front of the Conciergerie. A lady getting on spilled some oranges. The driver waited patiently while people rummaged around under their seats and passed them forward. The lady thanked the passengers as she gathered them up.

The doors hissed shut, and we continued past the Palais de Justice, Sainte-Chapelle, and Notre-Dame Cathedral. A baby started crying when the bus bounced hard going over a narrow bridge into the Latin Quarter. The mother rocked the baby in her arms as the Gallo-Roman baths, Cluny castle, and the columns of the Pantheon went by, one after the other.

Laura was grinning widely as we spilled out of the bus at the end of the line. "That was a pretty good tour for the cost of a bus ticket."

"That was the idea, and there's more," I said, leading her across busy Boulevard Saint Michel and into Luxembourg Gardens.

A tree lined lane winding past statues, flowerbeds, and fountains brought us to an octagonal pond in front of Luxembourg Palace. We sat in green metal chairs watching children sail model boats until clouds began to move across the sun. Then we wrapped scarfs around our necks and left the park through another gate near the Medici Fountain.

We were about to cross the street in front of the Odéon Theatre when my eyes were drawn to a Capadocian kelim displayed in a storefront window on Rue Racine. The sign read *Antique Rugs and Textiles,* and a middle-aged man was sitting behind a desk piled with books examining a bottle of wine.

I introduced us in my clumsy French, and he replied in perfect English. "It is always a pleasure to meet an American dealer. I am a retired English teacher who likes old wine as well as old rugs. Would you care to join me in a taste?"

"Certainly," I said. "What is it?"

"It's a ninety-nine Saint Aubin from Burgundy. It has a slight taste of the wood, but wine is like a man, it can have a flaw and still be pleasing."

"Sometimes it's even more pleasing with the flaw," I said.

He smiled at that as he filled our glasses. "Are you here on business?"

"Not entirely. We plan to spend a week in Paris and then go to Spain. I've got a Spanish rug I'm researching."

"Is that something I could help you with?"

I signaled Laura to get the photos out of her purse.

He adjusted his glasses as he studied them. "I've never seen one like this, but early European pieces sell quite well here. You might want to show your photos to Gaston Leroux, the rug and textile expert for the Paris auctions. His office is near here on L'Ile Saint-Louis."

"Might he be serving such fine wine?"

"Only if you're having a very lucky day," he said, the light of amusement glimmering behind his glasses.

192

40

Half a block down the street, the flowered murals, beveled mirrors, and Art Nouveau-stained glass of the Bouillon Racine brasserie drew us inside for a café crème pick-up.

"Shall we go see what the Paris appraiser has to say?" I said, nibbling at the little cookie that came with my coffee.

Laura nodded. "We might learn something useful."

After checking the route, we climbed aboard a 96-bus, and rode it to the Pont Marie stop across from L'Ile Saint-Louis. Open-roofed *bateaux mouches* loaded with waving tourists glided beneath us as we crossed the bridge and paused to take in the iconic view of central Paris: the Hôtel de Ville, the Conciergerie, the Louvre, and the Eiffel Tower.

Leaving the bridge past an amorous couple locked in a kiss, a left on the Quai de Anjou brought us to a narrow storefront with a wooden door that looked to be hundreds of years old. The door opened to a small office lined floor to ceiling with bookcases where a tall man in his fifties was seated at a desk typing on a laptop. Gaston Leroux motioned for us to sit in a pair of armchairs, finished typing, and let his dark eyes glide over us.

"How can I help you?"

"A local dealer told me you might be able to tell us what our table cover could bring at auction," I said, gesturing for Laura to pass me the manila envelope containing my photos, and a piece of paper with the inscription translation.

A veiled look came over his face when I handed him just the photos and slid the translation into my shirt pocket.

He studied them for a moment. "With these, the age is the key. I cannot determine the age from a photo, but they rarely date earlier than the sixteenth century. If yours is earlier, it could be worth significantly more."

He glanced at the pocket where I had put the inscription translation. "Do you know what the writing says? It looks like an old form of Hebrew."

"It may be sort of a poem," I said, not wanting to say too much.

He paused, as though reflecting, then leaned forward. "It is not necessary to sell a desirable artifact through the auction. There are enthusiastic collectors in Paris who would be very discrete cash buyers."

"I need to do more research. We're not quite ready to sell."

His smile faded, and he thumbed through the photos again, this time more slowly. "Could I keep one of these?"

"I'm sorry, they're the only ones I have."

The silence was thick as he handed them back. His hooded eyes followed my hand when I passed them to Laura and lingered as she slipped them into her purse.

"Could you give us some idea what it might sell for if we did put it in the auction here?" I asked when his eyes met mine.

He tapped a pen on the table, as if playing for time. "It does have an unusual design. This is the first time I've seen a crown or an inscription in one of these. If the inscription refers to an historical event that excites the marketplace, it could have a great deal of value."

"So, the key to its value is whether the inscription excites the marketplace?"

"That's right. If the historical event were something of historical significance, the value could shoot up like a rocket."

"How high could it go?"

I got a strange feeling that he knew more than he admitted when he dropped his pen and leaned back in his chair. "For a front-page kind of event, the value could be in the millions."

My surprise must have showed, because he smiled and slid one of his cards across the table. "As you well know, Mr.

Shepherd, an appraiser can never give a final opinion without seeing a work of art in its entirety."

It wasn't until we went out the door that it hit me—how the hell did he know my name?

Laura didn't say a word as we crossed the bridge to the bus stop. I picked up what had to be on her mind.

"You're probably wondering how it could be worth so much more than I thought it was."

She smiled.

"I've never handled one before and Leroux knows that market way better than me."

She poked me playfully. "I'd say you got a pretty good deal on your forty-seven-hundred-dollar investment."

"There was no way for me to know that. And don't forget, you own the other half."

She kissed me on the cheek as our bus was pulling up. "We wouldn't be together in Paris if you hadn't bought your half."

What she said struck deep. The mysterious table cover had delivered me to a woman I was learning to love.

After turning north at the Louvre, our bus stopped so abruptly that we were thrown against the seat in front of us. Outside, the white glare of camera lights lit up a horseshoe of TV reporters. They were interviewing a man beneath a green on black neon sign reading *Duluc Detective.*

"What the heck's going on?" Laura said, brushing back her hair.

"It looks like someone made it onto the evening news," I said. "Are you alright?"

"I'm alright, but I hit my head."

It wasn't until a crescendo of horns began honking that the bus jerked forward several times and managed to break free.

41

Nothing caught my eye during the auction previews next morning, but I realized I should have been far more attentive seconds after stepping onto the escalator down to the lobby. Face-to-face at the bottom, Gaston Leroux was shaking hands with tough guy Vincent.

I was trying to think of a clever way to greet them, when the pale-faced bald man walked up accompanied by Sisko Riloni. Cursing silently, I pulled out my camera, and zoomed in for a photo, just before they turned away and followed Vincent out the main entry.

I couldn't risk running into them on the street, so I led Laura out a side door, and hurried us onto a bus that had just opened its doors. My mind was racing. In one instant everything had gone wrong.

"Is something the *matter*?" Laura said.

I was groping for words.

She touched my arm. "Are you feeling all right?"

"No, I'm not feeling all right."

"Well, what is it?"

"Did you see those people at the bottom of the escalator?"

"I saw Gaston Leroux and your rug dealer buddy."

"He's not my buddy."

"What's got you so uptight?"

"It's the two people they were talking with."

"What about them?"

"The big man came to my gallery asking about the Spanish piece. The bald guy is Sheena's art appraiser."

"How do you know he's Sheena's art appraiser?"

"We heard her talking about him when Sammy and I were doing the heist."

Down came the brows and she looked at me hard. "What would Sheena's art appraiser be doing here in Paris?"

"I have no idea. It might mean we're dealing with some clever adversaries."

"Adversaries?" she said, studying my face. "Maybe they're just friends."

"People like that don't have friends."

She narrowed her eyes. "How come you never told me about any of this?"

I had no good answer to that.

The green on black neon sign of Duluc Detective was blinking at me from across the street when our bus was stuck in slow moving traffic outside the Louvre. On impulse, I hurried us off the bus, and into their building.

Marble stairs with a bronze railing brought us to a second-floor landing and a polished oak door with *Duluc Detective* inscribed in gold and black letters on frosted glass. The door opened to a reception area where an ash blonde wearing a white blouse and a black jacket greeted us from behind an ultramodern workspace. I started to say my name, but chose discretion, and pulled out the Fleet Detective card I had found in my back room.

The woman put on the gold rimmed glasses that were hanging from her neck. "So, Monsieur Fleet, what can we do for you?"

"I'm hoping you can help me with a case I'm working on."

She studied our faces for a moment, then picked up a phone and spoke in rapid fire French. Handing back my card, she pointed at another polished oak door. "Monsieur Duluc will see you now."

A man in his sixties with black hair turning gray at the temples was seated at a wide mahogany desk with nothing on it but a computer and a telephone. We sat across from him in a pair of soft leather chairs, and I pulled out my camera.

"I came to see you because I need to identify some people in a photo and get background information on them."

"We always try to give special consideration to our friends in the trade, Monsieur Fleet, but I need more than just a photo."

"I've got some names to get you started."

He took a five-hundred-euro retainer after downloading the photo and writing down the names.

"You should check in at least once a week," he said as he led us graciously to the door. "Someone is always in the office during normal business hours."

Neither of us said a word while we rode the bus back to the auction. My mind was overflowing with conflicting ideas about what might have brought those four unsavory characters together.

Sisko Riloni was standing by the escalators talking to a blond man with a beaked nose and a pock-marked face when we came into the lobby of the Hotel Druout. I changed directions and took the stairs to the second-floor showroom where the roundel was to be sold. Maybe Riloni saw me. Maybe he just pretended he didn't.

The seats were all taken, so we stood in back watching an impeccably attired auctioneer call out bids from the podium. Three people took bids from phones on his right, two women on his left were writing it all down, and stewards in long black aprons took turns holding up the objects to be sold.

Furtive movement drew my eye to the furniture dealers huddled in a corner when the auctioneer called out *adjugé* and banged down his ivory hammer on a Louis XV bombé chest. A big-bellied man was brazenly dividing a wad of hundred-euro notes among his cohorts. The auctioneer knew they were running a ring, but he couldn't do anything about it.

Riloni came in with a covey of carpet dealers a moment before the oriental rugs began selling. Forming a solemn line along the rear wall, they stood with their hands in their pockets while Riloni bought nearly everything.

A hush fell over the room when a steward held up the tiny ninth-century roundel. I had little hope of buying it but enjoyed watching it soar from an opening bid of 10,000 all the way up to 200,000 euros and a roomful of applause.

We were exiting the crowded salesroom when a man stepped from the wall, followed us onto the escalator down to the lobby, and stayed close behind as we went out the door.

I glanced his way when Laura stopped to look at a painting in one of the art galleries lining Rue de la Grange Bateliére. He turned away, but I got a good enough look. It was the same blond man with a pock-marked face who had been talking to Riloni.

When we continued down the street, he did too.

The open arched entry to Le Passage Verdeau, a glass-roofed arcade lined with quaint 19th century store fronts, was a few doors away. Ducking inside the first shop we came to, I hurried Laura behind the bookcases of an antiquarian bookstore.

"What are we doing?" she said.

"Someone might be following us," I said, sneaking a look just in time to see the blond man scurry by, scanning both sides of the marble-floored passageway with a worried look on his face.

"Who is it?" she said.

"Nobody we know, but he's been behind us ever since we left the Drouot."

"Maybe he's just going the same direction we are."

"He was talking to Riloni when we went into the auction.

She looked at me for a moment with raised eyebrows, then began examining the books on history that were right in front of her.

I kept my eye on the arcade while Laura looked through the books. When she held up a tattered, but potentially useful, copy of *Les Chemins de Saint Jacques Pendant le Moyen Age*, I went outside while she bought the book.

After making sure the thin man wasn't lurking anywhere in the Passage, we followed it to the far end and crossed the street for a bus that would take us up Rue des Martyrs.

We were taking a seat on the bus when I turned to look out the window. The blond man with the pock-marked face was staring back at me from the archway into the Passage.

Loud voices ricocheted off the walls of the narrow street when we were walking hand in hand toward our flat. Half a block ahead of us, three men were standing outside our apartment with their heads tipped back. The one speaking into a cell phone had the all-too-familiar face of Sisko Riloni.

I started forward in anger but felt a sudden yank as Laura pulled me into a doorway. Then we watched from the shadows as Riloni gestured in an agitated manner, pocketed the phone, and walked away followed closely by the other two.

I started to step out of the doorway, but Laura pulled me back at the brutal sound of motorcycles revving their engines. Seconds later, two chopped Harleys blasted by, leaving the stink of exhaust fumes hanging in the air. Both drivers were wearing black, Nazi-style helmets.

"Was that man on the phone who I think it was?" Laura said.

"Yeah, it was Riloni."

"It can't be just a coincidence that he was standing outside our apartment door with those two bikers."

"No. There are no coincidences like that."

"I hate missing more of Paris, but maybe it's time to start following the pilgrimage route."

"First thing in the morning, we'll take the rug to the restorer and then get ourselves on a train to Vézelay."

"How could they have found out where we're staying?"

"I have no idea, but it's not safe here anymore."

42

We left the apartment early and walked down the street to catch an 85-bus to the center of town. I nearly froze when we passed a newspaper vending machine. A grisly headline proclaimed that auction expert Monsieur Leroux had been brutally murdered during a nighttime burglary of his office.

It rattled me, even though I had no reason to think it had anything to do with us. I got even more spooked when the same, blue-helmeted motor scooter rider cruised by for the third or fourth time while waiting for the bus. I had us stay on past our real stop, get off at the next one, and then cross over to catch the first bus going back to the Palais de Justice.

Behind the venerable courts building, a provincial looking square was just waking up. A solitary waiter had begun setting up his outside tables, but Place Dauphine was nearly deserted at this early hour. An old man sat on a bench reading Le Monde, a young boy chased elusive pigeons while waving a stick, and an amorous couple stood cheek-to-cheek while their dogs sniffed each other.

On the other side of the tree-lined square, a narrow storefront was sandwiched between a hat boutique and a place selling Provençal textiles. Its milky-white facade had a sleepy, 19th century charm, and the window contained a minimalist display. Coils of colored yarn hung from dried tree branches above shallow bowls containing the leaves, roots, bark, and fungi that were the source of the colors.

The closest thing to a sign was '*Isabelle Maziére*' stenciled in black letters on the base of the window. Seconds after tapping on the door, a gray-haired woman peered through the lace curtain and opened it.

"Bonjour Madame," I said. "I'm Tony Shepherd. Our mutual friend Alaydin sent me to see you about an old Spanish rug I'd like to have restored."

She nodded. "Alaydin sent me an e-mail about you. Please come in."

We followed her down a dark corridor to a well-lit workroom where skeins of yarn in every color were stored in small compartments on the walls surrounding a polished worktable. Madame Maziére pulled an overhead light closer to the table, and we laid the panels out side-by-side so she could study them.

"Yours has more variety and detail than other table covers I have worked on," she said. "Fortunately for you, I just finished restoring a tapestry of the same age and have some of these colors on hand. That will save you some money because the dyes of this era are difficult to match. The cost to you will be about a thousand euros."

"Sounds good," I said. "How long will it take?"

"It's mostly a matter of replacing the missing knots along the edges and rejoining the panels, so I might have it ready by the end of the week."

"We're going to the northern part of Spain for a week or two."

"With your approval, I could have it delivered to the workshop Alaydin uses in Spain."

"We should be stopping near there. I'll let you know by phone. In the meantime, I prefer that nobody knows about this."

"All my restoration work is confidential. It's part of the service."

"How did you learn so much about natural dying?" Laura said, turning to take in the rainbow of colors around us.

"My father was a pharmacist," she said, removing her glasses and rubbing her eyes with an expression like she was concentrating on images in her head. "Making dyes from natural pigments used to be part of that profession. He saw my fingers stained with brown when I came home from school one day after gathering walnuts and showed me how to make a chocolate-colored dye from their husks. Later, he showed me how to make a golden color from moss, a violet from lichen, and a rusty red from wild mushrooms. It thrilled me to see the colors materialize in clear water and I always wanted to learn more."

"You must have learned everything by now," Laura said.

"One can never learn everything. There are no recipes, and the old dyes are difficult to reproduce."

"Didn't they use known formulas?"

"In those days, the master dyers kept their recipes to themselves. They only passed them on by word of mouth to a trusted apprentice. Most of their formulas have been lost forever."

"Isn't there some way to reconstruct what went into them?"

"Only by trial and error."

"Does that work?"

"Not so well as you might think."

"Why is that?"

"It's not simply a matter of boiling some dye materials in water. Blue, for example, has been made from indigo leaves for thousands of years. But before you begin, the leaves must be fermented. Then the wool is treated to an alkaline process to open the fiber so it can absorb the dyes."

"How did they do all that?"

"They used whatever they had available. Sour milk for fermentation, things like sheep urine, wood ash, and lemon peels for the alkaline process."

"Have you tried any of those old methods?"

She smiled. "I've tried them all. If I leave out a single step, or don't leave the yarn in the dye vat long enough, I get a different color."

After leaving the rug with Madame Maziére, we descended into the Metro and rode it several stops to the Gare de Lyon. An escalator crowded with people pulling suitcases carried us up to the soaring metalwork and hollow sounding resonance of the Grand Hall. Beneath the gigantic glass roof, a dozen tracks were lined with trains waiting for their passengers, and an aura of adventure was in the air.

"Are we going to take one of those fast ones?" Laura said, as we threaded our way past throngs of travelers gazing up at reader boards.

"We could. But it would be more scenic to take the TER, the Train Express Régional. It's not a bullet train like the TGV, but it passes through lots of small villages."

After standing in a short line at a *Billetterie Automatic*, we bought tickets to Avallon, not far from the Vézelay pilgrimage route.

"We've got an hour to kill and there's something I want you to see," I said, leading Laura to a monumental double stairway at the rear of the departure hall. Marble steps with an ornate bronze railing led to lace-curtained windows and an Art Nouveau sign reading *Le Train Bleu*.

"It's an expensive looking restaurant," Laura said.

"We can splurge on coffee and a dessert," I said, opening the door for her.

Crystal chandeliers hanging beneath gilded arches illuminated a masterpiece of Beaux Arts architectural detail. Majestic mirrors lining the wainscoted walls reflected baby-faced cherubs, nymphs, and angels cavorting across a crème and amber ceiling.

After stowing our bags in the foyer, a hostess wearing a formal black dress led us to a table covered in white linen and set with polished silver and sparkling crystal.

We sat studying the menu. "Their *Baba au Rhum amber Saint James, Chantilly à la vanille de Madagascar* is supposed to be pretty good," I said. "How about a couple of those, and coffee?"

"It's your treat," Laura said.

A silver-haired man in a waistcoat took our order while people were being seated at a nearby table. Judging by their clothes and their voices, they were Americans. Somewhere in the room a cork popped, people laughed softly, but those sounds were drowned out by the self-confident newcomers.

Scraps of conversation floated across while the waiter was taking their orders. "...her family, of course...mercenary marriage...better at giving headaches than head."

Laughter around the table was followed by a louder voice. "Look, they've got *Cervelle d'agneau*. I haven't had brains in a long time."

I was trying to hide my laughter when another waiter appeared carrying a silver tray and a bottle of Martinique rum. After pouring our coffee, he put two shiny sponge rolls crowned with whipped cream in front of us and splashed them with a generous amount of golden liquid.

Laura took a bite, wiped whipped cream off her lips, and smiled blissfully. I did the same.

"You seem a lot more relaxed," she said. "Has something else happened you haven't told me about?"

This was the wrong time to tell her about Gaston Leroux. "No, nothing's happened. I'm just glad to be getting away from all those shady characters. We learned some things, but I never should have given Leroux so much to talk about."

"Most of what I saw of Paris was from the window of a bus."

"We'll see more when we come back for the rug. Whatever brought those people together won't keep them here forever."

"Maybe so, but I'm starting to wonder if I should be looking for the next flight home."

"You don't need to worry," I said, reaching across to take her hand. "I won't let anything bad happen to you."

"I trust you, Tony, but those people we've been running into are something I hadn't planned on."

"None of them know where we're going or what we're doing. In spite of all that's happened, I believe the worst is behind us."

43

A whistle pierced the air after we had settled into forward facing seats in a coach that was barely half full, and the train began grinding its way through the bleak industrial sprawl of Paris. It picked up speed when we emerged into the residential suburbs, and soon we were rumbling through an ever-changing panorama of small towns and green fields.

The scenery changed as we moved into the swelling glory of Burgundy's sunflower covered hills. Stone farmhouses mingled with stately chateaux, and small villages nestled around mossy churches with ancient graveyards. You could almost hear the moaning of cows, the bleating of sheep, and the crowing of roosters.

It felt so safe and reassuring feeling the rocking motion and watching the world go by, that I was lulled into a shallow sleep until a garbled voice from tinny-sounding speakers announced we were coming into Avallon Station.

The train squeaked, and groaned, before lurching to a stop. Then the door hissed open, and we stumbled out onto a deserted platform basking sleepily in the autumn sunshine. Nobody but us got off.

A lone taxi driver eyed us expectantly when we stopped outside the station to study a tourist information kiosk. An artist's rendition of medieval Avallon showed high walls and cone-roofed watchtowers encircling a city surrounded on three sides by near vertical slopes. The forty-foot walls circling the town were further defended by reinforced terraces descending all the way to the valley floor.

The text explained that this naturally fortified site was called Aballo when it was chosen to be the Romans' local capital. Now it is a quiet market town of cobblestone streets lined with half-timbered buildings dating from the fifteen-hundreds.

"I wonder why the name Avallon sounds so familiar?" Laura said, as we hiked towards the two towers rising above the town center.

"Because it's part of the King Arthur legend."

"But this can't be the legendary Isle of Avalon."

"Some people think so. No place in England has ever been called Avalon, and a British king named Arthur disappeared in this region back then. On top of that, a legend says Arthur was treated for his battle wounds at *Les Fontaines Salées*, the healing springs outside Vézelay that were run by women."

"Stories like that show how hard it is to separate myth from history."

Neither myth nor history penetrated the modern and functional Europe Car office where we picked up our little Renault Clio. The agent said the best way to get to Vézelay was to take the street outside their office and a three-mile drive along the Cousin River would take us to the road we wanted.

After adjusting the seats and mirrors, we started down a sloping road with the fortifications of Avallon towering above us.

The road narrowed when we passed the last of the half-timbered houses, and we entered the peaceful calm of *La Valée du Cousin*, a river gorge with rocky cliffs on one side, and tall trees closing in on the other. Beams of sunlight slanting through the forest canopy illuminated milky mists hovering above the dark water of a rocky river. It was the kind of atmosphere in which myths are born.

"This makes me think of the French phrase 'genie de lieu'," Laura said wistfully.

I gave her a questioning look.

"It's a place that emanates something special and unique."

The road narrowed even more when we began passing a series of mill houses and I slowed to take it all in. Some of them had been converted to private homes, but still had their water wheels and dark wooden sluice gates. Then we rounded a curve, and I hit the brakes for a sign reading *Hôtel Le Moulin des Templiers.*

"This looks like a good place to spend our first night in Burgundy," I said. "It's close to Vézelay so we can get there before noon."

A shaggy black dog rose from the entry and barked as I pulled to a stop in the graveled parking lot. Seconds later, a lady came out, quieted the dog, and invited us in. She switched to English when she heard my French, explaining that she and her husband were English and had owned the hotel for fifteen years.

"Where does the Templar name come from?" I said, as I began filling in the registration form.

"Our mill was part of their defensive system for this river valley," she said, as a boy of about eight burst through the door waving a cardboard sword. A mustache was penciled on his face, and he was dressed like a pirate in a red and black bandana.

"Slow down, Ben, can't you see we have guests?"

"I wanna show Dad the sword I made."

"He's in his studio."

The boy bolted out a door to the garden, and she handed me a key on a numbered keyring.

"Yours is the first room down the hall. Feel free to explore the grounds. My husband enjoys having company if you care to visit his studio."

A flagstone corridor led to a white-walled room raftered with age darkened beams. The window overlooked a withered flower garden and a low stone wall that flanked the river.

After getting settled in, we went outside and followed rumbling noises to a water wheel being turned by a steady flow of dark water. The air was damp, and a mushroom scented breeze ruffled the trees rising up the other side. Tap-tap sounds were coming from a building facing the terrace.

We crossed over and knocked on a carved oak door. The tapping stopped, and a man whose face and smock were covered in white powder opened the door. "Welcome to my studio," he said, gesturing us in. "You must be the Americans."

Pieces of white stone littered the floor, and a timbered ceiling rose to an apex above our heads. A statue resembling a Greek Island Cycladic figure stood on a work stand next to an empty bottle of wine.

"We're the Americans," I said. "We stopped here because of the Templar name. We're interested in all that history."

"You're standing on five thousand years of history," he smiled.

I glanced at my feet. "I visited Vézelay several years back, but I don't know much about the history."

"This region is rich in history, Celtic and Roman history, but to properly appreciate history, we should have some ratafia. One of our local specialties."

Reaching into a cupboard, he took out a bottle, and carefully filled three glasses with a dark red liquid.

Laura sniffed at hers before sipping. "What's in it?"

"Freshly pressed grape juice and *eau de vie* sit in glass jugs until Christmas. Then they bottle it."

"It tastes sweet, sort of like a port," she said.

"That's about right. Chin, chin," he said, raising his glass and taking a hearty swallow.

"Your wife said you've lived here fifteen years," I said. "You must know how Vézelay got to be such an important pilgrimage site."

He nodded. "It wasn't always that way. The Basilica wasn't drawing so many visitors until the Pope shared some pieces of Mary Magdalene with them back in ten fifty-eight. There wasn't much." He grinned. "Just a finger or two. But when the Pope was generous enough to give you the finger, you kissed his ring and said, 'Thank you, Father'."

Laura was smiling. "I read that the Vézelay hilltop was an important Celtic site."

"It was one of the most sacred sanctuaries for their Druidic priests. That was why the Catholics built their church up there. They liked to put them on sites the locals already considered to be holy."

"Are any remnants of the Druids still up there?"

He smiled. "The monks had to depend on local Celtic masons, and they discretely filled the place with their own Druidic imagery."

"Is any of it still visible?"

"If you look closely, you can find carved hexagrams, druidic spirals, and snakes biting their tails. They even managed to carve Christ's face in the image of a Druid deity named Lugh."

"And the monks never noticed?" Laura said incredulously.

"The Druids were more advanced than people realize. They wrote with Greek letters, portrayed constellations on their coins, and believed in the immortality of the soul."

He paused to drain his glass. "Here, let me top you off," he said, adding a bit to ours, and refilling his own.

"Vézelay was also where Saint Bernard preached the second crusade. Richard the Lionheart, following in his footsteps, launched the third crusade from the same spot. If all that history isn't enough to justify your visit, then you should try some of our local food. Burgundy's not just known for its wines. The restaurant in the next mill down the river serves some of the finest local cuisine."

Back in our room, I was so mellowed out by the ratafia that I began nuzzling Laura's ear. "Wouldn't it be great if we could just stay here forever?"

"I bet you say that to all the girls."

"You're the only girl for me."

She pulled me closer. "If you're going to say sweet things like that, you darn well better kiss me."

"You should try to watch your language. You know how sensitive I am."

I kissed her anyway, and we finished in a tangle of sheets, breathing hard in unison.

"Where'd you learn to do that?" she said.

"I didn't learn it anywhere I just made it up."

"Well, now I'm hungry. Let's go try that restaurant."

A wintry moon cast tree-shaped shadows as we walked hand in hand towards the golden glow coming from the Moulin de Ruats. When I pulled open the door, we were greeted by a murmur of voices, and the warm smells of cooking.

Laura pointed to a framed page displayed on the wall, while we waited to be seated. It was from *The Light of Day,* an Eric Ambler book.

His characters were reminiscing about home while visiting exotic Istanbul. One character asked the other, "If you could choose, where would you most like to be dining tonight and what would you eat?"

"I would dine in Avallon, at Le Moulin de Ruats. I would order Le coq au vin."

"With the Cuvée du Docteur ?"

"Of course."

The *Cuvée du Docteur* was no longer on the wine list, so we picked a local red called Irancy to go with steamed Bresse chicken stuffed with leeks, carrots, and truffles. Creamy Epoisses cheese cleared our palates, and we finished with a dessert of *Flamusse aux Pommes.*

After pouring the last of the Irancy, I raised my glass. "To a wine that tastes like you and a glass that's never empty."

Laura reached across to touch my hand as we drank it down.

Pegasus and Cassiopeia were burning brightly in an ink-black sky as we walked the moonlit road back to our hotel. Except for the echo of our footsteps, the night was so still we could almost hear the stars breathing.

Then a stiffening breeze brought a faint stirring in the leaves, and the night seemed suddenly full of movement.

Furtive scurryings and mysterious rustlings in the shadows behind the trees were followed by the sharp crack of a branch.

Laura gripped my arm. "What was that?"

For a moment, I found myself looking to both sides of the road, half expecting the shadows to move, or a ghostly hand to reach out.

"We must have startled a deer," I said.

It wasn't until we were entering the driveway for our hotel that I caught the faint scent of cigarette smoke in a shifting breeze.

44

Hammering and sawing noises coming from the courtyard woke us, and we went down to a breakfast room overlooking the garden. After helping ourselves to croissants, crusty baguettes, and strong coffee, we were climbing the stairs to our room when I remembered it was time to check in with Duluc Detective.

Laura gave me a questioning look as I jotted things into my notebook while listening to his report. She gave me a more pointed look when I didn't say anything after hanging up.

"He turned up a couple things. Riloni's bank closed his account because he bounced a twenty-grand check. A rumor's going around that he's so desperate for money that he's gotten involved with a biker gang that rips off vacation homes in the south of France."

"That's terrible," Laura said. "But it doesn't tell us very much."

"No, but he thinks he'll have something more in a day or two."

Despite the disquieting news, we felt pleasantly relaxed as we followed the curves of the river through the wooded valley. When the road rose from the trees, we turned left on a bigger road that would take us to Vézelay, a traditional starting point for the Saint James pilgrimage, and the home of Laura's ancestors.

"It feels like a good day for a drive in the country," I said, as a stone bridge took us over the Cousin River and into the sleepy town of Pontaubert.

I was going the fifty-kilometer speed limit when a black Mercedes van with tinted windows moved right up on my bumper. It stayed close, then accelerated past when there was a momentary break in traffic.

The logo on the side read *Pompes Funèbres Barsini*—a funeral company.

"Why do people drive like that?" Laura said, indignantly.

"Maybe they're late for a funeral."

Sinuous roads carried us smoothly past endless fields of sunflowers until we entered tiny Fontette. Our car rattled and shook so much on their roughly cobbled street that I had to slow to walking speed. Then we rounded a bend to a breathtaking view.

Bathed in a golden light from the morning sun, Vézelay Basilica roosted on top of a distant hill. The houses of the old town stretched along the ridge from the great building like a clutch of chicks straggling after a mother hen. Beneath those houses, sixty-foot-tall ramparts of gray stone separated the town above from vineyards lining the steep slopes below.

"I bet this looks pretty much the same as when your great-grandfather lived here."

"It must have been hard to leave a place like this," Laura said.

Ignoring the signs that encourage visitors to park and walk up the steep main street, I circled the base of the hill and parked in a deserted lot behind the double-turreted rear gate to the city.

"Are we taking the back way in?" Laura said.

"Exactly," I said. "It's still a serious hike, but we'll avoid the touristy commerce along the main drag."

A few drops of rain hit our faces as we slid out, and Laura reached for her umbrella before we began climbing a series of ramps and stairs leading up to the basilica. After pausing several times to catch our breath, we joined a crowd of people standing in front of the massive building. High above, a colossal figure of

Christ was carved into the weathered stone, surrounded by divine beings and other more worldly figures.

We were standing there with our heads tipped back when the crunch of tires and the low murmur of a big engine came from behind. People grumbled at the disturbance, but the crowd parted, and the funeral van that passed us earlier drove slowly across the plaza, and into the parking lot next to the church.

Laura was still looking up. "The tympaniums carved above the doors are one of the things this place is famous for."

"What's the deal with all the dwarves with dog's heads and pigmies with pig snouts and floppy ears?"

"Those are supposed to be the ungodly people of the world."

"You mean like God made some kind of mistake?"

She nodded. "Something like that. The Pope issued a proclamation. Muslims had to be exterminated and killing them was a path to Paradise. Since people had no idea what Muslims looked like, they depicted them as sub-human."

"Some of them have beaks and are covered with feathers."

"That's how they did it in those days. Centuries of bloodshed were sanctified by convincing one group of people that another group of people were inhuman monsters."

"It's enough to make you wonder what Jesus bothered to die for."

"What's worse is that they still do it that way."

"Except now it's about the price of oil."

Inside the entry, people with cameras were pondering the mysteries of another tympanium, and the sweet sound of Gregorian chant was coming from open wooden doors. We followed the singing into the nave where sunbeams slanting through the high clerestory windows illuminated a vast space of light and height.

A succession of soaring arches supported by thick columns were built with alternating ochre and cream-colored stone. Above them, the slender ribs of the vaulted ceiling spread and intersected like the lines of a curved universe.

The white-robed Franciscan group that had been singing from the choir was filing down the center aisle. Visitors who were leaving for lunch followed them out, and we had the place nearly to ourselves as we explored the ambulatory bays surrounding the apse.

"This is the big draw," I said, coming to a low door with a hand-lettered sign reading *Crypt*. "Mary's bones are on display down there."

"We wouldn't want to miss any illustrious bones," Laura said.

Ducking beneath the archway, we followed well-worn steps to a dimly lit chapel set on raw rock that had been polished to a glassy smoothness by centuries of faithful footsteps. Thin stone pillars supported the ribbed ceiling, and the only source of light was a rack of candles in front of an iron-barred niche.

Behind those bars, protected by heavy glass, a gold and glass reliquary contained bones alleged to come from Mary Magdalene. It was so quiet we could hear the candles flickering.

"There's not much in there," Laura said, leaning in for a better look. "Just some tiny things wrapped in dingy, old cloth."

"They could be anything," I said, squinting through candlelight. "But it's a big deal to some people."

I wasn't paying attention to footsteps coming down the stairs until I realized a man wearing a black suit with a white carnation was standing too close to Laura. A bigger man, dressed the same, was blocking our way out. If it weren't for the balaclava ski masks, both of them could have passed for morticians.

In one sudden motion, the man's arm shot out and pulled Laura's purse toward him. Whiplash quick, Laura yanked it back so hard she stumbled into me. Pulling her behind me, I stepped in front of her to face him.

Taking a step back, he reached in his hip pocket, flicked open a switchblade, and came at me making jerky thrusting motions at my face. I was slowly backing up when candlelight reflecting off the blade reminded me of the flashlight Sol had given me.

Pulling it out, I hit the button, and dazzling flashes of light made it seem like the pillars were dancing. When my adversary raised an arm to shield his eyes, it gave me the second I needed to smack the knife from his hand and send it sliding across the floor.

Shifting quickly into a karate stance, he came at me again making chopping motions with his hands. When he launched a poorly timed head kick, I used a move I'd learned in martial arts. Leaning to the side, I let his kick glance off my shoulder, and pushed his foot as high above my head as I could possibly reach.

He was hopping around on one foot, struggling to stand, when Laura brushed past me and hooked his ankle with her umbrella handle. He kept his balance for a few seconds, then he fell. His head hit one of the pillars with a sharp crack, and he sprawled across the floor, out like a light.

I had the luxury of a split-second smile before the bigger man started shuffling toward me with a determined look in his piggy little eyes. This one would not tip over so easily, so I steered Laura to the opposite side of the chamber where another set of stairs went up. These guys had blocked the way we came in but never noticed there was another way out.

Tourists gave us startled looks as we scurried down a narrow passage past a small chapel, and out a wooden door into the parking lot for staff and clergy. At the far end of the lot, a third man, dressed like the other two, was standing beside the funeral van taking quick puffs on a cigarette and looking the other way.

Grasping Laura by the hand, I hurried us into a walled lane leading down to where our car was parked. I didn't dare risk driving past the main entrance, so I squeezed the car onto a narrow dirt track running down the back side of the hill.

We were bouncing along beneath overhanging trees when our wheels caught in a rut, and we heard the sharp shriek of metal ripping. We heard another metallic crunch when I wrenched the car out of the rut and my head hit the ceiling. We hadn't fastened our seat belts.

"It's a good thing this car is insured," I said, feeling giddy from the rush of adrenaline.

"This road is for tractors," Laura said, as the car bucked and shuddered.

"I bet some people might pay extra for a vacation like this."

"I'm not one of them," Laura said.

"I've got to keep it out of the ruts. If we lose our oil pan, we'll be stuck."

"I suppose some people might pay extra for that, too," she said a bit more sharply.

The ruts flattened out once we reached level ground and I skidded to a stop at an intersection with the D951. A sign pointed west toward Clamecy, the direction I wanted, so I swung a hard left and burned rubber.

We drove in silence for several minutes before I turned to Laura. "Are you okay?"

"Just a little shaky."

"You did great, tripping that guy."

"It happened so fast I hardly remember doing it."

"We might never have made it out if you hadn't done that."

"I did it on instinct."

"It was damn good instinct."

She gave me a crooked smile. "You weren't so bad yourself, remembering Dad's flashlight."

"I took the path of least resistance until he tried to Tae Kwon Do me. Then I Jiu Jitso'd him."

"That was very Zen of you."

Now we were laughing.

"I hope you don't regret coming here with me," I said.

She rested the warmth of her hand on my knee. "I didn't plan on getting mugged by guys in ski masks, but I wouldn't miss this trip for the world."

"Did you see that funeral van in the parking lot when we came out of the church."

"What about it?"

"It was the same one that passed us after we left the hotel."

The heat of her hand faded fast when she took it away.

45

Autumn forests enflamed in shades of red, orange, and yellow streaked by in a blur of color as I drove with my left front tire hugging the white line. We saw more wildlife than people in this rural part of France. Long-eared rabbits and red-tailed foxes vanished swiftly into the undergrowth, while hawks and eagles circled constantly overhead.

I didn't lift my foot off the gas until we started passing staff-carrying pilgrims who were walking this section of the Camino. We hadn't spoken since leaving Vézelay, and both of us had the same thing on our minds.

"What kind of person would choose a heavily touristed church as a place to snatch a purse?" Laura said.

"Someone who wants something more than your purse."

"Are you saying they knew who we were?"

"I made a mistake in Paris when I let it be known that we were carrying a copy of the inscription and some excellent photos."

"Why would that be so important?"

"Because the inscription is the key to the imagery. If they can't get their hands on the table cover, the inscription and the photos would give them everything they need."

"You don't think someone else might have taken pictures, or done a translation?"

"Even with pictures, it would be difficult to translate. My expert was only able to do it because I had given him a close-up of the back side. I'm almost certain we're the only ones who know what it says."

"Okay, but if the funeral guys are connected to the people in Paris, that still doesn't explain how they knew we were in Burgundy. They couldn't have followed us on the train."

"No, I made sure nobody was following us when we went to see Madame Maziére."

"What are we going to do if they catch up with us again?"

After running that through my mind a few times I came up empty.

Driving through the Burgundian countryside was not like it used to be. No peasants clutching at their children and leaping for the hedgerows, no geese perishing beneath your wheels in a fountain of feathers.

Every twenty kilometers we passed through small villages, gray stone houses with red roof tiles clustered around venerable churches. The only visible signs of life were matronly ladies carrying home lunchtime baguettes, and old men in cloth caps sitting in the town square like they were made of stone.

Shadows rippled across our hood from plane trees lining the road as we circled the hillside town of Clamecy. Then a stone bridge across the Loire River took us back into open country where cattle grazed in green meadows and drank from streams up to their knees in mud.

I hit the brakes and stopped the car a few seconds after coming into tiny St. Martin-des-Champs. A lumbering herd of Charolais cattle was coming straight at us down the middle of the street. Prodded along by farmers with long sticks, huge white beasts with flaring nostrils towered over us as they swept past our tiny car as if we were a stick in a stream. The car rocked when the last one passing brushed against our front bumper.

Leaving that town, a road winding through orchard-covered hills brought us alongside mirror-like canals where pilgrims rested beside their backpacks, and locals fished with long poles.

We turned south toward Limoges when the dark spires of Bourges cathedral loomed in the distance. An autoroute tollbooth spit out a ticket, the barrier went up, and I pushed the little car to its limit as we swished past long lines of heavy trucks towing trailers.

A couple hours later, I pulled into a rest stop outside Brive-la-Gaillarde so we could gas up and take a whiz.

We were rolling down the ramp onto the motorway when a black Mercedes van shot by with *Pompes Funèbres Barsini* written on the side. "Did you see that?" I said. "Those funeral guys must be trying to follow us."

"If they're following us, don't you think we should be doing something differently?"

"They're not doing a particularly good job of it. Anyway, I think we just ditched them."

There was some truth to that, so Laura let it drop.

The evening sky had darkened to a pink and purple glow when we stopped for the night at Périgueux in the Dordogne region. After parking behind the old covered market, we hauled our bags through narrow medieval streets festooned with canopies of Christmas lights and checked into a small hotel in the center of town.

Hungry for something quick to eat, we went out to explore and found a small Italian restaurant called Café Louise. Laura ordered a salad Niçoise, and I went for a small pizza Marguerite.

"How would you like your pizza cut?" the waiter said when he brought our order.

"What do you mean?"

"Would you prefer four or six slices?"

"Better make it four. Six might be more than I can eat."

Laura was smiling after he cut it into four pieces with one of those little roller things. "Where did you come up with that one?"

"It's a Yogi Berra classic."

We were eating in silence when Laura gave me a pensive look. "What are you thinking about?"

"Nothing."

"You have to think something."

"I was just feeling."

"Then tell me how you are feeling."

"I'm feeling good that we made it this far."

She put down her fork. "I wish I could say the same."

"What do you mean?"

"This trip isn't going the way either of us expected it would. First it was Sheena's art appraiser showing up in Paris. Then it was those guys in the crypt. I'm starting to wonder what's going to happen next."

I felt, rather uncomfortably, that I would like to know that too, but I didn't want to add to her worries.

"Things hardly ever go the way you want them to on a long journey. But nobody knows where we are, or where we're headed, so I think we're okay."

Back in our room, we crawled under a fluffy duvet and snuggled up close. That seemed like a good time to kiss her, and one thing led to another.

Afterward, we lay breathing each other's breath until we fell asleep.

46

Laura was asleep beside me with a ray of sunlight brightening her face when the tolling of church bells woke me in the morning. I gazed at her a moment before kissing her awake, and then we went out to take our breakfast at a small café where everybody seemed to know each other.

I was thumbing through a local paper, watching people come and go, when I came across an article about the murder of Gaston Leroux. The police were calling it a sadistic murder disguised as a burglary. What made it sadistic was that he had been tied to a chair and two of his fingers had been cut off.

I folded the paper to the sports section and tried to think of a tender way to tell Laura. I couldn't think of any.

Leaving the café, we explored the Byzantine domes of Saint Front Cathedral, then wandered the historic center, full of honey-colored houses with ornate towers. One tower had copper drainpipes shaped like the mouths of angry fish and showed the time of day on a sundial.

A street lined with storefronts brought us to a sign reading *Taja-Sutara Meditation Center*, and a window displaying a large poster of the Swami. A dozen green-clad followers were seated inside, meditating on a circle of cushions. When several of them glanced up, we turned and walked away.

"I never expected to run into them over here," I whispered.

"I told you they have more followers in Europe."

"How many places like this do they have?"

"Lots. The Taja Sutara Foundation is a worldwide organization."

We slowed our pace and did a little shopping when we came to an outdoor vegetable market. Then we joined a group of people who were gathered beneath a clock tower with their faces tilted upward.

A big brass bell above the dial face was flanked by two humanlike figures poised to strike the time with tiny hammers in their hands. A man stood on the left wearing a frock coat and a flared hat. His wife on the right was wearing a blue dress and a white bonnet. Two little children occupied the space in front of the bell. After the parents took turns chiming out ten o'clock, the children struck the higher pitched quarter hours.

Their last note was hanging in the air when a woman wearing a green sari jostled her way through the crowd and took Laura by the arm. "Laura. Is that you?" she said, as a tall man with red hair and a short-clipped beard came to stand beside her.

"Indira!" Laura said, after a stunned silence. "What are you doing here?"

"I flew over to teach a yoga class. Can you come visit with us? We'd love to hear about your trip."

"We would if we could," I said, jumping in after another awkward silence. "But we're headed to Barcelona and have a train to catch."

Laura nodded. "That's right. It's great to see you, but we'll have to catch up later."

I glanced back as we hurried for our car. The woman and the red-haired man were huddled together. The man was punching numbers into a cell phone.

"I have a bad feeling about this," I said.

"You're not the only one."

"Are you sure you never told her anything specific about our trip?"

"Absolutely."

Running into Laura's ex-roommate the day after getting mugged in the crypt had unsettled both of us.

224

Minutes later, we were exiting the parking lot when the gaping mouth grillwork of a BMW 7 Series limo appeared behind us. It signaled a left when I did and followed close behind when I swung onto the main road. If I slowed, it slowed. If I sped up, it sped up, like I was towing the limo on an invisible rope.

Impulsively, I hit the brakes and swung a right into the backed-up exit lane.

"What are you doing?" Laura said.

"It's probably nothing, but a black limo is hanging behind us. Those high-powered road cars usually go zooming by, but this one just followed us into the exit lane."

Then I saw why the traffic was backed up. A line of cars was exiting into a grassy parking area for the Cirque Medrano. We followed them toward a huge red and yellow tent with the limo on our bumper until a man in a reflective yellow vest directed us into a parking spot and sent the BMW somewhere else.

This was a chance to lose them, so I took Laura by the hand and hurried up a muddy path towards the crowd of people clustered outside the entry. When I saw how slow the ticket line was moving, we blended in with a group of children and ducked in without paying.

Raucous bursts of circus music and the smell of popcorn filled the dome of a tent that disappeared into darkness above the trapeze. Wooden bleachers circling a sawdust-covered central ring were packed with people. I had to shout to be heard over the noise. "If we take seats high up where it's dark, we can hide ourselves in the crowd."

After threading our way up narrow steps, we sat with our heads nearly touching the canvas. Far below, a woman wearing a pink tutu balanced atop a prancing horse while a man in red tights, black cape, and a stove pipe hat cracked his whip. The man lifted his hat when the woman took her bow and released three snow-white doves.

I was keeping an eye on the entrance when the tempo of the music changed, and a small red car zoomed out. It circled the ring, chugging and puffing smoke, then lurched to a stop. More clowns than I could count tumbled out wearing big shoes and frizzy wigs in orange, red, and purple.

Spotlights followed the clowns as they went around restyling the hair of surprised spectators with giant combs and bursts of hairspray. I was smiling at the expression on people's faces when two men wearing silver-gray suits and sinister shades came through the entrance and paused to look around.

Suddenly, several clowns came bounding up the steps straight to me, and the bright finger of a spotlight dazzled my eyes. I could hardly believe it.

One clown danced around honking a horn while another draped a frilly white collar around my neck, fluffed my hair with a giant yellow comb, and sprayed me with bursts of hairspray.

Every eye in the tent was fixed on me until the music changed, and the clowns bounded back down the stairs.

A smile spread over Laura's lips. "What was that you were saying about hiding ourselves in the crowd?"

"The first clown I ever saw scared me half to death," I said.

I was wiping the sticky hairspray off my forehead when I glanced at the entry.

The men in the silver-gray suits were gone.

47

I made sure nobody was following us when I pulled out of the grassy field and headed for the autoroute. The time had come to explain things to Laura, and I began cautiously because I didn't know how she might react.

"There are a few things I never told you that I probably should have."

"You're married, with children?"

"No, nothing like that. But I've held some things back so we could have this trip together."

"That seems to be your pattern. You held things back about the table cover, too."

"In my kind of business, it's sometimes necessary to tell an incomplete version of the truth."

Her voice tightened. "What do you call something that's an incomplete version of the truth?"

"What do I call it?"

"Yeah, what do you call something like that?"

"Cautious communication, or maybe diplomatic discourse," I said, flashing a smile.

"Nice try."

"What's that supposed to mean?"

"It means that you haven't been honest with me. That I've only been given part of the picture."

"I haven't been dishonest."

"Leaving things out is not being honest."

"How honest do you want me to be?"

"How can you even ask a question like that?"

"Okay. I should never have kept things from you, but I did it for good reasons. Now I realize I've gotten you into a situation you might not have chosen if I'd kept you up to date on everything."

"And you think the best time to tell me a more complete version of the truth is when I'm strapped into a car thousands of miles away from home?"

I was seeing a side of Laura I remembered from our first meeting. "That sounds a little grim," I said.

"It feels a little grim."

"I'm doing the best I can under the circumstances."

"What's that supposed to mean?"

"It means I'd do it differently if I could, but I can't, so it's best to tell you everything now because we're in it together no matter how it goes down."

"Okay, let's hear it."

"It's kind of complicated."

"I'm listening."

"You don't have to talk so rough."

"I'm just knocking it back. Like tennis."

She wasn't about to let me off easy, so I took a breath to steady myself. "In the beginning, the only reason Sheena wanted the table cover was because the Swami fancied using it on the cover of his new book. Now we know she had her hand in his cookie jar all along, and it was probably her criminal associates who inspired her to go after the table cover for her own financial agenda."

"Why do you say that?"

"Because everything seemed to change after her art expert discovered the same table cover might be in a museum painting. Suddenly the monetary value was dwarfed by what it might lead to, and everybody wanted in."

"Birds of a feather?"

228

"More like flies to a feast."

"That's an unpleasant analogy."

"Unpleasant, but true. Strange things started happening after I bought the panel. The big guy who came to ask about old Spanish rugs wasn't the only one poking his nose around. A woman in green came in to distract me at the Buckaroo Bar while my car was being broken into. A couple days later, someone tried to break into my gallery."

"Your car and your gallery were broken into?"

I shrugged. "Things like that happen when you deal with valuable objects. That's why I take precautions."

"Are you always so blasé about danger?"

"I thought they were just random acts until my client got mugged."

"And you never considered telling me any of this?" she said, raising her voice a tone or two.

"I needed your help to get the panels back and I didn't want to upset your parents."

"You could have told me after we got them back."

"I didn't want to scare you away."

She was watching me coolly, so I continued. "Stealing the panels back must have ruffled Sheena's feathers. She sent her dirty tricks squad to search my house while I was at work and then had them smash out my gallery windows during the night. They let me know it was pay back by leaving sandalwood joss sticks on the window ledge."

"My god! What else haven't you told me?"

I hesitated long enough for the silence to get loud. "It's the part I feel the worst about."

"Are you saving it for later?"

"It's about Sammy. Two women from the ranch caught up with him a couple weeks after our caper. When they saw him wearing a Patek Philippe watch he'd taken from their office, they knew he was the one who'd stolen their Castafiori emerald."

She gasped. "He stole an emerald, and you didn't tell me?"

"I knew about the watch, but he didn't tell me about the emerald until it was too late. I tried to help. I went to meet him at the Ballard Locks to work out a deal with them, but by the time I got there, he'd been attacked and drowned."

She didn't make a sound. She just covered her face with her hands. Then she turned on me and shot out her words like bullets. "You had no right to keep any of this from me. You don't do that to someone you care about. Do you understand what I'm saying? Am I getting through?"

"You're getting through loud and clear."

"It's unbelievable that you would deliberately conceal these things from me."

"I thought it would help."

"You were wrong."

"Someone was watching your parents' house when we came back from the ranch. I was afraid they were about to go after you, too."

"You mean my parents were at risk?"

"I didn't think they would be in danger once I got us away, and I was afraid you wouldn't come if I told you all of this."

"Oh my god! Stop the car, Tony. Stop it right now."

She was reaching for her bag as I pulled to the side of the road.

"What are you doing?" I said.

"I'm out of here," she snapped.

"Where can you go? What will you do?"

"I'll find out the benefits of travelling light."

"I can't do this without you," I said, as she pushed open the door.

"You could have fooled me," she said, slamming the door.

I pushed a button to lower the window and paced her as she walked. "Can't you see? I did it to protect you and your parents. I figured we'd all be perfectly safe once we took the rug and were gone."

If that brought any measure of comfort, she didn't show it. A scorching silence stretched between us like razor wire. When she finally turned to me, her face was a mask of anger. "That's terrific. Now, everywhere we go, trouble is about thirty seconds behind."

"I never saw any of that coming."

A sideways glance was followed by a tight-lipped silence, and she walked even faster.

I accelerated to keep up. "I know it sounds bad, but we could try looking at the positive side."

"Don't you dare try to patronize me," she said, shifting the bag to her other shoulder.

"I'm not trying to patronize you."

"Then what do you mean by 'the positive side'?"

"Everything will be okay if we just stick together and play the cards we have."

She stumbled on the rough ground, then leaned down to face me through the open window. "What cards?"

"We've got the inscription translation and the rug patterns to guide us. Nobody else has that. We just need to keep going and find a safer place for the translation and our photos."

"A safer place?" she said, straightening and walking on. "What the hell is that supposed to mean?"

"Instead of carrying them around in your purse, we'll hide them in the spare tire compartment. But first we go over the translation, so we won't need it again."

"How do we go over it?"

"We do it together. I can't bear to lose you."

A heavy truck thundered by, and a blast of wind ruffled her hair.

"I promise to do things differently if you get back in the car."

She didn't reach for the door handle until her hair was ruffled by another truck rumbled by. Then she took her sweet time getting in. "Now what?" she said, rummaging in her purse for a tissue to wipe the dust off her face.

"We're so close to figuring this all out. We should go over the translation one more time and put it in our memory."

Without looking once in my direction, she took out the translation and read it in a slow monotone. *Midway on the journey of life, the path we walk has brought us strife. To protect our souls, and our bounty save, we set forth on the savage waves. A sternward wind carried us far, to the sovereign crown above the field of stars. Here we sleep in peace and pray, beneath the tower that guards the way.*

I almost smiled but thought better of it. Getting her back in the car had taken all the energy I had.

"See how simple that makes it sound?" I said. "We're heading to La Coruña, the crown, and we'll look for a tower that guards the pilgrimage route. In a few hours, we'll be crossing into Spain. I need your help to figure out our road options to get on the Camino Primitivo."

She wore a tense, brooding look as she studied the map in her guidebook. A delicate silence ruled until she turned to face me. "There's no way to justify keeping secrets like I'm some weak link."

"I'm sorry. I made a terrible mistake."

"You can keep your apologies. I don't want them."

"I understand."

"You don't understand the way I do."

"I realize I handled it poorly."

"I'm perfectly capable of helping you with all of these things."

"I know you are."

"We both stand to lose if I don't know what's going on."

"I promise I'll trust you with everything."

I thought she was done, but she wasn't.

"You aren't the lone wolf you think you are."

"I didn't plan it that way."

"You could use the help of a good woman."

"I agree."

She looked my way. "Do you want a woman in your life?"

"I do, so long as it's you."

There was a two second pause. "It better be."

We shared a more agreeable silence as the motorway took us through the vast vineyards surrounding Bordeaux. Teams of workers were pruning back the vines, and gray plumes of smoke drifted over the fields from rusty oil drums where they were burning the cuttings.

Two hours later, signs announced we were coming into Basque country. Laura was still studying the map. I tried to lighten the lingering tension.

"If we stop in Biarritz, we could do some casino gambling."

Silence.

"Maybe you'd prefer Bayonne? That's where they invented the bayonet."

She raised her head. "If I visited Bayonne, it wouldn't be because someone came up with a better way to kill people."

"Ouch," I said, "I'm getting the point."

That brought the sliver of a smile, followed by a summary of what she had learned from her guidebook.

"Saint-Jean-de-Pied is the traditional place to begin the Spanish section of the Camino. But that's farther south and it's getting late. Our best option would be to go by way of Hondaribbia. It's an old fishing village across the Bay of Biscay from the French town of Hendaye."

The sky had turned dark, and pulses of light were coming from clouds that were sweeping across the sky ahead of us.

"You better hang onto that map," I said, as water began streaming down the windows. "We're heading into heavy weather and I'm going to need all your help just to get us there."

48

It was a nerve-wracking journey with the rain hammering down, but we experienced a surge of excitement when we crossed the border into Spain. Minutes later, the brown stone walls of Hondaribbia came into view.

The rain was so heavy the wipers could barely handle it when we parked in a tree-covered lot across from the medieval gate.

"I hope it slacks off enough so we can find a hotel," I said, as we sat listening to the relentless drumbeat.

"We could share my umbrella," Laura said.

In answer to her offer, a gust of wind rocked the car.

"That settles it," I said. "Let's go."

Shouldering our bags, I followed Laura's bobbing umbrella through rain dimpled puddles toward the twin turrets flanking the Santa Maria Gate.

The archway led to cobbled streets lined with tall stone buildings brightened by wetness. A dripping eye-level sign directed us down a narrower street to the Txoko Goxoa Hotel. Two blocks later we were drying off in a top-floor room listening to the dwindling patter of rain on the roof tiles.

"If it's slackening off, we should go out and get something to eat," I said.

Laura looked up from her guidebook. "Restaurants here don't open until eight. We might find some tapas in the Marina neighborhood where the fishermen come in."

"I've never had tapas, but that would work."

"They started out as saucers of goodies served on top of a drink."

"I never heard that."

"The word is Spanish for lids, but you don't call them tapas in Basque country. You call them pintxos.

Laura pushed open her umbrella when we stepped into the street, but I was absorbing water from the wind driven drizzle. I reached for an umbrella that was standing upright in a planter box outside the hotel and found out quickly why it had been abandoned. It wouldn't stay open. The clear plastic decorated with pink flowers draped around me like a transparent tent.

Laura smiled at the sight of me, but it kept me dry as we hiked to the main square where a huge fortress stood guard above the harbor. Here, the air smelled of the open sea, and a string of flickering lights off in the distance marked the French coastline.

"Do you know what they call this harbor," I said.

"The Spanish call it the Bay of Vizcaya."

Hearing that nearly bowled me over. "Vizcaya? A famous carpet in the Prado is called the Vizcaya Carpet. It has Hebrew writing and a star design. Maybe ours was made near here as well."

"That's another thing you neglected to mention," she said, with a sliver of steel in her voice. "Would you like it if I didn't tell you that we're next to a Basque province called Vizcaya?"

There was nothing I could say.

Lightening flashed in the distance, and a whistling wind ruffled my jacket, so we hunched our shoulders and started down a cobbled street past colorfully painted houses with flowers in their balconies.

At the bottom, the street flattened out to become a tree-lined esplanade leading to a lonely lighthouse. A few fishermen were darning nets along the shoreline, but all the restaurants lining the waterfront promenade were dark. Only the bars were lit-up and welcoming.

"That one is in my guidebook," Laura said, pointing at a pastel neon sign for El Marino Cantante. "It means The Singing Fisherman."

Two men wearing black aprons stood behind a zinc-topped bar covered with tiny plates of colorful pintxos. Chairs and tables filled the right side where a group of people were huddled together watching a soccer match on a large-screen TV. The only other customers were two craggy-faced fishermen wearing black wool sweaters and stocking caps. They weren't singing, just drinking beer and playing an intense game of checkers.

We ordered by pointing, and in a wink, we were carrying trays of food and glasses of Txakoli, a spritzy greenish-white wine, to an empty table.

"We should be celebrating making it to Spain," I said, when a cheer went up from the soccer fans.

"How might we do that?"

"We could try some of their sangria?"

"We haven't even started on our wine."

I took a large swallow. "This bubbly stuff won't last long."

"Sangria means blood. Do you know what's in it?"

I grinned. "Red wine, chopped fruit, and lots of brandy."

She looked skeptical, but I got up after polishing off my Txakoli, and brought back tall glasses of blood-red sangria.

Laura took a hesitant sip. "It is good, but there's no way I'm going to drink all of it."

She had a point. Cool and soothing going down, the sangria was hot and furious once it got there. I reached for hers after finishing mine. Soon, I was feeling pleasantly unbuttoned.

"Did I ever tell you about the two rug merchants who hated each other?"

"I don't think I've heard that one."

"Ali and Baba had small shops on opposite sides of the street in a small village surrounded by lemon orchards and date palms. They were drinking tea in the shade of their respective verandas

236

when a tourist lady came down the street. When she turned toward Ali's shop, Baba whispered to her. 'You shouldn't go in there. That man's a swindler and a thief.' When she turned to head for Baba's shop, Ali whispered. 'Be careful. That man's a remorseless liar.' The woman stopped in the middle of the street, glanced from one to the other, and said, 'Now that you have so kindly introduced each other, I think I'll find some other place to shop.'"

Laura smiled. "That's a funny story, but I bet Ali and Baba are just fictional characters in someone's imagination."

"Maybe we're all fictional characters in a book Life is writing," I said, downing the last of Laura's sangria.

My words came out slightly slurred, and she raised an eyebrow. "Are you planning to order another one of those?"

"Nope. One is my limit," I said, as the two fishermen came toward us on their way out.

Eager to try some of my high school Spanish, I blurted out, "What do you catch around here?"

I knew right away it didn't come out quite right.

Without pausing, one said, "Pescados."

Laughter hung in the air when the door closed behind them and Laura patted me on the arm. "Maybe we better get you back to the hotel. We've still got a three-day drive to La Coruña."

I didn't try to argue.

I was floundering up the rain-slicked street when I found myself listing. Laura caught my arm to steady me as I struggled to balance myself with the umbrella. Something about that affectionate gesture touched me so deeply that I embraced her in the middle of the street.

"Being with you helps me to be a better person," I said, burying my face in the scent of her hair.

Soft fingers brushed my cheek. "Maybe there's hope for you yet."

If it hadn't been raining, the tears in her eyes would never have been mistaken for raindrops.

"All that sangria is making me sleepy," I said, as we climbed the three flights of stairs to our hotel room.

Before taking off my clothes, I washed and cleaned my teeth, then I nestled under the covers. I was lying there with my eyes closed when Laura bent over.

"I'm going to take a shower," she said, tickling my lips with the warm tip of her tongue.

"You better not be long."

"A big boy like you should be able to wait five minutes."

"I'll wait, but you better not take more than six."

The sweet scent of talcum powder, and steamy air wafted over me when she came out of the shower. Wrapped only in a towel, she stood before the mirror combing out her hair.

After tying it back, she let the towel drop and turned to me with a mischievous smile.

She remained motionless in the soft light until I tossed back the covers.

Wet hair fell around my face as she straddled me and guided me inside.

One thrust became a steady rhythm, then a rocking motion accompanied by our simultaneous gasping of breath.

Outside, gusts of wind shook the shutters, and rattled the windows.

49

Bayonet-like rays burst through puffy white clouds as we circled past the mountains surrounding San Sebastian. We were heading southwest toward Burgos after enjoying a Basque breakfast—split loaves of toasted bread spread with olive oil, a sprinkle of sea salt, and a fresh tomato puree.

In the hills above, ribbons of woodsmoke curled into the sky from whitewashed Basque villas surrounded by leafy trees in shades of yellow and gold. Slopes became steeper as the hills slid by, and the villas were replaced by prodigious farmhouses surrounded by green pastures and brown cattle. The land was so deep in peace that I had stopped thinking about the characters we had left behind.

"It's a great day for a drive in the country," I said.

"Last time you said that I got mugged." She said it without looking up from the map.

"Those houses up there look like Swiss chalets."

Laura blinked up a glance. Then went back to the map.

"These hills are so steep that the cattle evolved with longer legs on one side so they can graze without tipping over."

She squinted up at the distant cattle. "I suppose you're going to tell me they're brown because they got a suntan."

"I'm only trying to get you to look at the scenery. You'll miss it all if you only look at the map."

"If I don't look at the map, you won't know what route to take."

High mountains and big road signs were coming up ahead of us.

"Okay, which route do we take?"

"If you stay left at the next interchange, it will take us through the mountains toward Vitorio-Gastiez."

The mountains looked impassable but were pierced by a series of tunnels joined to bridges spanning the deep gorges between the peaks. After popping out of a dark tunnel, a sunlit bridge above a rocky chasm would take us into another tunnel, out onto another bridge, over and over.

It was beginning to feel like the light at the end of the tunnel was just the entry to another tunnel when the last one took us past the mountains and onto a straighter road that would allow us to bypass busy Burgos.

An hour later, we began seeing road signs for Burgos. I was getting tired, so I asked Laura to drive. I tipped my seat back and must have dozed. When I looked up again, we were rolling beneath a luminous arc of never-ending pale blue sky, and the landscape had changed.

The farmhouses and pastures we had passed earlier were replaced by an arid landscape bathed in a golden luminosity I had never even dreamed of. Ancient olive trees with gnarled silvery trunks grew in abundance on terraced groves surrounding scattered adobe hamlets.

Low hills colored in infinite shades of tan and brown surrounded the hamlets. Some hills were being farmed, but most were barren fields. Every few miles a rustic adobe village could be seen off in the distance with an austere church steeple pointing up at the sky. It was a poor-looking landscape, but one that conveyed a feeling of purity.

"Where the heck are we?" I said, rubbing my gummy eyes.

"We're on a windy plain called the Meseta. You were sleeping when we passed the point where all paths of the Camino merged into the Camino Primitivo."

"I wasn't sleeping, I was meditating."

"You've been meditating for over an hour."

"That's what I do."

"You were making sleeping noises."

"People mistake my Oming for snoring."

She rolled her eyes but didn't say anything.

"It's your turn to talk," I said.

"How can I talk when you leave me speechless?"

Thirty feet away, groups of hikers hauling rucksacks were trudging along a rock-studded trail parallel to the road. Their heads were bowed, their shoulders slumped, and dust rose around their knees.

"This stretch of the Camino must seem endless to the people who are walking it," I said.

"It's the most challenging part. The never-ending flatness messes with people's sense of time and distance."

"What's that up ahead?" I said, as a town with three huge churches came into view on top of a low hill.

"That's Astorga."

"Then we must be getting close to Val de San Lorenzo."

"I saw it on the map. Do you want to stop there?"

"It's a famous weaving center with a textile museum. It might be a good place to spend the night."

Soon we started seeing signs for hotels as we passed a succession of small businesses lining the road into Val de San Lorenzo. *La Posada de Toriba*, a two-story building with a restaurant next door, looked good, so we took a room with a balcony view of the old church.

Laura was setting her travel clock on the nightstand when the booming strokes of four o'clock resonated from the church tower.

"We better check out the town before it gets too late," I said.

"Good idea. This might finally start to feel like a vacation."

"There might be a package for me at the Textile Museum."

"I should have guessed there was something else you didn't tell me about."

"I wanted it to be a surprise."

241

She arched her eyebrows. "You think I haven't had enough surprises?"

Indolent cats stretched lazily in the shadows as we meandered the narrow lanes of an adobe village bathed in the cool light of a drowsy afternoon. After perusing several quaint little shops, we explored the weaving studios surrounding the main square where women were tatting lace or weaving with wool on upright looms. A dark-haired woman rose to greet us when we crossed over to the Museo Textil. She was wearing an ankle-length blue skirt, a white blouse embroidered with flowers, and a crescent-shaped cap held on by a white lace scarf

"Buenas dias, Senora. My name is Tony Shepherd. I've come to pick up a package from someone named Aurora Sinatora."

Her eyelids flickered in surprise. "Why, that is me. The work you ordered arrived only yesterday. It is in our office."

She returned from a back room carrying a cylindrical parcel wrapped in tan paper and tied with brown twine.

"Do you have time for a tour of our museum?" she said, slipping it into a shopping bag. "We show a chronological history of our local weaving tradition."

"We'd love to. Especially if your costume is an indication of the quality of the work done here."

Her face lit up. "What I'm wearing is the traditional dress of our La Margeteria region. One of the pleasures of working here is that I get to dress for the occasion."

Laura glanced my way a couple times on the way back to our hotel, and I sensed what must be on her mind. "It's so well-wrapped that I don't want to tear it open right now."

She started to say something but was distracted when a bodega owner began opening his doors after the siesta. Laura picked out a multicolored ribbon for her hair, and I splurged on a twenty-year-old *Cardenal Mendoza* brandy and a couple bottles of *Ribiera del Duero* wine.

We were climbing the stairs to our room when I remembered to check in with Duluc Detectives. After his secretary put me through, I jotted things down. Then I sat staring at what I had written.

"Is something wrong?" Laura said.

"Sorry," I said, snapping back. "You might not want to hear this."

"Why would I not want to hear it?"

"Some is good news. Some is bad news."

"You could start with the good news."

"The good news is he found some things."

"What's the bad news?"

"We're dealing with unforeseen forces."

"What's that supposed to mean?"

"The big American guy we saw at the Paris auction is Vinnie Mingaloni. Interpol has him on their radar because he's a high-ranking member of an organized crime family."

"What would a mafia guy be doing hanging out in Paris?"

"He might be fencing art. One of his associates is Boris Balakov, a disgraced professor of medieval history and a master forger who's wanted in thirteen countries."

"That sort of thing would have shocked me before I met you, but now, none of it is really surprising."

"Maybe you should sit down to hear the rest."

"Do you really think it's easier to hear bad news if I'm sitting down?"

I took a deep breath and began reading from my notes.

"Then there's the pale-faced bald guy with the missing fingers. His Serbian name is Janko Radic, but he likes to be called Johnnie. He came to the attention of Interpol when an antiques dealer he'd been working with in Sarajevo was found murdered in his shop. Money was missing, along with a painting that had been hidden under the floorboards. Janko vanished like a ghost, but the painting turned up when police in Marseille intercepted a shipment of heroin hidden in antiques. Since then, he's been implicated in a string of church robberies where he posed as a priest."

"What happened to his fingers?"

"A rival gang tortured him by cutting them off. Some kind of Serbian message about the Hand of God and their three-fingered salute called the Tri Prstra."

She clutched at her fingers. "Maybe we should find someplace to hide out for a while."

"We can't quit. We're on to something, and it must be something big."

"But we're all alone and there are so many of them."

"Pitching it in when we're so close just doesn't feel right. I still think we lost them in Vézelay."

"We may have lost the funeral van, but if they're working with Sheena, they'd know we were spotted leaving Périgueux."

"That's true, but I told them we were heading to Barcelona, and we've gone five-hundred miles in a different direction. Anyway, we can't be certain who anybody is working with anymore."

"We can't be certain about anything. I've had a bad feeling since leaving Périgueux."

"Why do you say that?"

"A net could be closing around us, and we won't know about it until it's too late?"

"Why would we not know about it?3

"For one thing, the car we're driving is one they can recognize immediately."

That had been constantly on my mind since putting down the phone.

"I agree. We'll exchange it in for one with Spanish plates first thing in the morning."

Laura didn't say a word as I started uncorking a bottle of wine.

"Now that we're so close, we just need to keep following our leads. Your dad thought the circle with the X might be a compass pointing southeast from La Coruña. Let's try to see it his way."

After filling two glasses, I opened the map and sat down beside her. "The main road follows a forty-five-degree angle all the way from here up to La Coruña. That's the same angle your dad noticed between the crown motif and the cartouche shaped like a church."

"It does make sense," she said pensively.

"The three cities we should check out along that road look to be Lugo, Betanzos, and Ponferrada."

"That's right. I also read about a smaller village called Ambasmestas that might be good place to use as a base."

Feeling relief that Laura was back on board, I folded up the map as the church bell began chiming eight o'clock. "It's dinner time," I said. "Why don't we try the restaurant."

"Let's go, I'm starving."

Our hotel manager was checking in guests when we came down the stairs. A tall man with curly red hair and a short-clipped beard, and a woman wearing dark glasses with a heavy scarf around her neck. They had their backs to us but were dressed like pilgrims and carried rucksacks.

La Lecheria, the restaurant, was housed in a rustic stone building that used to be the town creamery. After seating us at a table polished from years of use, the waiter brought a ceramic pitcher of Tempranillo wine along with an appetizer of anchovies and fat green olives.

"We should try their gazpacho," Laura said. She said it with such self-confidence that I had to agree.

The gazpacho came in an earthenware pot with a plate of sliced bread and bowl of warm olive oil. The expression on Laura's face told me she liked it immediately. Eating and drinking in silence, we let our spirits piece themselves together after the unsettling news from Duluc Detectives.

I was mopping up the last of my gazpacho with a hunk of bread when Laura set down her spoon. She smiled at me a little, but her face was troubled. "You don't talk much at meals, do you?"

"I can't talk and eat at the same time. What's on your mind?"

"I'm thinking about all those people we saw."

"What are you thinking?"

"I'm thinking that creepy people may be gathering around us like an army of shadows."

I reached for my wine glass and took a sip while I tried to come up with something to lighten the mood. "It's good to be aware of possibilities like that."

"Aren't you worried?"

"Would it help to be worried?"

"I suppose you think I'm being paranoid."

"A little paranoia is a reasonable thing. We just need to have the courage to finish what we came here to do."

"I had courage when we started, but I lost it somewhere along the way."

The village was so quiet after dark that we were asleep in each other's arms by 10 p.m. I was jolted awake at midnight by the clanging of church bells. Then, at the very moment of dropping back to sleep, a sharp metallic sound jerked me awake. Hearing a murmur of voices and the barking of a dog, I got up and crossed the room to open our window.

As my eyes adjusted, I could make out the church tower and a shadowy graveyard enclosed by a stone wall. Then the moon sailed from behind the clouds and the graveyard became visible, its headstones gleaming palely as if exuding a mysterious light of their own.

A motionless figure stood on one of the gravel paths. Starkly silhouetted by the moonlight, he cast a long shadow and seemed to be gazing up at me. It wasn't until he turned to walk away that I saw by his robes that he must be a priest.

I watched until he was swallowed up by the darkness, and then went back to sleep.

50

The couple who checked in the night before got up quickly when we came into the breakfast room next morning. Something about the man with the curly red hair seemed familiar, but I lost it when the owner of the posada came to our table. "Would you like tea or coffee with your breakfast?"

"Coffee," I said.

Laura nodded. "Same for me."

He returned from the kitchen a couple minutes later with our breakfast on a tray. "I apologize for the inconvenience, but you'll have to use the side door when you leave. Our entry gate was damaged during the night."

"I heard some odd noises last night," I said. "Voices, a dog barking, and a loud metallic sound."

"Our teenagers were probably celebrating La Noche de Brujos. Some of the older ones have gotten into trouble, but most are from good families."

"That would explain it," I said.

"I do not wish to butt in on your holiday, but many of our guests who follow the Camino by car don't know that the most scenic route runs parallel to the main highway. When you're leaving our village, just take the smallest road out of town."

For a small fee, we were able to exchange our Renault Clio for a bright red Seat Ibiza with Spanish plates at a nearby Europcar agency. After hiding the translation of the inscription, the photos, and the package from the Textile Museum in the spare tire compartment, we followed the older road the patron had suggested. It was potholed and narrowed in places to the width of a country lane but allowed us to experience grand vistas and rustic villages where life went on much as it had centuries ago.

Coming into one village, we had to slow behind the rhythmic clip-clop of a pair of russet-colored draft horses pulling a wagon piled with firewood. The white-haired man holding the reins sat on a high bench with a young boy at his side. Both wore black woolen jackets and wide-brimmed hats that were fashion from an earlier century.

The hills grew steeper after leaving that town, and signs of civilization became less prevalent. Long stretches of road were walled on both sides with jagged rock, and the peaks were covered in dense tracts of pine trees and low brush.

I shifted into low gear when we began climbing steep switchbacks. A black mountain rose over us, menacing in its naked bulk, and huge boulders littered the slopes. Rockslides had made some sections of the road not wide enough for two cars to pass. The higher we went, the wilder and more rugged it got, like we were entering a land of enchantment and mystery.

I slowed to a crawl when we became enveloped in fog so dense I could only glimpse tree branches that seemed to be reaching out like twisted fingers from the milky white vapor. Feeling we had come to a crossroads, I pulled to a stop beside a cone-like stone shelter.

A face materialized in the mist outside Laura's window as she was unfolding our map. A small man with a face like a time-worn boot was beaming a blue-eyed smile from a growth of white stubble. Laura glanced my way before lowering her window.

"You folks need some help?" the man said.

"We're heading for Ponferrada," Laura said.

"That's where I'm headed. You want to take the right fork."

"You sound like an American," I said.

"I am an American."

"Us too, we're all a long way from home."

"For me, home is a place in my mind."

248

I pondered that for a few seconds. "Are you walking the Camino?"

"I walked it all night. I had to rest because this uphill part is hard on my legs."

"Why do you walk at night?" Laura said.

"I see all kinds of things I'd never see during the day."

"How long have you been walking it?"

"It feels like forever."

"If it's so hard, why do you do it?"

He smiled into her eyes. "I discover things I already know."

I nodded when Laura glanced my way. "We could give you a lift over the pass."

"That would be great."

He wasn't wearing the usual camino gear when he climbed in back. Just a red stocking cap, a green jacket, and a gnarly knobbed walking stick covered with tiny silver medals.

"Are those saints' medals?" I said.

"I'm collecting the ones for Saint Ferghana."

"I've never heard of her."

He beamed another smile. "She's the patron saint of people needing a cheap place to stay."

The climb was long and slow. but gave us a panoramic view when we emerged from the mist at the top of the pass. Tall peaks still rose above us, but what took our breath away was below. Downward through a series of valleys, rugged hilltops rose and fell, revealing an endless succession of rocky slopes gleaming in the bright sun.

"Our map calls this the Valley of Silence," Laura said, as I pulled over and parked.

A cool breeze carried the pungent aroma of wood smoke and pine trees as we crossed the road and stood gazing down a tortuous path leading to Santiago de Penalba, a medieval hamlet looking like something out of an old black and white movie. Women in black were herding milk cows in a steep meadow beneath low houses built of rough stone, their slate rooftops held firmly in place against winter wind by heavy rocks.

The silence welling up around us was punctuated by the muted clanging of cattle bells and the cawing of crows. Then a falcon wheeled across the sun, and a flock of small birds swooped and dove, the flicker of their wings twinkling in the crisp air.

For a moment, I tried to imagine what life must be like here in the winter snow, and I thought of the solitary monks who had made this tortuous journey on foot as early as the sixth century.

Going up a mountain is easier than going down. The road dropped fast after passing the summit, and the twists and turns made for tricky driving. My hands stayed locked on the steering wheel dodging potholes, dangerous drop-offs, and boulders that had rolled down from the slopes above.

After half an hour of intense concentration, the road levelled out and we were swallowed by urban squalor. Gas stations, tire stores, and apartment buildings with cluttered balconies in the outskirts of Ponferrada were a huge let-down until we rounded a bend and saw a massive castle standing guard above the road.

Our guest touched me from behind as I stared in wonder. "If you drop me off here, I can get back to walking away my sins."

"Are you planning to visit the castle?" I said, pulling to a stop at the side of the road.

"No, but you should. It's a Knights Templar castle and legend says that secret tunnels connect it to other historical sites. The museum alone is worth a visit."

"A Templar Castle, "I said, glancing in amazement at Laura. "The Templars are one of the things we came to learn about."

He turned to face me after sliding out of the car. "There's always more to things than meet the eye. But the truth is closer than you think."

I turned left to park across from the castle. When we got out of the car, our hitchhiker was nowhere to be seen.

"That guy must be lucky with rides," Laura said.

"He was lucky to get one with us," I said. "But how come we didn't know this was a Templar castle?"

"I had just started reading about Ponferrada when we picked up that man. Then we got busy talking to him."

Wind flapped my jacket and leaves skittered across the tarmac as we crossed the street to a ramp leading up to a wooden drawbridge over a deep moat.

The forbidding entry gate beyond the drawbridge was protected by two crenellated defensive towers and flanked by brooding walls of tan-colored stone. The tops of those walls provided a path for armed sentries, and even taller walls rose behind them.

Suddenly police cars were screaming toward us from different directions, sirens wailing and blue lights flashing. They blocked the drawbridge entry when they skidded to a chaotic stop, and police rushed up the ramp with their guns drawn.

"I wonder what's going on," I said.

"Oh my god!" Laura said.

"What is it?"

"Don't you see?"

"See what?"

"Up there," she pointed. "Above the gate."

Then I saw it. A Tau Cross was carved into the stone directly above the entrance.

"Let's find the tourist office so we figure out what's going on," I said.

An agitated looking woman was hanging up the phone when we came into a small office adjacent to the castle.

"Why are the police blocking the entry to the castle?" I said.

"I'm sorry, but the Castillo de Los Templarios will be closed for two days while they investigate the theft of Templar manuscripts from our museum."

"When did that happen?"

"It must have happened last night. We discovered the broken display cases when we came to work."

251

There was nothing else to do, so I joined Laura who had started looking through their display of guidebooks.

"Listen to this," I said, reading from one showing the Tau Cross and a coat of arms on the cover. "The Cross of Tau is an ancient symbol for resurrection. It's presence on the castle is attributed to Pedro Alvarez Osorio, the Count of Lemos. The Cross of Tau was also used by the Castro family, the most powerful family in Galicia. Their well-known Coat of Arms depicts golden orbs on a red field."

"Castro?" Laura said, leaning closer to read over my shoulder. "That was the family my ancestor worked for."

"That might explain why the red and gold colors of the Castro Coat of Arms show up as alternating bands on the back of the table cover."

"That clinches it," Laura said. "We'll find a hotel in Ambasmestas, check out the other towns on our list, then come back here on Sunday when the castle reopens."

A forty-five-minute drive along a road winding through a placid river valley brought us to a sleepy town embraced on three sides by steep, protective hills. Signs offering beds for pilgrims were everywhere, but the only people we saw were a blind man walking his dog, an old lady sprinkling sawdust on her doorstep, and a woman resting against her backpack on the church steps.

The streets got quieter the farther we went, so I turned back to the first hotel we'd passed, a stone building called *Posada Camynos*. The *patron* was out front mowing the lawn, but he shut off his mower when we pulled into the parking and led us to a reception desk at the bar.

After showing our passports and filling out a form, we climbed wooden stairs to a sparsely furnished room. An iron-railed balcony running along the side of the building gave a view of a lushly green field and milk cows grazing along the river. When a thick fog began to cloud our view, I uncorked a bottle of wine and poured each of us glass.

"We've got a long drive ahead of us tomorrow if we're going to check out all of those cities," Laura said.

"How long is it?"

"It's two hundred kilometers each way on small roads."

"We better eat now so we can get an early start."

The dining room resembled a medieval inn with its stone floor, smoke-blackened beams, and heavy oak tables. An open log fire, hissing and crackling in the river-rock fireplace, filled the room with its resinous scent. At first, we were the only customers, but it wasn't long before the tables filled with tired-looking hikers.

We lingered after our meal to enjoy the warmth of the fire until I realized a line of people had formed inside the entrance. I signaled for the bill, and Laura went up to our room while I waited to pay.

There was an unpleasant disturbance at the door when the waiter handed me the bill. A tall man with curly red hair and a short-clipped beard had boldly pushed his way inside. It was the same man we'd seen at breakfast in Val de San Lorenzo. He scanned the room like he was checking to see how full it was, then pushed his way back out into the fog.

I was pondering what to make of it as I climbed the stairs to our room, but my train of thought took a detour when I pushed the door open. Laura was lying in bed covered only by a thin sheet. Playfully, I pulled down at the sheet. Laughing, she pulled it up. Then she threw it aside and pulled me into bed with her.

Afterwards, we fell asleep in each other's arms, comforted by the faint bursts of laughter coming from below. I knew no more until Laura was hammering at me and shouting something I couldn't understand.

"The door to the balcony! Someone is trying to get it open."

I got up to check it, but all I could find was a loose shutter that must have been banging in the wind.

I went back to bed, and was almost asleep, when I realized there was no wind. The night was unnaturally calm.

51

A feeble sun was filtering through the morning haze as we left the hotel. "We've got a lot of ground to cover today," I said.

"We can do it. Just keep your eyes peeled for more towers that guard the way along the road up to La Coruña. Then we'll swing by Betanzos and Lugo on our way back. A church in Betanzos is famous for its tombs of Spanish nobility, so we might be able to find something relating to the Count of Lemos or the Castro family."

The northwesterly road took us through a series of small villages separated by forested hills and vineyards. Streams of people making their last big push for Santiago were more plentiful when approaching or leaving any of the villages.

I slowed to pass a crowd of pilgrims who were overflowing the plaza in front of a church. "This place looks like a backpacker convention."

"Villafranca del Bierzo is a traditional resting place for the final leg of the Camino," Laura said, as I caught a glimpse of a man wearing a red cap and a green jacket.

"Hey, I think I saw that guy we gave a ride to yesterday."

"I saw him, too. But he was gone when I tried to look closer."

"I wonder how far a person has to go to walk away his sins."

"You'd probably have to do it to find out."

Twenty minutes later the hills had become noticeably greener. When a sign announced *Entrado a La Provincia de Galicia,* I turned to Laura. "Any idea why they call this province Galicia?"

"It was named after a Celtic tribe called the Gallaeci."

"A Celtic tribe?"

"All of western Spain was settled by Celts."

Relishing the comforts of our car, we rolled through one small town after another—Pedrafita O Cabreiro, Becerrea, San Pedro, Laxosa, and Narela. Then, seemingly out of nowhere, a curl of dark stone walls and turrets stood silhouetted against a pale blue sky.

"Whoa," I said. "What's the deal with all those walls and turrets?"

"That's Lugo, the only city in the world still surrounded by Roman walls. It's the last town on our list. We'll stop on our way back."

A surge of excitement washed over me when we started seeing signs for La Coruña, but my enthusiasm went out like the tide when we slowed to a stop-and-go crawl in the gritty suburbs of a grimy port city of a quarter million people.

An hour of slogging from stoplight to stoplight past billboards, smokestacks, and railyards, with one eye on the car ahead and the other on the car behind, brought nothing but the faint smell of the sea and fleeting glimpses of a stone column rising above the busy port.

After parking across from the tourist office near the tower, we went inside to browse through their maps and guides. Then we wandered around the harbor with the lamenting squawk of seagulls rising above us. We weren't sure what we were looking for, just hoping something might jump out. Nothing did.

"That tower we keep seeing is the only thing here that looks half-way interesting," I said.

"It's no help to us. They call it the Tower of Hercules, but it's actually the only Roman lighthouse still in operation."

"How come they call it the Tower of Hercules if it was built by the Romans?"

"A local legend says Hercules founded La Coruña for the Greeks."

"You want to know what I think?" I said.

"What do you think?"

255

"This place is a big disappointment."

"It is, but now we have plenty of time to check out the last two towns on our list."

After freeing ourselves from the tentacles of La Coruña traffic, a two-lane road winding through fields of pampas grass and vineyards brought us to the medieval gate of Betanzos, a smaller port city on a river estuary inland from La Coruña. The old town welcomed us with a tumbled heap of houses with glassed-in balconies rising uphill from the gate. The twisting maze of streets was so hard to squeeze through that I grabbed the first underground parking we came to.

Exit stairs brought us to an outdoor market pungent with the mingled aromas of fruit, cheese, honey, and spices. People selling food tempted shoppers with samples while shouting out praise for their products. Others hawked pottery, knives, baskets, and leatherwork.

Laura picked out some chocolate chip cookies, and a sack of Mandarin oranges. I couldn't resist buying her the white lace scarf she was admiring.

An uphill hike brought us to Plaza de Garcia Hermano, a central square surrounded by the sheltered arcades of gray stone buildings. The Celtic wail of Galician bagpipes was coming from the open window of a music school as we crossed the plaza to a cobbled street leading down to a church surrounded by palm trees.

Laura bounded up the steps to Santa Maria de Azogue, the church that's famous for its tombs of Spanish nobility.

"Look at this," she said, pointing at two circles a foot in diameter that had been crudely chiseled into the weathered rock on either side of the doors. For a moment, I was too stunned to speak. One enclosed a Maltese Cross, the other, a Star of David.

"This is very strange," I said, running my fingers over the grooves. "More symbols inside of circles."

Laura covered her head with the scarf and reached for the door. "We're getting so close I can feel it."

The darkness of the interior was pierced by rainbows of light shooting through the stained-glass windows. Up on the altar, a priest wearing a fine brocade was preparing his service while an assistant perched on a ladder wiping dust from a life-sized wooden effigy of Christ.

As our eyes adjusted, we made out the sumptuously adorned medieval sarcophagi built into every available space on the inner walls of the church.

"I've never seen so many fancy sarcophaguses," I said, hearing my voice resonate.

"You're supposed to call them sarcophagi," Laura whispered.

"I looked it up. Both are correct. Same goes for hippopotamuses. You could even say sarcophaguses for hippopotamuses."

"I don't feel like saying it."

"Fine by me."

"Let's check the names," she grinned. "Maybe we'll find some sarcophagi for the Hippopotami family."

Votive candles illuminated most of the shrines as we wandered past reading the family names, but none were the ones we were looking for.

We were headed for the exit when the priest's assistant intercepted us near the door. "Is there something I can help you with?"

"We wanted to know if the Castro family, the Osorio family, or any of the Counts of Lemos are buried here."

He looked thoughtful for a moment. "Those are well-known names, but none of them are here that I know of. There used to be another shrine over there," he said, pointing to an empty space along the wall. "If you'd like, I could ask the priest."

"Please do."

He returned with a more serious expression on his face. "Father Francisco says the tomb of another noble family used to be there, but it was moved many years ago to a church in Ponferrada."

Laura and I exchanged a look.

"Father was surprised you would ask about those particular families. Are you by any chance an historian?"

"No, just an interested tourist. We were also wondering why a Maltese cross and a Star of David are carved on your entrance."

He took a deep breath. "Other people have asked about that. All we know is that someone chiseled them in centuries ago. Many Jewish people left Spain through this port during the Inquisition. I suppose the Star of David could relate to that unfortunate history, but the Maltese cross is inexplicable."

"So much history," I said.

"Are you by any chance a Catholic?"

I shook my head. "Too much kneeling for my taste."

He nodded as if in agreement.

Laura took my arm as we headed outside. "You seem to have a dark view of organized religion."

"It must be all those paintings I've seen."

"Paintings?"

"The ones showing people being roasted alive with their eyes gouged out."

52

The slanting rays of a low sun cast their soft light across the dark walls and eighty-five evenly spaced towers of Lugo as I pulled into the parking outside San Pedro Gate. I was opening the door when a gray car drove in and parked a few rows away. Two men in gray suits got out seconds after we did. Both had short black hair, neatly trimmed mustaches, and shiny black shoes.

They followed us at a distance when we went through the gate but went somewhere else when we started up a stone ramp to check out the view from the top of the walls. Nestled beneath us, narrow streets running between the red tiled roofs converged on a central plaza surrounded by the columns and arches of a medieval arcade. Beyond the plaza, the double towers of a church rose over the town. Laura pointed. "That church would be another place to look for tombs of Spanish nobility."

After descending the ramp, we picked our way along the cobbled streets to Lugo Cathedral where the smell of old stone and incense worked its magic. A merry-go-round of martyrs and saints looked out from between stone columns, and ladies in black tended their favorite saints in small chapels illuminated by votive candles. None of the family names were ones we were looking for.

When we exited onto sun-drenched Plaza Santa Maria, the rhythmic sound of American rock 'n' roll was coming from one of the bars tucked inside the arcades. We followed the sound to a bar called La Penalba and were transported back in time to the 1950s. Brando biker posters and pictures of rock music icons looked down from the walls while a vintage Wurlitzer jukebox pulsated pink and purple to a Chuck Berry beat.

"It's a Retro club," Laura said, pulling me towards the long mahogany bar that ran down the right side of the dance floor. After a refreshing glass of tinto, we were heading back to our car when the gleam of tarnished silver, inlaid chests, and Oriental porcelain drew me to an antique store window. The door was locked, so I pushed the buzzer and waited until a white-haired man with skin like tanned leather came and opened the door.

Laura wandered off into the cluttered maze of merchandise while I paused to examine a display of Crusader armor. I was admiring a double-edged sword with a two-handed grip when I heard a muffled, "Tony."

Threading my way through the narrow aisles, I found Laura standing before a life-sized wooden horse. The horse was wearing a leather saddle on top of a quilted caparison, a medieval battle cover. Laura was pointing at the coat of arms embroidered on a velvet cloth draped behind the saddle.

The design showed a gray castle tower topped by a golden crown with the Cross of Tau at its center. Two white circles outlined in blue were positioned on either side of the tower. One circle contained a red Maltese cross, the other, a red X. Both were colored exactly like the circles in our table cover.

The shopkeeper came to join us when he saw me examining the cloth. Not wanting to let on what I was after, I said, "How much is the saddle?"

"It's an old one, from the fifteenth century. The price is four thousand euros."

"How much are these?" I said, pointing at the boot-shaped stirrups with gold inlay hanging from the saddle.

"The stirrups are twelve thousand euros."

He smiled at my look of surprise. "Fernandez de Castro, the tenth Count of Lemos, took them as booty from the Sultan of Morocco during the Battle of Salado in thirteen forty."

Laura squeezed my arm from behind. "That's more than I have with me," I said. "How much is the velvet embroidery?"

"The banner is twenty-five hundred," he said, removing the cloth. "The Coat of Arms for Monfort de Lemos is on both sides."

"Too bad it's got these little holes," I said, poking my finger through the biggest one and wiggling it around a little bit.

He smiled. "It would be more expensive without the holes."

"That's a lot of money. Would you take a thousand?"

He looked at me like a hawk, crossed his arms, and shook his head. I dug out my wallet and made like I was counting my money. "How about fifteen hundred?"

His eyes flicked from my face to the wallet. Then back to my face. "Seventeen hundred," he said, making a horizontal slash with one hand. I dug out the cash.

Laura was hugging the banner like a child holds a Christmas present as we headed down the street. "It's amazing to find something decorated with the same symbols that were used in our table cover," she said, just as the two men in gray suits came around the corner, walked briskly past without looking at us, and climbed the steps to the antique store.

I took a quick look inside the gray car before unlocking ours. A police radio was tucked under the dash, and a roll of yellow and black crime scene tape was on the floor. I figured they must be detectives working on the theft of manuscripts from the castle museum.

Laura was still cradling the banner when we pulled into our hotel parking an hour later. Knowing how good she felt about spotting it, I said, "Let's open it up while there's still some natural light."

I was holding it high by the corners so she could take it all in when a bright yellow panel truck with *Correos* written on the side slowed to a near stop, then accelerated away with a throaty roar.

53

The joyous sound of Sunday morning church bells woke us at eight and we were parked across from the Templar castle by half past nine. After handing in our tickets at the entry beneath the Cross of Tau, little yellow arrows directed us through a seemingly endless series of chilly bed chambers, hushed corridors, and chapels full of shadows.

It felt strange to be in a place with so much history, like you half expected the former inhabitants to still be there. Laura stopped in her tracks when we turned down a chilly hallway lined with life-sized mannequins wearing medieval costumes.

"What's the matter?" I said.

"Do you believe in ghosts?"

"No. Do you?"

"I'm starting to."

At the end of the corridor, long swords and armorial trophies were hung above a stairway leading down to a wooden door. The entry was blocked by a chain, and a sign reading *No Dejar Entrar.*

I glanced back the way we had come. "Maybe we should take a quick look at what's behind that door?"

"What would we be looking for?" Laura said, as I reached to unhook the chain.

"Those mysterious tunnels beneath the tower."

She grabbed me by the arm. "It might be dark down there."

"We've got Sol's flashlight," I said, pulling it out.

I had to shake the lever handle a couple times before the door opened with a rusty groan. Cool air hit our faces as we brushed away sticky cobwebs and followed s a corroded iron railing down slippery stone steps to a narrow, arched tunnel.

Laura gripped the back of my shirt as I led the way along a cramped passage that seemed to twist back on itself. We heard the drip of water when we came to an intersection with a much larger tunnel, and a musty-smelling draft of air chilled the sweat on my neck.

"Why has it gotten so much colder?" Laura said.

My breath stopped in my throat, and I drew back with disgust when my light swept across a cave-like cavity filled with human skulls and bones. "It's an ossuary," I said.

"I know what it *is*. I think we should go back."

"Okay, but first let's see what's inside that opening up ahead."

I could tell by the feel of the air that something was different as we inched our way into a cavernous chamber with a ceiling so high my light barely reached it. Cockroaches skittered across the floor when my flash lit up alcoves piled high as they could be with moldy rope, rotted sailcloth, and blackened barrels.

"This stuff looks really old," I said, hearing my voice resonate off the stone walls.

Suddenly we were surrounded by the flutter of bat wings and scurrying sounds erupted from an opening in the middle of the floor.

"This must be how they brought things in from the river," I said, moving closer to moss-covered steps leading down into darkness.

Laura's grip on the back of my shirt tightened when my light reflected off the red eyes of rodents who squeaked and squealed as they scurried for cover.

"I'm going to start screaming if you don't get me out of here."

I'd seen enough. Ducking beneath the frenzied bats, we hurried back down the tunnel and up the stairs to the door we had come in through. In my hurry to get it open, I pulled too hard, and the rusty old handle came off in my hand.

Laura didn't need to say a single word for me to know what she was thinking.

"Shit," I said. "The humidity's got it jammed in the frame."

"There must be some way to loosen it," Laura said, as I groped around the edges for any opening to cling to.

After a couple broken fingernails and a couple solid kicks, nothing had moved and there was blood on my hands.

"There's no way I can do this without tools," I said, playing my light over the heavy, wrought-iron hinges. "Maybe we can find another way out through the tunnels."

Distant squeaking sounds put an end to that line of thinking.

"That's it, I give up."

"I don't believe it."

"Don't believe what?"

"That you've given up."

"What else can I possibly do?"

"Maybe it's time for brains over brawn."

"We can't very well wait for it to dry out and shrink."

"No, but we can take stock of what we have to work with."

She was right. Sol's flashlight had beveled edges for self-defense. Using it like a tiny lever, I moved methodically around the edges of the door. After what seemed like an eternity, I managed to pop it loose.

When I pulled it open, two tight-lipped security guards were glaring down at us from the top of the steps. "What are you doing down there?" one said in accented English.

"We thought there might be a toilet," I said.

"Toilets are on the museum level," he said, pointing at the ceiling.

Then I saw the security cameras and realized they must have been watching when we went into the tunnels.

The guards stepped aside to let us pass, then followed close behind as we retraced our steps. I heard a radio crackle when we started up the stairway to the Templar Museum. One of them was talking to somebody.

Entry to the palace was by way of the Grand Hall, a stately gallery containing suits of armor and gilded manuscripts in display cases. Some display cases were shattered and draped with yellow and black crime scene tape.

At the end of the gallery, more yellow arrows directed us into the palace dining room. Moth-eaten deer heads lined the walls of a long room with a beamed ceiling and a fireplace big enough to stand in. The hairs on the back of my neck rose to attention when I saw the gilt-framed portrait that was suspended above the fireplace.

An opulently dressed lady and gentleman were staring out at us from either side of a table covered with a rug that looked exactly like ours. A globe of the world was positioned between them.

Laura clutched at my arm. "That looks like ours!"

"It is ours. It's got the same star design, the same colors, you can even see part of the inscription."

"Look at the man's hand," Laura said incredulously. "His finger is pointing at the crown."

Indeed, it was almost as if the people in the painting had looked out and spoken to us.

We moved in closer to read the tag.

*Denis of Briganza and his wife, Beatrice de Castro Osorio,
the sixth Countess of Lemos, 1578.*

"This must be the painting Sheena's art expert saw," I said.

"We've got to explore this town," Laura said. "Every cell in my body is telling me we're getting closer."

54

We were crossing the upper battlements on our way to the exit when Laura paused to take in a view of the town below. A huge basilica loomed over the central square where people were moving around like miniature figures on a large chessboard.

"Maybe we should look inside that church." I said.

"It doesn't fit the description, but it may be our last option."

Suddenly, shouts and laughter erupted from directly below us. Children were kicking a soccer ball around next to a tiny church nestled up against the castle walls.

"I can hardly believe it," I said. "If you hadn't stopped to look, we would have missed the only church that fits the words of the inscription."

A rope railing steadied our descent down a tight circular stairway to San Andres Church, a chapel-like building that was dwarfed by the walls of the castle.

Next to the door, a blue and white enameled plaque displayed a floorplan of the church that was shaped precisely like the cartouche in our rug. The text beneath it read: *The temple at the foot of the castle is the most important monument in the old quarter.*

"My god," Laura said. "They even call it a temple."

An ancient brass plate said the church was supposed to open at 10, half an hour ago, but when I tried the door, it was locked.

"I can't believe we've come this far and won't to be able to get inside," I said, as a soccer ball hit the side of the church with a resounding *thwack*.

Laura caught the ball on the rebound, tossed it to the children, and asked if they knew how we could get inside the church. A boy of about eight offered to take us to the sacristan's house.

We followed him down a roughly cobbled street that was marked on either side by massive medieval doors. When he stopped and pointed at a humble old house, Laura mounted the low steps and knocked.

The door was opened by a wrinkled woman dressed in black who nodded once when Laura explained we wanted to see the church and disappeared down a dark hallway. A minute later, an elderly man, brown as a nut and dressed entirely in white cotton, emerged from the shadows carrying a key ring that would have been the envy of any medieval jailer.

The man led us up the roughly cobbled street at such a brisk pace, we could barely keep up. When he stopped at the church door, an orange tabby cat came and rubbed against his ankles. Choosing a key that was almost a foot long, he fit it in the lock. There was a metallic clunk, the lock turned, and the door creaked softly as it swung open.

After beckoning us inside, he explained that the priest would be along shortly, and left us alone to explore the cool and musty space.

Sorrowful statues of saints stared down from above as we explored dim little chapels with the friendly cat following close behind. Votive candles flickered in the gloom as we read family names and the dedication of the chapels to specific saints.

Laura breathed deeply and rested a hand on my arm when we came to the last alcove. My skin seemed to tighten on my body as I took in the pattern of the floor tiles. A lattice of yellow stars on a green background surrounded by a blue border of white scallop shells. The same pattern as our table cover.

Unlike all the others, this alcove was empty, except for a white marble altar and a stone sarcophagus in the form of a recumbent knight. A name, obscured by a layer of dust, was carved into the sarcophagus.

Not even a fly was moving as I leaned over and brushed away the dust.

Pedro Alvarez Osorio, 1320-1380
The Count of Lemos

The expression on Laura's face told me she was thinking the same thing I was—we had found what we had been searching for.

Then my eyes were drawn to a wooden chest that was sitting on the altar with its lid hanging askew. The circled T symbol of the Count of Lemos was carved into the side facing us.

I was struggling to take it all in when the cat meowed once, made a beeline for the door, and a pink-faced priest wearing a floor-length cassock came gliding into the alcove.

"I apologize for being late," he said. "Can I help you?"

"This is a tomb of local nobility, but the chamber is nearly empty?"

He smiled benevolently. "We tried to keep all the old shrines during the renovation, but this one had been neglected for too many years. The chest was all we were able to keep."

"It looks like it's been opened."

"The lock and hinges had rusted off."

"Was anything inside?"

He flicked his hand "Nothing of value. Just an old terra-cotta goblet, and a crumbling roll of nautical maps that we tossed in the trash."

I nearly choked. "You threw them away?"

"They were falling apart from dampness."

"You are a Catholic, aren't you?"

He reached to touch his crucifix. "Certainly."

"Yet you threw away historic documents that had been carefully preserved in your church?"

His cheeks reddened. "They seemed rather ordinary at the time, though, come to think of it, they were marked up with old French writing that nobody could read."

"What about the goblet?

"I can show you that. We have it stored in the rectory."

268

I tried to compose myself as he went to get it. "Nothing of value," I said, as sarcastically as I could. "I feel like telling him those maps could have solved one of the world's longest running mysteries."

Laura looked at me with a soft expression in her eyes. "Sometimes kindness is wiser than the truth."

I was giving that some thought when the priest returned carrying a small chalice with a pedestal foot. It didn't glow—or vibrate like a flying saucer—but a decoration of palm leaves was artfully incised in the red clay, and there was gold leaf around the rim.

"It's chipped," he said. "And it has some small cracks, but it's the perfect size for passing out communion wafers."

I was stunned, but not too stunned to go to work. Picking it up reverently, I looked him in the eye. "Household artifacts like this are an obsession of mine. This one would be perfect to round-out my collection."

"I'm sorry, but the Church is not interested in selling."

I widened my eyes. "But think of the benefit to your church treasury if I took it off your hands, say for five thousand euros? Cash, of course."

"I don't have that kind of authority."

Talking to this guy was like trying to light a wet match.

"I apologize, Father. I'm forgetting it is better to give than to receive. How about if I make it ten thousand, as an act of Christian charity?"

I held up a cautionary hand before he could reply. "I know, it couldn't possibly be worth that much. But it would give me a chance to contribute to the preservation of your fine church."

He rested his fingers on the rim of the chalice. "For something like that you must contact the Church administration. All I can do is give you an address to write to."

If this priest ever had an original thought, it probably died of loneliness.

"But that would take far too long," I said, pulling it gently towards me. "There must be someone you can call."

Puckering his lips, he twisted it out of my hands. "There's a donation box near the entrance if you would like to make a contribution."

I could feel the priest's eyes on the center of my spine when I tossed a noisy handful of coins into his donation box.

"Maybe I should have offered him the extra five-grand as a finder's fee," I whispered.

"Sometimes you're about as subtle as an avalanche. I suppose bribing church employees is another trick of your trade?"

"I wouldn't have to bribe him if he didn't have such a deplorable lack of faith in his fellow man. Whatever happened to Christian generosity?"

"Just remember, Tony, life's greatest treasures only exist inside of us."

"Maybe so, but thick-headed priests tossed the maps to the world's biggest lost treasure into the trash. Now I know how that king felt when all the Templar vaults turned out to be empty."

Laura took me by the arm. "Isn't it sort of wonderful to think of them passing out communion wafers from the Holy Grail."

"It is ironic."

"Maybe it's not too late to tell them what we know?"

"It's too late. Without the maps, it would be impossible to link the chalice to the Templar treasure. Besides, I like the idea that they're using it for communion without knowing what it is."

"Don't sound so glum. It's not like nothing has been found."

"What do you mean?"

"We had a terrific adventure."

"We'd still be having one if we'd gotten to see those treasure maps."

55

We were in for a gloomy ride, until Laura began peeling some mandarin oranges, and their sweet tang filled the car. When those were gone, the heady bouquet of chocolate chip cookies cast its spell.

Half an hour later, we washed it all down with the bracing bubbles from a cold bottle of San Pelligrino.

"I didn't know how thirsty I was," I said, passing back the bottle.

Laura patted my knee. "There are times when water is more precious than gold."

I was surprised how such simple things rekindled my spirits. Maybe it was the mingled scent of oranges and chocolate, or Laura's affectionate touch, but a soothing stillness had settled my mind.

A wispy veil of purple-colored clouds was cloaking the horizon when we pulled into our hotel parking, like even the cosmos was drawing a final curtain on our adventure.

"We're out of wine," I said. "I'll run down to the village for a bottle."

"Okay," Laura said, sliding out. "But don't be long."

"I'll only be a minute."

She smiled suggestively. "I might go straight to bed."

I considered getting out of the car.

"I'll be back before you're under the covers."

Following the river road into town, I parked beneath the corona of a streetlamp, and hurried inside a small store. When I came out, blue lights were flashing from an unmarked police car, and a man in a gray suit was shining a flashlight into my window. I was struggling to ask him what I had done wrong when headlights washed over me, and a second police car pulled up. The man who got out asked for my passport in English and handed me a card identifying himself as Inspector Javier Carvalho of La Brigada de Patrimonio Historico. The Spanish art police.

"What's this all about?" I said, digging out my passport.

"We've had reports that you and your lady friend have been making unusual inquiries about objects of Spanish heritage. What exactly is your interest?"

I knew I had to keep it simple as my mind flashed images of the security guards at the castle, the suspicious priest in Betanzos, and the testy one I had just tried to buy the chalice from.

"We're just tracing some family history. One of her ancestors worked as a tutor for the Count of Lemos."

A look of recognition passed over his face, and he nodded. "Spain has suffered the loss of many important objects in recent years. Laws are now in place regarding property of cultural interest. Fortunately, the banner that you purchased is not on our list. Otherwise, the Ministry of Culture would have the right to acquire it."

"I'm glad to know that we've done nothing wrong," I said, thinking of Laura and watching him methodically transcribe my passport information into his little notebook.

"Is there any way to speed this up?" I said, "My lady friend is waiting for me back at the hotel."

He stopped writing and stared at me until I threw up my hands.

It was only a two-minute drive, but I got there in one. The lobby was deserted, so it wasn't anything I heard or saw that made me stop at the foot of the stairs. It was the sharp chemical smell hanging in the air, and a stillness as silent as an ambush.

Taking the steps two at a time, I froze when I saw Laura's white lace scarf laying discarded in a wedge of light coming from the door to our room. I called her name, and the dead air sunk me.

Fear slammed into me like an arrow when I looked inside. Our cozy little love nest had been savagely devastated. Dresser drawers were upside down, the mattress was ripped open, and the contents of our travel bags were strewn all over the floor. Worst of all, Laura was gone.

I gripped the doorframe to keep from going under until something clicked inside of me. Then I bounded down the stairs to the lobby and pounded on the ringer until the patron's puzzled face peered out of a back room. After blurting out what had happened, he followed me upstairs.

A screaming storm of dark thoughts flooded my mind as we stood gaping at the wreckage. It wasn't until he saw the broken fire escape door at the end of the hall that he hurried off to call the police.

Not knowing what else to do, I stepped cautiously into the chaos and started putting things back in order. A tiny black object cracked under my foot when I stooped to pick up Laura's hairbrush and her travel clock. It had *Minitracker* printed on the side and had been concealed in the clock. That was how they had been able to follow us!

The town police arrived twenty minutes later. A skinny one with pimples, and an older one with a pot belly and a mustache. The patron interpreted while they asked the routine questions. Was Laura unhappy? Was she alone because we had a fight? Might she have done this herself? Was anything of value missing? And so on.

I told them nothing of value had been taken except for Laura, but they didn't seem keen on doing anything until they wrote it all down and filed a report. I lost all hope they would be of any help when they spent more time talking with the patron about his broken door than they did talking to me.

I didn't mention the tracking device, or the people I was thinking of. These small-town cops could never make a case with what I had. Besides, the kidnappers hadn't gotten what they wanted. The photos, the translation, and the package from Senora Sinatora were safely hidden in our car. I figured I'd be hearing from someone, sooner or later.

A terrible sense of dread welled up inside me when the police left me alone. I had gotten Laura into this and failed to protect her. Scenes of darkness were snaking their way through my mind as I paced the room, clutching her lace scarf, and smelling her scent.

My emotions cooled as the clock ticked. When all I felt was the chill of the room, I pulled the cork and poured myself a dose of twenty-year-old brandy. When I finished that, I had another. The alcohol warmed me, but too much would cost me the clarity of mind that I needed.

Whoever had taken Laura was betting they could use her as a lever to move me any way they wanted. And they were right. I missed her more than I ever imagined I could miss someone.

What they did not know, was that my response would be in accord with one of the most fundamental laws of nature.

We all know that law. For every action there is an equal and opposite reaction.

I didn't need another shot of brandy to know what I had to do. All I needed was the opportunity.

56

An empty brandy glass was hanging from my hand, and I was thinking hard about a refill when the phone rang. It was the desk.

"Someone wants you to come down."

"What kind of someone?"

"Someone on a motorcycle. What shall I tell him?"

"Tell him I'll be right there."

I splashed cold water on my face and hurried down the stairs. The patron was signing in guests, he pointed to the front door. I pushed it open to the throaty rumble of a chopped Harley Davidson motorcycle parked on the edge of the tarmac.

The monster riding it had a bush of a beard, a nose like a beak, and shaggy black hair held in place with a blue bandana. No helmet. Just a black leather vest over a black T-shirt, faded jeans, and wrap-around sunglasses.

Without saying a word, he extended a tattoo-covered hand and wiggled an envelope. I took the envelope, feeling something hard and small inside, and watched him slam the bike into gear and wheel away with a screaming blast of noise.

I started to turn away when his taillight disappeared around the bend but paused to listen. When I heard him downshift at the crossroads, veer left, and accelerate up into the mountains, I knew which road he had taken.

I ripped open the envelope. One of Laura's earrings was inside, along with a crude note written in block letters. *ANSWER YOUR PHONE AT MIDNIGHT OR THE GIRL DIES.*

I read it fast, and I read it slow. Either way I didn't like it, but whoever sent this had hell coming their way.

I got our map out of the car and interrupted the patron by opening it on his counter. "Do you know what's up that road?" I said, pointing.

He looked at me with wide eyes. "That's just an old mountain road. The only thing up there is a deep-pit mining operation that closed years ago when the work became too dangerous."

This wouldn't be the first time I played a lone hand, but I had to move fast. When the patron went upstairs with his guests, I ducked behind the bar for a Bic lighter, a bar rag, and a bottle of vodka. A swift sweep of the kitchen got me a serrated knife, a squeeze bottle of dish soap, and a cannister marked *FireShield Cooking-Fire Extinguisher*. All of it went into a mesh shopping bag that was hanging on the wall next to the door.

My intentions were cold and clear as I followed a footpath to the weathered woodshed behind the hotel. Garden tools were inside, along with a lawnmower and a can of gasoline. I took the gas, a short-handled ax for splitting kindling, and carried everything back to my room by way of the metal steps leading up to the broken fire escape door.

Taking each step as if it were meant to be, I filled our two empty wine bottles with gasoline, squirted in a few ounces of dish soap, and shook the contents. After soaking the bar rag in vodka, I tore off two strips, and stuffed them into the necks of the bottles with a couple inches hanging out. Dr. Molotov's time-honored recipe would act like a flammable gel every bit as potent as Napalm.

The serrated knife and the Bic lighter went into my hip pocket, the aerosol fire extinguisher went into my jacket, and the two bottles went inside my travel bag.

Feeling an unnatural calm, I loosened my belt to make room for the ax, made sure my shoes were tightly laced, and headed for my car.

The roughly paved road wound upwards into an endless sea of hills and dark trees. Fifteen minutes later, my headlights swept across a dirt road leading into the forest and the faded sign of a mining company. I caught glimpses of light as I drove by, so I swung around and parked on the opposite side of the road, pointing downhill.

The night air smelled of pine trees as I hoisted my bag over my shoulder and began following a rutted path that angled upward into the darkness beneath the trees. Glittering galaxies lit the way, but the farther I walked, the more the branches closed in and blocked what little light there was.

After stumbling a few times on protruding rocks, I reached for my flashlight just before the earth disappeared from beneath my feet. For a split second I registered that I was falling into emptiness. Then a painful jerk from the shoulder strap of my bag left me dangling in space, turning slowly back and forth. It was only the nylon strap getting hooked over a small tree stump that had saved me from a hundred-foot plunge into a rocky grave.

Praying the strap would hold, I clawed around for something to grab onto. The cliff edge was undercut and ready to fall. Tree roots were sticking out, but they didn't have enough strength to support me. By twisting around, I managed to get one foot onto a protruding rock before it dislodged and clattered into the pit below with a terrifying noise.

For a moment, even the trees seemed to be holding their breath, but all I heard were the soothing sounds of the night, the odd cricket, and my own rasping breath. Then the popping and ripping of threads reminded me I was running out of time.

My only option was the rapidly weakening strap. Pressing my feet against the decaying cliff wall, I tried pulling myself upward inch by inch, hand over hand. Dangling brambles tore at my face and arms, but I was finally able to hoist my upper body, and then my legs, onto the edge of the cliff.

My hands were shredded, my pants were bloody and torn, and yawning below like a gaping mouth with jagged rocky teeth, was an abandoned mining pit.

Half expecting to be attacked, I glanced around, but there was no one. The noise in my head was the sound of my heart hammering in my chest. Then I heard the sharp snap of a twig and looked up into the barrel of a shotgun. The man holding it was wearing night vision goggles and military style camos.

"What's in the bag?" he said.

"Just some hiking gear," I said, reaching to unhook the strap. He poked me with the gun. "You better let me do that."

Keeping his eyes on me, he bent to grab the strap. As he moved his feet, and stretched his fingers to reach it, the cliff edge fell away with a sudden sucking sound, and he vanished from my sight.

I waited for the clatter of falling rocks to taper off and peered cautiously over the edge. The man lay spreadeagled on the rocks below. For a second, the muscles in his body tensed, and his fingers moved. Then he was still.

After unhooking my bag, I took big gulps of air to calm my frazzled nerves and moved deeper into the forest. Fifty yards in, the trees cleared around a two-story wooden building. Its windows were blazing, and black figures moved around inside.

I was inching my way forward through the low brush when the wind picked up, rattling the leaves. Then the sound of a car door slamming startled me. Dropping to my knees, I waited for my heart rate to slow, crawled like a wolf to where the forest ended, and cautiously raised my head.

Two motorcycles and a yellow mail truck with *Correos* written on the side were parked outside the entrance. One motorcycle was the same chopped Harley ridden by the monster who had delivered the note. The funeral van we had seen in Vézelay was parked next to them with its rear doors open.

I watched as two men removed what looked like a body from the funeral van. It wasn't until they carried it into the lit-up entry to the building that I realized it was a painted wooden statue.

When the door closed behind them, I crept to the rear of the funeral van, dropped my bag, and squirmed beneath it on my back. After finding the fuel line with my flashlight, I sawed at it

278

with the serrated knife until my hand was soaked with gasoline. Then I wiggled back out.

Shouldering my bag again, I crawled on hands and knees through thorny bushes toward the lighted windows. Had I been standing, or moving any faster, I would have triggered a tripwire for an alarm that was strung low across ground.

I paused to listen. Casual chatting voices were coming from one of the windows. Balancing myself with one hand on the ground, I stepped cautiously over the tripwire, sidled up to the side of the building, and peered through the curtains.

The pale-skinned bald man was seated inches away with his back to me. I knew with blinding certainty he was the one who killed Sammy when he waved a handful of gilded manuscripts and the diamond encrusted Patek Philippe sparkled on his wrist.

Ducking back down, I edged my way to the rear of the building where steps led up to a back door. The door was locked, but I could see into the hallway. Two doors on the left were secured with padlocks, and the door at the end opened to a room where three muscular men sat with their feet propped on a low table littered with beer cans. I was badly outnumbered, but I would have the advantage of surprise if I could create a diversion.

Scuttling back to where the vehicles were parked, I lit the rag on one of my bottles, and pitched it as hard as I could at the side of the funeral van. It worked perfectly. A fireball exploded upwards with a blast of heat that momentarily blinded me.

Reeling away from the flames, I ran to the back door just as the fuel tank in the funeral van let go, rocking the air like a thunderclap. Now both motorcycles, the van, and the truck were ablaze in a hellfire of heat.

A frenzy of activity erupted at the end of the corridor as the three men rushed out to see what had happened. Hoping no one had stayed behind, I rested my bag on the top step, smashed out the window, and opened the door from inside.

The first padlock fell away with a stroke of my ax, and I kicked the door open, eager to see what was inside.

57

DYNAMITE.

Firelight flickering through wraith-like curtains lit up wooden boxes stenciled with markings that identified them as explosives left over from the mining operation.

Turning quickly to the other door, I slashed off the second padlock and flung it open.

A crimson glow from the fire outside illuminated a roomful of statues casting long shadows. Life-sized saints holding up their hands in benediction. Jesuses with welcoming arms. Sorrowful Madonnas. Gilt-winged seraphim ascending to heaven.

Every one of them seemed vibrantly alive in the quivering light.

But where was Laura?

An unlit stairway was down the hallway. Steps went down to musty smelling darkness, and up to gray gloom. I was running out of time, so I had to guess. Groping my way forward, I found the first step by tripping on it and took the stairs two at a time to a second-floor landing.

Two doors opened easily to the sharp smells of dirty bedrooms and stale cigarette smoke. The third door was locked, but a key had been left in the deadbolt. I turned the key, pushed at the door, and a blade of light split the blackness.

Leaning cautiously inside, I whispered, "Laura."

She sprang from the shadows, wrapped her arms around me and squeezed. "Thank God. I knew you'd come."

Breathing in her scent, I took her by the arm. "We've got to get out of here."

She touched the side of my face. "You're all bloody."

"I had a little fall."

A floorboard creaked.

Laura's eyes shifted past me.

I wheeled around.

A man, looking mean and dangerous with a gun in his hand, was standing at the top of the stairs.

For moment, we stared in silence.

"Look what we got here," he said, moving closer and prodding me in the chest with the pistol.

I retreated, taking little steps until my back collided with the wall. It was then I saw the gun was a World War 2 Government Model Colt 45. These have a safety mechanism that keeps them from firing when pressed against something.

Taking a chance, I pushed back against the barrel with the palm of my hand.

Showing me his nicotine-stained teeth, he pushed back.

I smiled into his eyes

He sneered into mine. "I'm gonna waste you and laugh."

Wrinkles of bewilderment creased his face when he pulled the trigger, but they disappeared when the side of my ax met the side of his head.

We were halfway down the steps when another man poked his head into the stairwell. His face clouded and clenched just before my foot caught the tip of his chin in a sweeping motion that was like kicking a football.

Hand in hand, we scrambled down the hallway and out the door. I was bending for the bag I'd left on the porch when two more men came running down the hallway. Flicking on the Bic lighter, I lit the rag, and flung my last bottle through the entrance.

A blast of flames filled the doorway and cast dancing shadows as we sprinted into the forest.

The trees provided cover until the moving beam of a powerful light stabbed the darkness, lighting the branches above our heads and sending twisting shadows across the forest floor. When the light briefly found us, shots rang out from a large caliber gun. There was a singing whine as a bullet ricocheted off a rock.

I paused to listen when we came to the edge of the forest lining the road. Angry voices were moving towards us. It crossed my mind that it was only a matter of time before the dynamite would explode.

After hurrying Laura across the street and into our car, I was about to open my door when she screamed, "Tony, look out!" Wielding a pipe wrench like a medieval mace, the big-nosed biker who had delivered the note was almost on me.

I ducked my head a fraction of a second before his weapon crunched into the metal roof. Something about the violence and finality of that sound stopped time. A second became infinity, and when it moved again, I stood to defend myself.

Quick as a striking snake, he feinted at my head, but kicked me in the groin instead. Gasping at the sudden pain and nausea, I went down all fours.

"Where do you think you're going?" he said, pounding the wrench into my ribs as I covered my head with one arm, and tried to crawl. "You don't really think we'd let you get away."

The blows kept coming until I managed to roll myself away and scramble to my feet. Both of us were breathing heavily, but he twisted his face into a toothy grin, and came at me again with surprising agility.

Half in shock, I was backing away when I remembered the aerosol fire extinguisher in my jacket pocket. Fumbling blindly, I pulled it out and pointed it at his face. He froze at the sight of it just long enough for me to blast his eyes with a jet of soapy foam.

The reaction was immediate. He lurched around trying to wipe the stinging liquid out of his eyes, lost his balance, and toppled to the ground. I moved in so fast I hardly knew what I was doing.

A kick in the ribs knocked the air out of him, but he started to push himself up. A harder kick knocked him sideways, but he was still gripping the wrench. Switching to his head, I kicked him again and again until he slumped face down on the tarmac. He was barely conscious, but I had to keep him down.

Jumping in the air, I came down on one of his legs with both of my feet, and it snapped like a toothpick. He was jerking around so much, it took me two tries to break the other one. It was crude stuff, but these were crude people.

I must have been a hell of a sight, bent over, gasping for breath with my lips drawn back from my teeth. Part of me felt like taking a bow, but loud voices were coming closer. I was turning towards the car when a bullet whistled past my head. I felt a burning sensation when the next one brushed my jacket.

The car started with a roar, and spit gravel as I accelerated down the hill. I took the first curve so tightly that my wheels started to slide, then the road straightened. I was driving as fast as I dared when a flash of yellow light lit up the sky. Seconds later, a shockwave shook the car.

Laura was looking at me in an odd way when I skidded to a stop at the bottom of the hill. When she spoke, her voice was distant, and slightly off key. "I hope I never end up on your bad side."

"Why do you say that?"

"Did you really have to kick that guy so much when he was down?"

"He was too big for me to fight if he got up again."

Then it hit me. Her hands were gripping one another, and she was taking short, rapid breaths. "I never expected anything like this to happen," I said, wrapping my arms around her, and pulling her close. "I must have been out of my mind to get you involved."

Suddenly she was sobbing, and tears were all over my face. "I lost sight of everything when they took you," I said. "Everything except getting you back. What happened? Did they hurt you?"

The sobs slowly changed themselves into words, incoherently at first, but coming clearer as she regained control. "There were four of them…it was like a bad dream, but it was real …I've never been so terrified. That creepy bald guy…he was waiting in our room. His buddies had torn the place apart and were furious because they hadn't found what they were after."

"Did they say what they were after?"

She wiped tears from her face. "What do you think they wanted? They wanted the table cover. They were driving by when you held up the banner with the coat of arms. They thought that was it. They asked where you had gone. I lied. I told them you went to pick up some friends. Then they tied my wrists and forced me to breathe something awful. When I woke up, I was in that funeral van. I tried not to tell them anything, but the bald guy kept poking me with a gun."

"He threatened you with a gun? What was he trying to find out?"

"He wanted to know what we were doing. I got confused and let too much slip. I told him that the designs in the rug made us think something might be hidden in a temple by a tower. They got me to admit that we've got the table cover. How did they ever find us?"

"I hate telling you this, but a tracking device was hidden inside your travel clock. It fell out when they ransacked our room."

"What do we do now?"

"We've been through too much to risk making any rash decisions. We need some rest. We should go back to the hotel."

"You must be out of your mind," she said, shoving me away with both hands. "No way am I going back to that room!"

I held up my hands as much to defend myself as to placate her. "Thanks to you, they think I brought back some friends. We couldn't find a safer place at this time of night."

"We wouldn't need to find a safer place if you had listened to me a little bit more. Now I just want to be done with all of this and go home."

"I can't tell you how sorry I am, but they can't try anything tonight because their wheels are all fried. Are you still with me?"

For a moment, she looked at me like she was seriously considering the question. Then she sighed. "Of course, I'm with you. This has been the most terrifying day of my life, but I can't think of any place I'd rather be than with you. Crazy, huh?"

Crazy or not, that really got to me. There was more to be said, but I could say none of it. All that mattered, was Laura was still with me.

She was still shaky when we got to our room, so I wrapped her in my arms, conscious of nothing but the relief of her being there and my overfilled heart.

Parts of me were stiff and sore, so I took my jacket off to take an inventory. When my finger caught in a small hole on the upper sleeve, I felt around and found an exit hole on the other side.

Baring my body to the bathroom mirror, I found my arm was smeared with blood from a bullet wound, red welts crisscrossed my back, and my ankle was swollen purple. The bullet wound was a tiny red groove, an inch long. A classic graze.

After turning the water on hot as it would go, I scrubbed myself with bath gel. Then I covered the wound with a Band-Aid and put on fresh clothes. When I was done, I felt oddly refreshed and relaxed. Maybe it was because we had narrowly escaped something terrible.

Laura was brushing her hair at the mirror, so I excused myself and returned the gas can to the shed by way of the rear door. The cook was finishing up in the kitchen when I came back in through the lobby. I asked him to bring some food up to our room while discretely slipping the serrated knife, the dish soap, and the aerosol can back on the counter.

We drank brandy until the meal came, then ate everything the cook brought us. Afterwards, Laura went to take a shower, and I plugged in the electric kettle to make some tea.

I was in bed when she came out with a bath towel wrapped around her. "Why don't you put out the lights," she said, dropping the towel and laying down beside me.

Seconds later, the kettle started bubbling and trembling, but nobody bothered with it.

58

The phone rang just before midnight and the gravelly growl of Vinnie Mingaloni bent my ear. "You've caused me a lot of trouble."

"There seems to be a lot of that going around."

"You played it pretty smart. You fooled us."

"Fooling people like you doesn't make me smart."

A moment of silence. "Nobody gives a shit what you say if you don't have the guts to say it to our faces."

"It sounds like you've got one of those anger management issues. They've got programs for things like that."

"I've got my own anger management program, but you wouldn't like it very much."

"I hope you're not planning to bore me to death by telling me all about it."

A pause: I could hear him lighting a cigarette. "It wouldn't be boring at my end," he said, in a voice that had gone dangerously soft.

"Look Vinnie, you lost your leverage, and I'm running low on popcorn. If all you want to do is give me a hard time, I'd rather get back to my movie. And you can tell your team of thrill seekers I'm ready for them if they want another taste."

"You're in a tight spot."

"What do you mean?"

"What's your next move? Run off into the hills with the girl over your shoulder?"

There was nothing I could say. We were outnumbered, and our only escape was a narrow road through a heavily forested river valley.

"Don't feel so bad," he said, in a more conciliatory tone. "My guys are willing to put an end to this. They want to do a deal for everything you've got."

A little voice told me to just say no, but with the treasure out of the picture, I was curious how far I could push him.

"A deal for everything?"

"Yeah, the rug and the translation."

"I might be willing to do a deal now that we've got an appraisal. Let's say four hundred thousand euros. Cash, of course."

"We heard about your appraisal. The most we can pay is a hundred thousand dollars."

"This is euro land," I said. "We don't want dollars. Make it three hundred thousand euros."

I heard a rustling sound like he was putting his hand over the phone, followed by a silence that was so long it made me think he might have hung up.

"Okay," he said when he came back on. "We thought you'd like dollars, but if you wanna insist on euros, we can come up with two hundred thousand."

"That won't cut it after what your buddies did to Laura. My last offer: two hundred and fifty-thousand euros. Take it or leave it."

"Hold on."

The phone was muffled again, and when he came back on, he sounded different—like he had been laughing.

"Okay, pal. If you're so keen on euros, you've got yourself a deal. But that means we get whatever else there is, too."

"I can live with that, especially now that we're pals."

"That's right. We can be pals so long as you go away. If you stay around poking your nose into things, you're gonna be on the receiving end of my anger management program."

"I wouldn't want you to have to overexert yourself."

287

A pause. "I wouldn't like that either. How about we do the exchange at noon tomorrow in a secluded place outside of town?"

"No way. We want people around. We'll do the exchange in Lugo. There's a Retro Bar on the square called La Penalba."

"I'll have to run that by my team."

I heard muffled voices. Then Vincent came back on the line.

"We're good with Lugo."

"I'm glad to see you made the right decision."

"It had to happen sometime."

"One other thing. Don't be late. The guys I work with would take it badly."

"You know such lovey people."

"I take them as they come. You're gonna have to do the same."

"Don't worry, we'll be there. I wouldn't want to miss our last get together."

Another pause. "I guess we'll see about that tomorrow."

The line went dead, and I put down the phone.

"Do you really think it's a good idea to be so rude?" Laura said.

"It pays to look strong when the other guy is expecting you to be weak and afraid."

"Maybe they have good reason to expect us to be afraid."

"They might be suspicious if I rolled over too easy."

"Maybe we're the ones who should be suspicious. We could be walking straight into a trap."

"Monday's a market day in Lugo. There will be lots of people around."

"I guess we have to do something dangerous just to get out of this mess."

59

My internal radar began scanning as soon as we left the hotel. I was almost certain no one was watching, but the vague sense of menace felt like a clenched fist in my stomach. Laura was feeling it too when we pulled into the parking outside the walls of Lugo.

"I can't do this," she said.

"Can't do what?"

"I don't want to see those people again."

"We'll be perfectly safe in a busy restaurant."

"We should have talked about this earlier."

"We did talk about it."

"You talked to Vincent more than you talked to me."

"You've got to trust me on this. It's a chance to put an end to our problems."

Rockin Around the Christmas Tree was playing on the juke box when a bearded guy leaned in, scanned the room, and disappeared when he spotted us.

Seconds later, Vincent came in, followed by Johnnie Radic. A brace supported Radic's bald head, and dark glasses accentuated the paleness of his face.

I was caught off guard when a tall man with a shock of white hair followed them in and gave the room a sweeping, raptor-like gaze. I didn't blink or look away when his eyes fell on me, but it felt like I was being illuminated by a hot searchlight.

People at nearby tables were either staring, or trying not to, as the three innately suspicious characters settled into the chairs directly across from us.

"What a pleasant surprise to see all of you together," I said. "Let me guess, one watches football while the others do the dishes?"

Laura jabbed my leg beneath the table.

"I see you've got that smart mouth again," Vincent said. "But let's find out how smart you really are. Johnnie wants to see the rug."

"Can he see? He looks like a blind guy in those Roy Orbison shades."

Radic showed a neat row of tiny white teeth. "I see you just fine. You're the one who blew up my art collection."

"Storing your loot next to a room full of dynamite was a dumb idea."

The eyes behind the lenses became narrow slits.

Vincent leaned closer to my face. "Mavis, our big guy, isn't so happy about the busted legs you gave him."

I almost smiled. "Some people can't be happy no matter what you give them."

"He's thinking a nine-iron would do a better job next time."

"I'm not much for golf."

"He's going to remember your face."

"I'm trying to forget his."

"You were lucky."

"I was also very quick."

Now they were looking at me like a trio of undertakers measuring me for a coffin, so I pushed the tableware aside, removed the rug from the museum shopping bag, and spread it out as best I could.

Radic flipped a corner, frowned, and seemed to be irritated about something. Then he shrugged his shoulders. "It looks like what I saw."

The Professor, patient as spider on a web, leaned in for a closer look. After an uncomfortably long inspection, he delivered the faintest of nods.

"Okay," I said. "Now let's see what you've got for me."

Radic shoved a brown paper sack across the table. I took out one packet of hundred-euro notes, counted ten thousand, then riffled through the rest. The paper, ink, and serial numbers looked good, and twenty-five packets was the right amount.

"It looks like we've got a deal," I said, handing over the translation of the inscription.

Radic unfolded the paper with his long, pasty fingers, and grunted with satisfaction as he read it.

Vincent put his elbows on the table. "You better not spoil things by mousing around anywhere near the edges of this thing."

"You can have the cheese. We just want to get out of the trap."

He held my gaze while he folded the rug, then looked at The Professor.

The Professor ticked his head at the door, and they filed out without another word.

I smiled at Laura when the door closed behind them, but my brain was stabbed by a dark thought. Clutching the money bag, I headed to the restroom, latched a stall door, and riffled through the bills more closely. I was looking for the security strip, the tiny metallic band with a code printed on it. They didn't have any.

I slumped against the stall door with my eyes closed. When I couldn't take the sound of toilets flushing any longer, I went out, signaled the waiter for two glasses of tinto, and sat at the table considering how to tell Laura.

"Things never turn out like you think they will," I said.

"What do you mean?"

"Fate can always stick out a foot and trip you."

She gave me a questioning look.

"The bills are counterfeit. They don't have any security strips."

She gasped. "Counterfeit! Are you sure?"

"I can hardly believe it," I said, thumping the table and causing a few heads to turn. "We came all this way, did what we had to do, and we've got nothing to show for it. Nothing."

As if on cue, a tinkle of coins tumbled into the jukebox, there was the scratchy hissing sound of a needle on vinyl, and the room filled with that persistent organ riff and those classic lyrics of "I Got You Babe."

An intuitive recognition leaped the distance between us like heat lightening as our eyes met. Sonny and Cher were singing about how their money's all gone, they don't have a pot, but they're still glad for what they've got.

The smile began in Laura's eyes and then lit up her face. I smiled too when it sunk in that a simple song could be so magical. The treasure our quest had led me to was sitting right in front of me.

Regardless of all that had happened, we were going to be okay. When Sonny began his *put your little hand in mine* line, I drew Laura to her feet, vaguely aware that other dancers had made space around us.

We held each other close like teenagers in love until the song came to the concluding *I got you Babe* chorus. Then I led Laura into a careful little twirl that brought a flurry of applause from a nearby table.

Afterward, I went over in my mind all the things that had brought us to this place in time. How we clashed the first time we met. How unlikely it was that I would ever see her again. How fate had given me a second chance. How I came close to squandering it. How she was stolen away. How I fought to get her back.

The way we had overcome all those obstacles could be seen as a pathway of events fashioned to lead to this very moment.

I reached across to touch her hand. "I think we've found something more important than what we were looking for."

She closed her eyes for a second and nodded. "That's true, but I still have to cope with losing my family heirloom."

I couldn't help but grin. "It's not lost."

She gave me a lingering look. "What do you mean, not lost?"

"I knew how much you wanted it, so after all those crosses, I figured it was time for a good old-fashioned double cross."

"What are you talking about?"

"I didn't plan it that way, but I wanted to nail those bastards for what they did to you. Your family heirloom is safe in Paris with Madame Maziére. I sold them an illusion. All they got was a copy Alaydin had made for me in Spain."

Her eyes tightened. "That's another thing you neglected to tell me!"

"I wanted it to be a surprise."

"I can't believe it. You cheated them with a forgery?

"It wasn't a forgery. It was a reproduction I had made for myself."

"Remind me to never get into a business deal with you."

"Maybe I could interest you in a different kind of proposition."

"What do you have in mind?"

"Would you like a chance to be my widow?"

"What kind of a question is that?"

"Would you prefer the subject to be about love?"

"I do."

"Then all you have to do is say those two words at our wedding."

She looked like she was about to cry.

I wrapped my fingers around her hand. "Don't you realize I love you? I never want to lose you."

She picked up a paper napkin and dabbed at the corners of her eyes.

"What's wrong?" I asked.

"Nothing we can't fix together," she said, crunching the napkin into a red ball and setting it down on the table between us.

I watched in wonder as the napkin slowly unfurled, becoming a ruby red flower opening its petals.

60

They were waiting outside when we left the bar. Two detectives in gray suits, and a team of men with binoculars watching from a rooftop across the square. Inspector Carvalho smiled at my surprise as he took the bag of counterfeit money from my hand.

"Did you really think we would take no interest when an American woman was kidnapped for no apparent reason?"

"The local police didn't seem to be overly concerned," I said.

"That's because they report to us."

"If you'd told me that, I might not have had do it all by myself."

"Nonetheless, you owe us a full explanation as to why you were meeting with suspects in an active investigation immediately after a massive explosion at a site we had under surveillance."

The rest of the afternoon was spent in a cramped office of the *Policia National*. The tape recorder in the middle of the table was surrounded by thick files and 8 x 10 glossy photographs of our key adversaries and their known associates. Laura and I sat on one side. Three detectives sat across from us.

Inspector Carvalho made notes as he talked. "How did you become acquainted with Vincent Mingaloni and Johnnie Radic?"

"They came to my store separately, asking about the table cover. Later I saw Radic doing some kind of business with Sheena, the woman who runs the Rancho Sutara ashram."

"What did the people at the ashram have to do with it?"

"All I know for sure is that Radic was appraising and buying things from them. Valuable things that had been donated by their members."

"Where were Mingaloni and Radic when you were doing all your looking around?"

"They were completely invisible."

"So how did they catch up with you?"

"A tracking device was hidden in Laura's travel clock. They could follow our movements."

Inspector Carvalho shook his head in frustration as he scribbled away. "What do you expect they will do, now that they have the inscription translation?"

"They aren't likely to just give up and go home. They think a lot of money is involved."

Laura was yawning. We'd been talking for hours.

"My guess is they might try something in the San Andres Church," I said, hoping this might put an end to it.

After our statements were typed up and signed, they were faxed to Interpol, and San Andres Church was placed under twenty-four-hour surveillance.

Two nights later, four in the morning, infrared cameras picked up suspicious movements inside the church. An Organized Crime Squad working with the Spanish Guardia Civil moved in and cordoned off the streets around the historic building. Minutes later, Vincent Mingaloni and Johnnie Radic were arrested while chiseling open the sarcophagus of the Count of Lemos.

They were initially charged with grave robbing and desecration of an historical monument. When a search of their Mercedes uncovered bundles of suspicious euros stuffed in the door panels, they were also charged with counterfeiting.

The local TV news broadcast a short video showing Vinnie and Johnnie handcuffed together while being led into the back of a police van. Vincent wore a faint smile on his face, but Johnnie Radic had to be restrained when he kicked and spit at the cameras.

A third man, referred to in the tabloids as The Professor, demonstrated his genius for survival by slipping through police barricades seconds before the signal was given to move in. He remains the prime suspect in a worldwide investigation amid speculation that he was the mastermind behind all of it.

Sightings of people matching his description have been reported from Thailand, Mexico City, and Medellin, Columbia.

In the days that followed, Johnnie Radic's fencing network made headlines across Europe amid lurid stories about how he used his ties with unscrupulous antique dealers to peddle art that was stolen out of European churches.

A link between stolen art and the profits from heroin trafficking emerged when an underboss in one of the Sicilian crime families was caught importing huge quantities of the drug into New York City by using pizza parlors as fronts.

Turning informer to lighten his sentence, he implicated Johnnie Radic in the theft of a twenty-million-dollar Caravaggio painting that has not been recovered.

If our testimony contributes to the recovery of the painting, the $500,000 reward will go to Sammy's wife and children.

Epilogue

Two weeks later, we were back in Seattle hanging decorations on our Christmas tree when Laura handed me the morning paper.

"Take a look at this," she said, folding it to the front page.

MASS ARRESTS AT RELIGIOUS CULT

Walla Walla—State and Federal authorities converged on Rancho Sutara and charged fifty of the group leaders with multiple felonies: attempted murder, wiretapping, conspiracy to fly a bomb-laden plane into the county courthouse, and the largest bio-terrorism attack on U.S. soil.

The mass poisoning of 800 people resulted from cult followers spiking the salad bars of ten popular restaurants with salmonella as part of a plot to take over the local government by incapacitating voters. Several of their group leaders have turned state's evidence and gone into the Federal Witness Protection Program.

According to court records, after their schemes to skirt land-use and immigration laws collapsed, the ranch leadership decided the only way to save their utopia was to take over the entire county. Justification for their crimes was reportedly found in the words of their swami who taught that any action in furtherance of his vision was spiritually correct.

Investigators also discovered a powerful sedative had been injected into beer kegs used to serve the homeless, and that Sheena's headquarters was a hive of secret doors and hidden tunnels with listening gear tapping into every room on the ranch.

The swami, whose luxurious quarters had nitrous oxide spigots by his bedside, entered a guilty plea to charges of immigration fraud for performing false marriages. He left behind ninety-three vintage Cadillacs with low mileage after paying a $500,000 fine and being deported from the United States.

"What a story," I said. "I wonder if any of those people got close to what they were looking for."

"We'll never know the whole truth about all the things that happened," Laura said.

"Things in this world seldom finish with the loose ends all neatly tied up."

"I bet that's not the last we'll hear of it."

It wasn't.

While awaiting trial, Sheena appeared on a series of TV talk shows, cheerfully admitting that their entire operation had been a scam to dupe affluent young Americans.

"We blended religion with capitalism and sold them enlightenment."

Swami responded. "Sheena was just a waitress. I made her a queen, and she stole millions."

If I figured Sheena right, she had always spelled 'Swami' with a capital $.

After pleading guilty to carefully planned poisonings, widescale wiretapping, and setting fire to public buildings, Sheena spent two years in a state prison before moving to Switzerland to be closer to her money.

Sammy's death continues to weigh heavily in my quieter moments, but, in a curious way, those who were responsible may have gotten their just desserts. The mysterious table cover has become part of his memory and continues to send ripples across the surface of my life. Intrigued by how close it brought us to finding a lost fortune, I delved into the history and legends of Spain.

The Knights Templar moved swiftly before the crackdown in 1307. Their main fleet was berthed in La Rochelle, but fully crewed ships were stationed in many other ports. History is clear, the vast treasure disappeared and has never been found.

Equally intriguing is what became of the knights who escaped. Along with a flotilla of ships, thousands of men, women, and children simply vanished.

One legend says that the Knights Templar buried a great treasure in Spain under the protection of the Spanish king who persuaded Pope John XXII to allow him to regroup them into a military order called the Order of Montessa. The emblem of the Order of Montessa is a red cross.

History is also clear that the province of Galicia was in a constant state of civil war for more than a hundred years after the Templar assets were transferred to the Count of Lemos. During such troubled times, someone in the Count's powerful clan would have known that concealing a treasure was the only sensible thing to do. My guess is that the same person had the table cover woven to create a lasting record that keys to that treasure were hidden in the family tomb.

Further research turned up a tantalizing legend about underground passages on the northwest coast of Spain leading to caves filled with treasure. That tempted me to go back until it crossed my mind that legends of lost treasure may involve a parable, or a lesson of some kind—and my lesson had already been learned.

After all, the long arm of coincidence withdrew the tell-tale contents of the Lemos chest at almost the same moment Laura and I managed to bring the two panels, and ourselves, back together. Our lesson was that life is a precious journey, and the greatest treasure is each other.

So, in the end, there's no secret, no pot of gold, or holy grail. There's just what's in front of all of us. And that's no small thing. Just go outside and look at the stars.

As for Laura and me, the beautifully restored artifact of our escapade will be a source of stories we can tell our grandchildren when they are old enough to appreciate them.

And perhaps, one of these days, I might figure out a way to tell her about that Castafiori emerald I have tucked away.

Better yet, I'll just hang it on the Christmas tree and see if she notices.

About the Author:

John Goodall studied Fine Arts in college, graduated with a Bachelor of Arts, and went on to take a Juris Doctor degree from the University of Washington. For more than thirty years, he practiced law in Seattle while directing a gallery specializing in the sale, restoration, and appraisal of rare tapestries, rugs, and textiles. He has written for international art journals, exhibited in major American and European cities, and traveled widely. He is currently living in France.

Made in the USA
Columbia, SC
02 March 2022

57076787R00186